# Her Name is

# *Hazel*

## Sarah Forester Davis

PO Box 224
Sharon Center, Ohio 44274
SarahForesterDavis@gmail.com

For more about HER NAME IS HAZEL, follow Instagram @SarahForesterDavis #KillianAndHazel

Cover by Sarah Forester Davis

Paperback ISBN: 979-8-42077-942-2

## Dedication

To my husband, my mom, and Chelsea.
Thank you for always encouraging my eccentric
behavior, for being my people, and for not committing
me when I tell you my characters speak to me all day
long in my head.

This book deals with some topics that might be triggers for certain people. If reading about sexual assault is a trigger for you, I wrap you up in the warmest of hugs and ask that you not read my book. There are no books in the world that are worth triggering traumatic events that you have bravely overcome.

Much love always,
Sarah Forester Davis

# Hazel

## -during-

Keep it together, Hazel. Keep it together. If you stay quiet, he won't find you. If you hide here long enough, he'll probably just give up looking. He'll move on to someone else. He'll forget all about you ... for now.

My name is suddenly being screamed from a distance. I grab at coats that have been thrown onto the closet floor, covering my entire body with them like that might help. I can't let him find me.

I need to be invisible.

"I know you're in here somewhere!" he shouts. "Just come out so we can talk! I promise, we'll just talk!"

Talk?! Bullshit. He doesn't want to just *talk*. He wants to control me. He wants to control every little thing about me. He wants to own me. That's what his plan was all along, to own me, to feel as if he's the reason for all my success. He wants me to forever be in his debt, even if by doing so I lose myself in the process.

"Fine!" his sharp voice pierces the walls around me. I slam my hands over my ears to cover the noise. "If this is how it's going to be, good luck making it in this world! Acting like this will only ruin you! I'll make sure of that!"

Ruin me? I'm already ruined. He's already ruined me. He accomplished that a while ago.

My heartbeat is rapidly thumping in my ears. It's obnoxiously loud, like it's trying to drown out all other sound. It's trying to protect me from him, from all that could possibly happen, but it's not working. I can hear the footsteps getting closer even over the steady rhythm pounding in my head, and then I abruptly hear nothing. Absolute silence.

I wait for it, because I know he's coming.

Three.

Two.

One.

And the closet door flings open.

# chapter one

Before and after. I've always thought of my life as a before and an after. I'm not sure where to put the split, where the before came, and where the after started. All I know right now is that the before was definitely better than the after. I prefer the before, because the after is just ridiculous.

You know what else is ridiculous? London in the late spring. It's a goddamn joke. There's no sun, just constant gray clouds and rain drizzle. I glance around at the pale-faced patrons who are pretending they don't recognize me as they guzzle down their drinks in this elaborate pub hidden in the heart of the city. But I see the way they hold their phones up as if taking a selfie. They recognize me and they think they're being clever, but in reality, I know it's me they're taking a photo of. There's no goddamn selfie.

They're not clever. They're simply foolish.

Everyone here looks like they just crawled out of an underground shelter. No color, dark rain slickers that look perpetually wet, hair that hangs down limp around their faces because of the endless fog. Living in this city is like being in a low budget vampire movie, all the time. The only good thing about London in the late spring is the nightlife, because you can just drink away the misery.

"Killian!" my name is shouted. That voice could only be

coming from one person. I turn to see my agent heading toward me, the flash of cameras can be seen from outside of the rainy windows.

*Jesus.* I roll my eyes in frustration. Can't a guy get a drink in peace around here?

"Killian!" Blake shouts again. His English accent is much stronger than mine and sometimes it's hard for other people to understand him. Sometimes I purposely ignore him with the pretext that his accent is just too insufferable to try to hold a conversation. "You're wanted outside! Huge crowd of reporters, all in the rain, for *you*. What the hell are you doing in here by yourself?" He grabs at my drink, chugging it in one gulp and dropping the glass down loudly on the counter.

"Was just taking a break," I mumble under my breath.

"You're nineteen," he reminds me. "You shouldn't be drinking by yourself, it's bad for your image. At least get caught surrounded by your devoted fans or something. I'm not letting you sneak away tonight. Get out there, talk to the press. It's good for the movie."

London, the last stop on our press tour and the city I call home from which I've been away all spring. I haven't even had the chance to go to my apartment since I've been back in town. Blake has kept me too busy with absolute nonsense. It's good to be home, but at the same time, I don't feel like I'm home. I feel like this is just another random city, and tomorrow I'll be getting on another plane forgetting where I was just a couple days ago.

"The movie can carry itself," I reply, which is true. It's probably the best movie I've ever been in. "I'm tired. I'm practically forcing my eyelids to stay open. It's after midnight. Can we just wrap this up already?"

"Ugh," groans Blake in utter annoyance. "Don't be like this again. You've been like this for a year now. Ever since last spring. All moody and miserable. Get your spoiled ass out there, suck up to the press, find some girl to take back to your hotel room tonight so you can relax, and let's end this press tour on a positive note."

I turn my nose up at him. "How is shagging up with some random fan ending this press tour on a positive note?"

He waves at the bartender for another drink. "It will end *her* night on a positive note and might put *you* in a better mood. Be grateful for your fans."

"I am grateful for them." I grab the shot that slides my way, tossing it back before Blake can take it. "But I don't need to sleep with them all to show them my gratitude."

"Fine," Blake's lips form a tight frown. "I'll sleep with them all. You keep acting like you're better than them, and see where that gets you in this life."

"I *am* better than them," I hop off my stool, pointing at the empty shot glass as I catch the bartender's attention. He refills it one last time. I swallow it down and wave it in front of Blake's pissed off face. "They spend countless hours tracking me down, to just simply sneak a picture of me as I sit here enjoying a drink. They don't even talk to me. They just shriek in my face and start crying like I saved the life of their dying family member. I'm grateful for them, but after tonight, I'm done for a while. I need a break from this life."

"A break?" he nervously laughs. "You're Killian Lewis. You don't take breaks, remember?"

"Consider this your warning," I slam the empty shot glass onto the wooden counter. "Cancel my auditions for the summer, and see if the start of my next project can get moved to the fall. I'm leaving for a while. Going to find somewhere to disappear. Where no one will find me. Got it?"

Blake squeezes his hands on the counter as if forcing himself to remain upright. "You want me to tell the director of your next movie to *push* back the start date? How much did you drink tonight?"

I get right up in his face and stare into his glossy brown eyes. "I. Need. A. Break. From. This. Life." Then I walk past him and toward the door that will take me outside.

"This will ruin you!" Blake yells after me. "Actors like you aren't allowed to take breaks!"

The whole pub seems to stop talking. I can hear ice popping in glasses, it's so quiet. People start pulling out their phones again, thinking they're about to record the famous Killian Lewis make an ass out of himself. Typical, privileged actor is what they think I am. But I've been doing this for a really long time. I know the rules. I call Blake over with my finger. His cheeks turn bright red and he adjusts his bowtie as he struts his way over to me.

I then lean into his ear and whisper so that no one around us can hear me. "If taking a break after more than ten straight years of making you millions ruins my career in this field ... then *fuck* it all."

Then I put on my fakest smile and walk out to the flashing cameras and fans screaming my name.

# chapter two

The mind is a funny thing. It brings up memories and old conversations at the strangest times. It just throws shit at you, no warning, just a sudden flash of the past.

As I'm sitting here, my half-brother's voice is ringing out in my head. His voice is always ringing out in my head. He's a good ten years older than me, but he's also an actor and I find myself calling him all the time for reassurance that this type of life is actually worth living. His advice is quite possibly the only advice I actually listen to, although I'm starting to believe he has a severe drinking problem. It actually might be beneficial to start searching for a new mentor soon.

"You want to quit everything?!" he asked me, shocked, through my cell early this morning. "Just abandon acting after all your success?"

"No, Theo," I responded. "I just want to have a few months off to think. To just not be an actor for a little while. I need a break from the insanity of this life."

"Do it," he surprisingly agreed. I could hear a glass hit his teeth. My morning is his night, and I was pretty sure he was drunk as we were talking. "Do it now while you're still young and can use your immaturity as an excuse. Come hang out with me for the summer. I'll be a good role model."

I laughed because between the two of us, I'm definitely the

more mature one. "Thanks, but I need to be somewhere a little less under the microscope. California for a summer definitely sounds intriguing, though."

"Come back," he begged. "Remember how much fun we had last year while you were here?"

"Actually, I don't," I recalled. "My memories of those two days with you are all a big blur. Except for your black eye. That still stands out."

He snickered loudly. "And if you came to visit for an entire summer, I'd make sure we'd have *just* as much fun as we did before," he promised.

Other voices suddenly enter my mind, loud and shrill. "Killian! Killian, we're here to try to talk you out of your insane idea to take a break at the peak of your career!" this voice breaks through my train of thought. "Will you focus, please?" I shake away the conversation with Theo and blink hard to bring my mind back down to reality, because it's obvious I had slipped away into my comfort zone again.

I'm at the head of a table surrounded by my team of highly professional individuals that all care so intensely for my well-being, they set up this impromptu lunch meeting behind my back. First, we've got Blake who lives solely off the percentage he gets from every single project I do. I'm his only client, and the only reason he's my agent is because my mom was intrigued by his memorized promises and slept with him a decade ago to secure my success.

Next to him is his assistant, Madison, who's only a couple years older than me. She started off as one of my diehard fans but I never gave her the attention she desperately craved, so she jumped to Blake. Apparently, she has major daddy issues. Sadly, the only reason she's his assistant is because this is who he's *currently* sleeping with. Then we've got my publicist, Carol. She might be the only one here who actually cares about me. I keep seeing her shoot me sympathetic smiles over her large wine glass.

And last but not least, the cold-hearted bitch that runs my entire life: my manager, my mother.

"Baby," my mum grabs my hand, her fake English accent sounding extra absurd today. She's American, but refused to leave London even after my British dad walked out on us twelve years ago. "We just don't want to see you make a rash decision and regret it. You have your choice of auditions all summer long. After this last movie, everyone wants you. You don't want to go to any of them?"

"I don't," I boldly state.

They all start laughing at me. I haven't missed the chance to go on auditions since my mum threw me into acting when I was five. And now that my name is turning heads, I'm in demand and being pulled in twenty different directions by every director in the U.K. My entourage is pissing me off, though. I fold my arms over my chest and watch them all as they share nervous smiles amongst each other.

"I think you just need to sleep on it for a day," my mum continues, tipping her wine glass back to swallow the last couple drops. "I'll cancel your meetings for this evening. We'll reevaluate tomorrow after you've gotten some sleep." She waves down the waiter who's standing off in the corner of the room, scared to be in our presence. "We're ready to order!"

He quickly rushes over, his face pinched in fear. He walks straight to me first. This is how it always is when I'm out with other people. The youngest person at the table has gained the most respect.

"Sir?" he looks down at me.

I bring my hand up to his shaking arm. "You don't need to call me sir," I smoothly say. "In fact," I look up at his name tag, "Paul, do you think you can give us a few more minutes? I'm not quite ready."

"We're *ready!*" my mum barks at the two of us.

Paul stands there, not sure who to listen to. I squeeze his arm in reassurance and look back at the four—three, if you take away Madison—adults staring at me in exasperation. "I will not be sleeping on it for a day," I say to them all, smooth and calm. "I've thought long and hard about it. I've made up my mind and I will *not* be changing my mind. I'm taking the summer off, and that is that."

"The hell you are, Killian!" my mum glares at me. "As long as you are here, under our watchful eyes, you will be doing what we tell you to do this summer!"

"I'm nineteen and actually, none of you can tell me what to do," I point out.

"As your manager," my mum grinds her teeth and says, "I *will* tell you what to do while you are here."

"Paul, I'll take the bolognaise," I kindly say, then I turn back to everyone else. "Well, then it's a good thing that yesterday I booked my plane ticket to Ohio, so I won't be under your watchful eyes all summer where you find the senseless need to control every little thing I do."

Blake's glass slips out of his hand, spilling dark red wine all over the crisp white tablecloth. It soaks through like blood would on a wounded soldier's army shirt, yet no one does anything. "You did what?!"

"I'm taking the summer off," I bluntly say again. "Carol! When's the last time I've had more than two consecutive days off in the last, oh, let's say, five years?"

Her face turns bright red as I put her on the spot, but I see a smile forming on her thin lips at the same time. "Never, Killian. You've never had more than two consecutive days off in the last five years."

"Paul?" I question him. "If you worked pretty much every day for five years, at the ages of fourteen through nineteen, how would that make you feel?"

"Bloody miserable, sir."

"Bloody miserable," I repeat. "Thanks, Paul."

"My pleasure, sir."

"I'm burnt out!" I cry to them all. "I'm screaming from the goddamn London Tower that I'm mentally not here anymore! I can't even remember what it's like to not be working! To not be waking up in hotel rooms or when the sky is still black because of early call times! I get chased by fans just walking into a goddamn drugstore! I will not be throwing myself into another pointless role just to please you all, until *I* fucking feel like it. Understand?"

Madison grunts under her breath. "You just want to disappear, Killian? Remember that American actress who did that last year? She was your age. What was her name?"

"Birdie," Blake quickly says. "Prime of her career and suddenly she slips off the radar, right before she's set to walk out on stage for some awards show. Pretty certain she bailed on a movie, too. I think she ended up in rehab. Drugs. Last I heard, she's making underground indie films because that's all she's being offered now."

"She was amazing," Madison sighs. "I cried like a baby during her last film. And she was so beautiful, in this natural girl next door way. Could have done anything she wanted, and now no one even remembers her name."

"I'm sure she had her reasons," I roll my eyes, vaguely remembering who they're talking about. "Not everyone has to continue down this path if they don't want to."

My mum dramatically wipes at her eyes with a cloth napkin. Her mascara is leaving a black rim under her eyelashes. I swear she does this on purpose to make herself appear overly theatrical. "This *path* is the right path for you!"

"The right path for me, the right path for Theo ... what if we just wanted to be normal? You didn't seem to care much when Theo spent most of his childhood in America and far away from you! Or when he left London for good when he was only nine—"

"He was filming a TV show!" she cries out. "One that he was a part of for seven years! And he had his father to guide his career all that time! I didn't need to worry about him!"

Theo and I don't have the same father. His father is an American director that cheated on his wife with my mum. Nine months went by, and he had the luxury of paying secret child support until his wife discovered his illegitimate child five years later. He then took Theo under his wing, throwing him into the world of acting until my mum suddenly moved him to London for bigger and better opportunities. As soon as Theo could, he got the hell out of here and away from her greedy hands. His father is the reason for his success, but I don't tell Theo that.

My mum tries to grab my hand but I slowly pull it away from her reach. She dramatically hiccups as she cries out, "I can't help but feel like you're making a mistake—"

"And I can't help but feel like as my manager, you're only thinking about yourself."

She loudly gasps. "Killian! I'm only thinking about you!"

"Bullshit," I laugh. "You haven't thought about me since my first paycheck cleared the bank when I was five. Which is why I'm spending my summer as far away from you as possible. As far away from all of you, actually. Though I *will* miss you, Carol."

She gives me a small smile. "I'll be ready when you get back. Ohio seems ... lovely."

I let out a snicker. "No, it doesn't. But I know none of you will follow me there, so I'll somehow manage."

"Killian!" my mum yells my name, causing everyone to jump in their seats over the shrillness of her voice. "If *this* is how you're going to behave, how you're going to treat us, then you're on your own. Good luck getting to Ohio without a mob of fans attacking you on your way."

12

I glare at her and then laugh under my breath. "Did you forget? I'm really good at pretending to be someone I'm not." I look back up at Paul. "Five minutes to let the shock wear off, and they should be ready to order. We might need another bottle of wine or two. Oh, and if you could do me a small favor and *not* tell the press where I'm heading, I would really appreciate it."

He grins and nods his head. "Not a problem, sir, but may I ask?" He brings his mouth down slightly. "What the bloody hell is in Ohio?"

I pat his shoulder hard. "My dad, Paul. My dad is in Ohio."

# chapter three

There's something magical about airports. It's like they're their own planet, separated from the chaos of the real world. I've lost track of how many airports I've been in, but they're all packed with the same type of people.

You've got travelers filled with adrenaline because they're about to embark on an epic holiday they've been planning for years. You can spot these kind from a mile away, bouncing in their seats with their overpriced coffees and travel bookbags, a permanent smile plastered on their excited faces.

Then you've got the opposite travelers, the ones returning home from their epic holidays. You can also spot this type from a mile away. Gone is the excitement and anticipation, and in its place is now pure depressed gloom over having to leave their relaxed selves behind and once again live life as they had before.

Then, thrown in the mix with those two, you've got a variety that we'll just call the leftovers. Business travelers, travelers heading to visit family whether they want to or not, travelers escaping life with their secret lovers, and then people exactly like me. The travelers who are just trying to disappear from life entirely.

I refuse to travel in luxury today even though I easily could. I refuse to throw around my name and the perks I get from being Killian Lewis. I'm leaving that Killian behind in London. The Killian I plan on being for the next couple months wouldn't know what it's like to sit in first class and have the entire world handed to him each and every time he entered an airport.

Today I boarded my flight with my baseball cap on, covering most of my features. I was hoping not to be recognized. I was hoping to blend in with my surroundings, and it worked. Once safely in my seat, I purposely took a few allergy pills knowing they would knock me out, and then made myself comfortable up against the window. I slept most of the way to New York, completely ignoring the older couple sharing the row with me. I was in an overmedicated, drowsy stupor as I went through customs here at JFK, but I kept my head down and no one acknowledged me at all. It was perfect.

But now ... my flight to Cleveland is delayed.

Thankfully, in America I don't get recognized nearly as often as I do in London. But I'm on my own for the first time ever in this country. There's no team to keep the fans at bay if I'm discovered. There's no one to shield me as we walk through the airport. No one to grab me food, no one to bring me a coffee. No one to simply reassure me that everything is fine. And the fact that I now have four hours before my flight leaves for my final destination has my heart jumping in my chest like it's playing a paddle ball game with itself.

I tug my baseball cap down firmly on my head and walk to my gate. It's packed. People look pissed, babies are crying with snot dripping down their sticky faces, kids are running in circles like trapped dogs. I start to sweat and scan the area for an empty seat in which I can barricade myself. I need a corner in the back of this room, away from life, away from everyone at this gate.

I need to be invisible.

I step over the legs of people lounging in their seats who

don't even bother moving their tripping hazards out of the way. I step over the bodies of toddlers rolling on the crumb-filled floor while their parents sit there staring at their phones. I walk right over to the only empty seat I can see. I walk right over to a girl who has her head resting up against the wall, her own baseball cap pulled down with her wild brown hair spilling out from under it as she reads a book.

*Who in the bloody hell reads actual books anymore?*

She doesn't look like a bloodthirsty fan as she carefully flips the page. I know looks can be deceiving, but I don't have any other options right now.

"Is that seat taken?" I point and shakingly ask.

She looks up at me over her book, her light gray eyes lock right onto mine. *Jesus Christ.* She's absolutely beautiful, and she's staring at me with this weird look on her face. Shock, surprise, fright. I've seen it all before and I'm almost certain she knows who I am. A lot of fans act frozen in terror when they see me in person for the first time. But this one is behaving differently, and my fear of the unknown is washed away with the sudden urge to pull this girl into my arms and whisper sweet nothings into her ear.

*As an actor, am I just predisposed to play out love stories in my head at all times?*

Her eyes don't move, and she blows a large bubble with the gum that she's chomping down on with her teeth. It pops and she carefully brings it back into her perfect small mouth. I'm ready to bolt, ready to run and hide in a storage closet for the next four hours before she alerts the entire boarding area who I really am, or before I ask her to run off with me into the colorful sunset that ends every love story movie.

"It's all yours," she suddenly says. Her voice is like butter, like sweet butter that melts over my entire soul as she speaks.

*Am I really swooning over her goddamn voice?*

I let out a loud sigh and instantly throw myself down into

the chair. If she knows who I am, she's not going to tell anyone right now and for that I'm eternally grateful. But now I have to sit here next to her, because if I quickly run away, I'll cause a scene. I'm not sure what's worse. Sitting here next to this girl who suddenly has me questioning my entire life and its worth, or running like a mentally ill quack straight down the terminal with all eyes on me.

"Rough day?" she asks, peering under my hat.

My heart lands directly in my throat. Obviously, I've been this close to girls before. But each moment with them has always been planned out so thoughtfully, all I've ever had to do is act my role. It's almost a curse being an actor during your puberty years. You know how to *act* in front of girls your age, but you don't know how to behave in front of girls your age unless the cameras are rolling. This is real life, not some script, and the longer her eyes are on mine, the harder it is to form an actual thought.

"*Long* day," I finally reply. Two words, that's all I can manage right now.

"Yeah?" She opens her tattered bookbag and throws her book inside. She pulls out a bag of pretzels and tosses it onto my lap. "I've learned the key for long travel days is to just keep snacking. And drinking. But people frown upon getting drunk at airports."

I laugh at her. She can't be any older than me.

*Stay cool, Killian.*

"How old are you?" I ask.

"Does it matter?"

"To the bartenders it might."

She waves me off like I'm insane. "No one really cares how old you are in airports."

"You travel a lot, I take it?"

She snickers, like I should already know the answer to this and she's shocked that I don't. "I can't remember how many

17

airports I've been in, but this one I guess is the one I spend the most time in lately. I should have my own lounge here at this point, or at least they could dedicate a terminal to me."

*Who is this girl?*

"Where you'd fly in from? London?" she goes on.

"What gave it away?" I grin. Just keep asking questions. Keep talking so she doesn't know you're already planning out your future with her in your mind.

"The accent, for starters. And you just look like you're from London."

"I didn't know we had a certain look."

"Tight jeans, black t-shirt with some garage band plastered on it, Manchester United baseball cap. You're literally screaming London."

"Okay," I smirk. "But *I'm* not the one wearing a London Underground t-shirt, am I?"

She quickly glances down at her herself and for a second, she looks like she might start crying. I question in my mind if maybe this was a gift from an old boyfriend. A *dead* old boyfriend, hopefully.

She then shrugs her shoulders over her clothing choice for today, and I breathe a little easier. "It's my favorite shirt. It was a gift. Can't get rid of it. I'll probably be buried in it one day, if I'm being completely honest. Besides, I'm sure you have the same exact t-shirt in a drawer at home."

"You're right. I actually think I do."

Her eyes light up and she stretches her arms above her head, forcing her t-shirt to ride up. This reveals a strip of her extremely toned stomach above her snug yoga pants. I'm staring at her skin and it doesn't seem to faze her in the slightest. Most girls I meet do this on purpose. They show me glimpses of their uncovered body in hopes they'll get caught by paparazzi leaving my hotel room the next morning. I'm ashamed to say it's worked quite a few times. But this girl, she's literally just stretching and would probably punch me right in my face if she discovered I was thinking it might be any more than that.

Why do I feel so protective over her? Why am I looking around to make sure no one else is watching her as she stretches like this?

She lowers her arms and yawns. "Well, strange boy from London I just met in the JFK airport, we aren't going to just sit here for the next four hours making fun of our taste in clothing, are we?"

My eyes go back to hers. "You have other plans?"

"*We* have other plans," she grins, standing and throwing her bookbag over her shoulder. She carefully looks at the strangers whose attention she's just caught by suddenly moving. She backs up a little to the wall and pulls her baseball cap down further. She then reaches her hand out for mine. "You coming with me?"

Her long fingers are covered in skinny gold rings, and there's a small black bird tattoo right where her wrist meets her hand. I have two options. I can sit here until it's time to board this plane, trying to hide from anyone who might catch on that I'm not your typical traveler. Or, I can spend the next few hours with this stranger who I find myself utterly infatuated with all of a sudden. This stranger who I will probably never see again after today, even though my mind has already planned out our wedding.

Fuck it. I place my hand in hers and let her pull me up. "Where to first?"

"That depends," she slyly smiles. "Where are you sitting on your way to Cleveland?"

"Uh, back of the plane, I think?"

She lets out a loud laugh. "No friend of mine is sitting in the back of the plane. You'll be in first class, with me. Let's go see if we can fix that."

She turns, pulling me along through the crowd of people that have taken over every inch of the waiting area of this gate. And as I watch the careful movements she makes as we trudge our way to the customer service desk, as I watch her avoid all eye contact, keeping her head down and her baseball cap pulled fully over her eyes, it hits me.

She's trying to be invisible, too.

# chapter four

Harold!" this girl cries out to the portly man behind the counter. He needs to lose some weight, for sure. He's also completely bald, like I could probably see my reflection on the top of his head if I stood on my tiptoes and peered down. "Will my friend here have any issues sitting in first class when we finally get the hell out of the city at some point today?"

Harold taps against his keyboard for a moment and then raises his eyebrow. "The only seat in first class still available is the one next to you, Miss. Hazel."

Hazel. A name. Her name is Hazel. I love this name. *Why do I love this name?*

She pauses for a minute. "Well ... there we go!" she then loudly announces. "He's all set. He'll sit next to me."

Harold gives me a cautious look. Like he's her father and doesn't trust me next to his daughter. I nervously look away from his piercing gaze. He turns to Hazel, surprised, and declares, "But you *never* let anyone use that seat."

She winks at him and taps him lovingly on his arm. "Today I am. There will be no problems, right?"

"No, Hazel."

"Wonderful!" She grabs my hand again and pulls me away. "Okay, London. Next, we're getting a drink."

"Who the hell are you?!" I quickly ask as we rush down the terminal. My thoughts of running away with this stranger have suddenly turned to high alarm. "Are you some sort of American princess?"

She abruptly stops walking and I collide into her. My entire body erupts into instant chills as we come in close contact with one another.

"Do I *look* like a princess?" she hastily asks.

She doesn't let go of my hand. She doesn't back up, even though my body is firmly pressed against hers. Her eyes are literally searching mine. I can feel nervous sweat drops glide down my back. I want to say yes, because I'm thinking she might actually be royalty.

"No," is what I end up gulping.

"Good," she instantly replies as she starts walking again. "Just trust me here."

She pulls me into a dark pub, one that's filled with men and women in business suits and a rowdy group of guys watching a baseball game on a big screen against the wall. I would never even fathom walking into this American bar, in an airport, at nineteen when I know for a fact that I've still got two years before I can legally order a drink here. But Hazel walks right up to the counter, ignoring everyone else. The bartender nods his head in her direction, finishes pouring beer for the guy in front of him, then walks right over to us.

"You've brought a guest," he says to Hazel. Just like Harold, he's also eyeing me in alarm. But I'm also eyeing *him* in alarm. He has piercings all over his face. Nose, lip, eyebrow, and a strange tattoo that trails the length of his neck that I'm afraid to ask questions about.

"That I have, Fred," Hazel answers him. "Treat him kindly, he's had a long day. We have a lot in common."

"Okay, but I'll be watching you," he warns me, his eyes narrow and I find myself looking down at the counter. "What will it be?" he asks quietly, glancing around to see if anyone is paying attention to the three of us.

Hazel throws me a look and shrugs her shoulders. "Rum and Coke good for you?" she questions.

"Uh, sure?"

"Two Cokes," she tells Fred. She then reaches into her bookbag and pulls out two tiny rum bottles. "We'll take them to my booth and be sneaky."

"You're always sneaky, Hazel," Fred laughs as he shakes his head.

I watch as he fills our glasses with Coke, and then watch as Hazel dumps the contents of each little rum bottle into them. She winks at Fred and then grabs the drinks. "This way, London." She walks us over to a booth in the back of the pub, hidden from literally anyone who might wander in. You would never even know this booth was here unless you had the privilege of claiming it as your own, like Hazel has. She throws herself down and immediately takes a large sip of her drink. "You going to join me?"

I cautiously sit across from her and then wave my hand in the direction of the bartender, waiting for an explanation. "What was that?!"

"Fred and I have an understanding," she simply says. And then she blurts out, "Don't ask questions, okay? I really don't want to answer questions right now. But I think you of all people can understand that?"

*What the hell does she mean by that?*

"I can," I find myself saying. "But how do *you* know that?"

She smiles and leans back in the booth, taking her baseball cap off and running her hands through her tangled hair. It's a mess, curls and waves falling in every direction but against her porcelain face, it looks beautifully perfect. Like she just had a whole team of stylists work hours to make her hair purposely look exactly like this. I find myself staring at every new feature

I can finally see. Her high cheekbones, her large, light gray eyes, her forehead that's covered in small barely visible freckles.

Why do I feel like I've seen her before? Why do I feel like we've met before?

"Will you stop staring at me?" she demands in a joking yet serious way.

I can feel my face blush. "I'm sorry. I just feel like I know you from somewhere."

She takes another sip of her drink. "You know me from somewhere, just like I know you from somewhere."

I let that sink in for a minute. I then take my own baseball cap off, immediately brushing my dark hair out of my eyes. She's staring at me now. We're both staring at each other. I'm suddenly aware that she probably knows exactly who I am, and she finds joy in the simple fact that I don't know who she is. That I don't *remember* who she is.

"There you are," she knowingly smirks. "No questions right now, okay?"

"No questions," I agree, although I seriously have a million floating around in my head.

"So, London. Cleveland?" she grimaces. "Have you even been to Ohio before?"

"Twice," I tell her. "But it's been a long time."

"You going to be there awhile?"

I sip my drink, trying to channel my inner conscience here, trying to figure out if I should trust this girl that I know I know from somewhere. "The summer," I finally say. "I'm going to spend the summer there. You?"

*Why does she look excited with what I just said?*

"Same. Pretty much. I go back and forth a lot between here and there. Like a ping-pong ball."

"How old are you?" I ask her again.

"I thought I said no questions," she reminds me, but then

she answers. "I'm nineteen. So are you?"

I nod my head. "You go to school at all?"

She leans forward on the table and almost laughs her response. "No. Neither do you, right?"

I press my chest into the firmness of the wood, scanning her features again as I feel my mind is *finally* getting close to figuring out who she is. "No. No time for school."

"Shame," she frowns, blowing a curl off her forehead. "Being normal sometimes sounds fun, right?"

"I would love to be normal." I catch myself off guard with how quickly that sentence just flew out of my mouth. I've never said it out loud before to anyone. "I don't know what it's like to be normal, though."

She looks at me with sympathy, with understanding, and I'm suddenly embarrassed with how I just shared my personal thoughts with this stranger who moments ago I wanted to marry. But she taps her finger on my wrist and says, "I know the feeling." She then goes back to her drink, her wild hair hiding the small glass as she leans in and takes a few sips through the thin straw.

I follow her movements, watching her the whole time, both of us sitting in silence for a little while. "Where are we going after this?" I finally ask.

"Figured we do a little shopping, my treat. I slept in these clothes last night and I think I'm starting to smell."

I choke a little on the fizzy Coke in my mouth.

"Plus, you'd look adorable in an I Love NYC t-shirt," she continues. "Maybe I'll get us matching NYC hats, too."

"You want us to come across as travel companions?" my heart races as I ask.

"No," she laughs. "I want us to come across as tourists who are heading home to Ohio after our mind-blowing honeymoon in New York City."

*Honeymoon? Is she planning out our future together like*

*I've been?*

"Role playing?" I grin. "Aren't we a little young to be honeymooners?"

She raises her eyebrow at me. "Not if you act the part well enough. You ready? Time is flying. No pun intended." She chugs what's left in her glass and nods to the crowded terminal, placing her baseball cap back on her head.

"How do I know you, Hazel?" I'm not leaving this booth until I figure this out.

She frowns at me and flicks my baseball cap across the table, where it falls onto my lap. "You don't, London. You don't know the real Hazel. You know who Hazel was before. Just like I know who you were before ... before today. But you made a choice to leave it behind, and you're living in the after now until you go back. And in the after we *don't* ask questions. We just live. We just be normal, okay?"

I slowly nod my head, but I need a little bit more than that. "Can I ask just *one* question?"

Her eyes squint. "One. Just one. For now."

"In the before, were you Hazel, or did you have a different name then?"

She lets out a sigh and stands up, taking my baseball cap off my lap and placing it firmly on my head. She then pushes my dark hair to the side and away from my eyes. This simple act is so personal and intimate, it's as if she has done it before.

"I've always been Hazel," she says. "But no one called me that. And no one calls me that when they talk about that part of my life, the before."

"What do they call you?"

"That's two questions," she tugs on my hand, trying to get me to stand up.

I tug back, staying in my seat. "I think if I'm going to be your husband for the rest of our time spent together, I deserve to know your alter ego, right?"

She growls. "If I tell you, no more questions?"

"Sure."

"And you'll still call me Hazel?"

"I'll call you Hazel," I confirm.

"Would you rather I call you Killian?"

My eyes grow large. Of course she knew all along who I really was.

*Be smooth, Killian. Act normal.*

"How about in JFK, you keep calling me London. But if I have the privilege of seeing you outside of this airport, you can call me Killian."

"You think we'll see each other outside of an airport one day?" she smirks, a secret smile suddenly appears on her lips.

"I'm starting to think there was a bigger reason for this four-hour layover."

"Yeah, bad weather in Pennsylvania."

"Hazel?" I shake my head.

"London?"

"Who are you?"

She tugs again, pulling me up so the brims of our baseball caps are practically touching. "I'm Hazel, but when I'm not Hazel, they call me Birdie."

# chapter five

I'm being pulled through the JFK airport by the American actress who dropped off the face of the planet last year. Birdie. I'm with Birdie. I try to let it sink in for a moment. I try to remember all the movies she had been in before she left that world behind. But there's no time to make a mental playlist, as we've now entered an NYC souvenir store filled with overpriced gifts that you pick up last minute for the loved ones you forgot about while you were away.

Hazel ... Birdie ... I'm not sure which name to associate with this vivacious girl anymore, this girl who I still find myself desperately attracted to in this weird *I must protect her at any cost* kind of way.

"This one," she pulls a black t-shirt off a rack, holding it out in front of me. It has a massive red heart on it, with *NYC* plastered below it and a cartooned taxi cab driving down a city street. "This one for sure."

"You want me to wear that?" I question in disbelief.

"Absolutely," she grins. "For the rest of the day, on the airplane, up until you crawl into your bed tonight and peel it off your exhausted body. Find something for me," she then says. "I'm going to get us matching hats."

I watch as she skips toward the hat selection, pausing by a magazine rack for a brief second. Her head spins to read the titles of the ones in the display case, and her face turns up in disgust. A pissed off look appears, and then she takes each and every one and flips them over so no one else can read the headlines plastered on the covers.

Hazel demands privacy and respect even if it's not for her, even if it's for other people.

*I think I'm in love.*

I go back to the t-shirts and find an obnoxious pink one. It's hideous and just downright ugly on so many levels. It's something you'd find in a thrift shop after having had three different owners and one round through a disgusting trash bin. It has the Statue of Liberty on the front, her torch replaced with an apple, the city skyline in the background and *I survived NYC* in chalk letters written like clouds in the sky.

I sense her approaching and look up to see her smiling with two graffitied *I love NYC* hats, one in black, one in pink, swaying from her hands.

"Does this not scream unforgettable honeymoon in New York City?!" she calls out.

I hold up the pink shirt and try not to laugh at the sudden repulsion that shows on her face.

"That?!" she cries. "Are you kidding me?! Geez, London. You hate me that much already?"

I look down at it. "I think you can pull it off, actually."

"I can pull off anything," she winks in confidence. "And it matches my new hat, so it's a win."

She takes everything over to the register, throws down a hundred-dollar bill, and tells the foreign man behind the counter to keep the change.

"Let's go find a bathroom," she then says to me. "Or as you Londoners say, a *loo*. What the hell is a *loo*, London? The name of some fat, sweaty old guy who gets drunk every night at the local bar in his no name town? Loo. Who the hell came up with that?"

29

I can't help but laugh as I follow her down the terminal to find the nearest restroom. "I don't actually call it a loo," I tell her. "In fact, I grew up traveling and acting so much, there's a lot of British slang that I never picked up on, much to the disappointment of my mum."

"Mum," she points her finger at me. "You picked up that one. I'm going to stick with *mom*, but I think I'll start calling the bathroom a loo. Just to be different."

I start laughing again, but then I find myself suddenly questioning if she was planning on us changing in a stall *together*, and I feel the sweat instantly form along the back of my body. Fat drops all the way down to the boxers hanging out of my jeans hidden under my shirt. What if it starts soaking through? What if my sweat stains create large, detestable spots all along my shirt? Now I'm sweating even more ... *why is she making me sweat*?!

"Dammit!" she suddenly cries out in annoyance. "Why is there always a line for the women?! Feel free to go," she points to the empty men's room.

*Okay, so she wasn't planning on changing with me.*

"I'm sure I'll still be here when you get done," she sighs.

I look at the line; there's at least fifteen other women before her. It's obvious that for every restroom devoted to a man, there needs to be two for women. Aren't women the ones usually tugging the hands of their two or three children into the stalls with them, while us guys walk in, carefree, by ourselves? We take a piss and we're in and out in one minute, while women are stuck waiting in massive lines, and then have to spend twenty minutes ensuring their kids wipe properly and wash their hands. The math doesn't make sense, if you ask me. Someone needs to get on that.

The terminal is suddenly packed like sardines with fast moving people who are all heading to baggage claim. There must have been five or six planes that all arrived at once. My anxiety has surfaced not only for myself but also for Hazel, knowing she's going to be standing here awhile. Now that I know who she really is, I find myself wanting to protect her even more than I did when I sat down next to her an hour ago.

"I'll wait with you," I say to her casually, like it means nothing when I know it really does.

She gives me a funny look and then playfully grabs at my hand and swings it. "I knew I married the right guy."

I can feel my face turn red as our hypothetical wedding once again plays out in my mind. The older lady in front of us suddenly turns around, her cane hitting my toes hard. "You two just get married?" she kindly asks.

"We did," Hazel smiles as she convincingly lies. "We were just on our honeymoon. Heading back home to our horse farm in Ohio today."

"Enjoy every second of it," the lady warmly says. "Life goes by way too fast."

"We will, thank you," Hazel says in return. Her eyes suddenly snap over my shoulder. "Dammit. Don't look," she whispers to me. "But I think we've been spotted."

*Shit.* "We? Or you? Or me?"

"How the hell am I supposed to know? I can't read their obsessed minds!"

The older lady looks to where Hazel's staring. "That crowd of people pointing at you two?" she asks, confused.

"Maybe," Hazel answers.

"You two famous or something?" she questions.

"Maybe," Hazel says again, staring down at the ground.

The lady takes a good look at the two of us. "You're so young and innocent. You don't want the attention right now?"

"I don't want the attention ... ever," Hazel mumbles.

A wrinkly hand suddenly appears on both of our shoulders, her cane now whacking me in my stomach. "Can I help?" this lady asks us. "Sammy!" she yells down the line to a man sitting on an electric cart. He gets up and slowly walks over to her. "Move it, Sammy!" she yells to him.

His feet move faster. "What can I do for you ma'am?" He then jumps a little when he notices Hazel. "Hazel! It's been a couple weeks!"

"Hi, Sammy," she quickly says. "How's the family?"

"Good, Hazel. Grandbaby is getting big. Walking now."

*Does Hazel know everyone in this goddamn airport?*

"I'm going to be here a while," the lady tells Sammy. "Get these two kids on your cart and further down the terminal. They've got stalkers, and nobody has time for that shit today."

Sammy only looks mildly annoyed. "More stalkers?" he then turns to Hazel and asks, raising his eyebrow at her.

"Fans," Hazel corrects. "I think they're just fans."

"Ah. Fans we can deal with. But who's this?" he points to me, once again giving me that evil eye I've gotten so used to seeing today.

*Why is it that everyone we run into looks at me like I'm going to abduct Hazel and murder her behind an abandoned airplane hangar?*

"A friend," she immediately answers. "One I trust."

"Alright then. I'll take your word for it. Let's go," he nods to his cart.

The lady gives our hands a firm squeeze. "Pleasure meeting you both."

Hazel quickly leans in and gives her a kiss on the cheek. "Pleasure was all ours. Thank you."

The cart moves fast through the crowds of people, as Hazel and I both keep our heads down and avoid all the curious stares and whispers.

"How about I drop you off by the family restroom at the pet service area?" Sammy suggests. By the tone of his voice, it sounds as if he and Hazel have done this before.

"Sounds good, Sammy," Hazel replies. "And if you can

32

drive around until that bathroom is unoccupied, I'll name my first born after you. Though I think I might have already promised you that."

He laughs. "No need for another Sammy, bathroom is empty. Looks like you're in the clear." He pulls up right next to it and Hazel and I hop down. "Enjoy your day. I'll catch you next time," he waves as he drives off.

Hazel flings the door open and I go in after her, locking it behind us in a non-creepy, not going to murder you behind an abandoned airplane hangar type of way. Her back is to me and I watch as she takes a few deep breaths before pulling her hat off and tossing it right into the open trash can. She then quickly spins around to face me, like she forgot for a moment that I was here with her. I've only known her all of one hour, but it doesn't take a genius to understand what's going through her mind right now.

"Are all your airport adventures this exciting?" I ask her, trying to lighten the mood.

She moves closer to me and slowly pulls my hat off my head, placing it on the wet sink. She then naturally runs her fingers through my hair. I suddenly feel as though electricity has traveled from the very top of my scalp all the way down to my toes.

"No," she gradually replies, her eyes frantically searching mine. "But I didn't want to bore you."

I try to bite down hard on my tongue to keep myself from saying anything embarrassing, but the pain in my mouth doesn't seem to do the trick. "Hazel, I don't think you could ever bore anyone."

Her eyes travel around my face. My eyes, my nose, my lips. Why do I have the sudden urge to kiss this person I literally just met? Sixty minutes after meeting her and my thoughts have already wandered to *this*? I could have any girl I ever wanted by just snapping my fingers, but I've never actually wanted anyone the way I suddenly find myself wanting her.

It's not in an intense sexual way either, although my mind *has* imagined a few blush-worthy scenes. It's in this desperate need to protect her way, and this scares the shit out of me. I've never cared about another human being the way I find myself caring about her. A stranger that I just met in an airport.

"Killian," I watch my actual name leave her mouth. "Don't," she simply says. "I'm not worth it." She then shoves the black t-shirt into my chest. "Turn around," she demands, and before I can even get my feet to move, she starts pulling off her shirt.

I quickly spin, yanking my own shirt off and throwing on my new NYC one in its place. I stall for a moment or two, just to give her enough time to change before I turn back around. I'm nineteen and I'm an actor, so seeing girls in their bras isn't anything new. But with her, I feel as if she deserves my utmost respect for reasons I don't quite understand.

She's standing there watching me when I finally look her way. Her eyes stay on mine while she shoves her London Underground t-shirt into her bookbag. Her new bright pink one that she's now wearing is making the bathroom walls look florescent in color. Like we're trapped inside the bubble from the bubblegum she blew earlier in her seat.

She lets out a humorous grunt. "We look ridiculous."

"We might actually attract more attention wearing these," I admit. "But pink is definitely your color."

"You think?" she looks at herself in the mirror.

I go and stand next to her and glance at our reflections. There's something so normal about seeing the two of us standing side-by-side. She lifts her hand, pushing her hair back at the top of her forehead.

I point to her wrist. "What's with the bird tattoo?"

She looks down at it. "It's my reminder," she softly replies.

"Reminder of ...?"

She turns her body into mine, her face looks pained like she's fighting back memories she doesn't want to remember. I look down at her hand and find myself rubbing the bird with my thumb. Why am I touching her? I don't touch girls who haven't thrown themselves at me with their pathetic sexual advances. I don't touch girls I just met in the JFK airport. But here I am, touching her. I almost pull my hand away but my conscience is screaming at me not to.

I stare into her troubled eyes, and they're *definitely* troubled, and I keep my thumb on her wrist the whole time. Her face softens with my touch and she carefully pulls up her shirt with her other hand, revealing another tattoo on the side of her lower back. It's a birdcage and it's empty, with the door swung open.

She allows me to run my finger along it, even though I can tell this intimate moment has her alarmed. She's afraid to be touched. She's afraid to let me touch her, which is perfectly fine because I'm literally a stranger she just met. But I can tell it's more than that. I can tell there's something about her past that has her afraid to let a beautiful moment like this into her life. Yet she's allowing my fingers to softly move along the ink that's a permanent fixture on her skin, and I don't know why. Why is she allowing a stranger to touch her so intimately?

*I* know I'm not a serial killer. I know I'm not some crazed, obsessed fan, but how does she know this?

"Hazel," I whisper into her ear. "What is it a reminder of?"

She pulls her shirt back down and I watch as a single tear drips down her cheek. "It's a reminder that no matter how many times they try to cage me ... I always have the ability to let myself fly free."

# Hazel

## -after-

I was warned that tattoos would hurt. That I would probably be wincing as the needle dug into my body, forever leaving its mark behind. But I find myself actually enjoying the pain. It's a bit psychotic, right? Each time the needle presses against my soft skin, it reminds me of Birdie, it reminds me of the pain *she* was in and how Hazel doesn't have to deal with that shit anymore.

A free bird on my wrist to look down upon to remember who I was before, and how I never have to be that person again. And then an opened birdcage on my back to remind me of what it felt like to be trapped, but also what it felt like to finally be free.

Trapped. Caged. Controlled. Worthless. All thoughts that were a part of my life at some point.

Free. How I feel right now. Just completely ... free.

"You doing alright there, Hazel?" the tattoo artist asks me as he works to finish the birdcage.

The pain shoots down my leg and I wince, but then I look down at the bird on my wrist. Even though it's just a simple black bird, I can almost feel the pain it had to endure to get there, to get to this point, to become a permanent part of my after. But now its wings are spread in flight and it's free. It will always be free.

A wise person once told me that no matter how often they try to cage us, we always have the ability to let ourselves fly free. These tattoos, my bird and the empty birdcage, they're my reminder. A reminder that I'm free but also a reminder of the owner of those words I find myself repeating in my head at least once a day, if not more. This person deserves to be remembered, even if they never remember me. Even if I never see this person again.

So, I allow the pain to wash over me knowing I'll never forget who actually spoke those beautiful words for the very first time, and then I smile and answer the tattoo artist, "Never better."

# chapter six

This way, London," Hazel pulls me out of the bathroom and straight to an empty gate. "Meredith!" she greets the lady behind the counter. "When's the next flight?"

I wait for it. I wait for this lady to realize that Hazel is not by herself.

Ah. There it is.

Meredith gives me the most impressive evil eye of the day, and then asks in the boldest New York City accent, "Who in the world is *this*?"

"Just a friend," Hazel warmly smiles. "No need to sound the alarm. I trust him."

Meredith points to me in disgust almost. "She *trusts* you? That says a lot. I hope you know that. What the hell are you two wearing?" she eyes our outfits in repulsion.

"We're incognito," Hazel whispers. "We're trying to fit in with the tourists."

Meredith hides her laughter. "You look like you stole this garbage out of a homeless man's shopping cart."

"Well, then maybe we're just trying to fit in with the locals?" Hazel grins. "When's the next flight?" she asks again.

"Next flight isn't for another five hours," Meredith says in return. "Should be empty for the next three, at least. It's all yours," she then nods behind her.

"Wonderful!" Hazel declares, pulling my hand yet again as she moves us behind the counter and to the empty seats. "Give the kiddos a hug from me!" she calls out to Meredith.

"Will do, Hazel!"

She then throws herself down into a chair, her back facing the terminal and her feet draped over the seat next to her. "Sit," she points to the one on the other side, as she pulls her hat off and gives her head a wild shake.

I do as she says and then gently tap her on the top of her shoulder. "Please, tell me why you have *so* many connections to the people who work at this airport?"

She looks up back at me and knocks my hat off with the tips of her fingers. "Don't you have people you trust? A family of trustworthy people?"

I think about it for a moment. "No, I don't. I trust myself, that's about it."

She pokes me in my chin. "That's a problem. When you're constantly running away from your life, you need to find a group of people that you can trust. People who don't care *who* you are. They just want to help, whenever they can."

"Your group of people all work at the JFK airport?" I ask with surprise.

She pokes my chin again and then abruptly sits up. Her body turns toward mine and she folds her legs into her lap. "They do," she then says. Sweet and simple. "They've all helped me at one point or another and I trust them, completely. They're my family while I'm here."

"Harold, Fred, Sammy, and Meredith have all helped you at some point?"

A huge smile appears on her delicate face. "You remember their names."

"I pay attention to the details," I say back.

She looks impressed and this excites me for some reason. "Yes, they've helped me and they continue to help me every single time I'm in this airport. And because you're with me, they'll help you now, too."

Interesting. "How many people have you journeyed around JFK with?"

Her finger rests on my chin. "Just you. Only you."

My eyes look down at her finger and I slowly remove it, keeping it in my hand. "Why me?"

Her head tilts and she pulls her finger from my grasp, pushing it into my chest. "Because when you walked up to me today, I saw myself in your frightened face. And there was this little voice in my head that screamed some pretty intense things at me."

"What did it scream at you?" I ask. I desperately want to know. I feel like I *need* to know.

"A few things, actually," she loudly laughs. "But most importantly, that I could trust you."


THERE ARE TWO new things Hazel teaches me before we finally board our plane for Cleveland. One, no matter how much time you have to kill, you will never run out of snack options in an airport as long as you're traveling during the day. It's endless, the amount of food you can consume all day long.

She proves this by taking me to the food court and forcing me to try one dish from each available place. I might throw up on our flight due to the simple fact that I've never eaten so much food at one time, but it was totally worth it.

And the second thing she teaches me? Even if you can board the plane first, don't do it if you're trying to be invisible.

"Everyone will see us," she told me with exasperation as the gate attendant called for first class and I eagerly jumped up. "Everyone will walk right past us, slowly staring as they make their way down the aisle. Bumping into our shoulders, whacking us with their carry-ons, apologizing and making eye contact. You want to keep your head down and avoid humanity for the next thirty minutes? Or do you want to go grab some pretzels and sneak on once everyone is already in their seats paying no attention to the people who get on last?"

She's obviously done this before. And she obviously has six stomachs.

We are the very last people to board this delayed flight, and as we sit down with our warm, buttery pretzels that I know I'll never manage to eat, the cabin door closes and I suddenly feel like a chapter of my life has swiftly ended. The pages have been read, never to be read again.

I look over at Hazel, who is swiping through text messages on her phone, and feel this stab of jealousy for everyone she has in there as a contact. Four hours of knowing her and I've already wanted to kiss her, protect her, marry her, and now I desperately want to be a member of her contact list.

She looks up from her phone and catches me staring at her. "What?" she gives me an odd look.

"Nothing," I quickly say.

"Damn," she yawns, ignoring my peculiar behavior. "I'm suddenly extremely tired."

Could it be the seven-course meal she just tucked away in the JFK airport?

She throws her phone into her bookbag and looks out the window as we start taxiing down the runway. She then takes off her NYC hat and attaches it to the straps of her bag.

"The flight attendants in first class know me," she says to my curious face. "They won't say anything ... about either one of us. No one will find out we're up here."

"More members of your family of trustworthy people?"

She smirks. "Leon and Claire."

I slowly take my own hat off, shaking out my hair as I can't imagine how stiff it must look after being under a hat for so long. "Exactly how many times have you flown from JFK to Cleveland?" I ask her.

"Too many," she responds.

"Ballpark figure?"

She looks deep in thought. "In the last year or so? Probably fifty times?"

"*Fifty?*" I shockingly repeat as the plane lifts off the runaway. "What the hell are you doing in New York?"

"That's top secret," she bluntly answers. "If I told you right now, I'd have to kill you. I don't want to do that. So tell me, who's in Ohio?"

"My dad," I immediately reply. "And my stepmum, and a half-sister I've only actually met a few times. I think she's seven? Or eight, maybe?"

"You sound like a really awesome big brother," she laughs. "I hope you buy her expensive Christmas gifts."

"Do you have any siblings?"

"Nope," she honestly responds. "I think my parents knew as soon as I was earthside that I was all they could handle."

"I have a half-brother, too," I blurt out, not sure why I'm telling her this. "He's older, an actor, lives in California. Moved there permanently a year ago. Different dads. He's American. I haven't seen him in over a year."

She pauses for a moment and almost looks lost in thought. She blinks hard. "Geez, London. Your family tree is all over the place."

I lean my head back on the seat and close my eyes. "My brother is the only one I actually talk to on a regular basis. But I think he needs to spend some time in rehab. He has issues. My mum is my manager and she stopped treating me like her son when I started bringing in six figures for each project at the age of five."

Hazel doesn't say anything back. I pop my eyes open and catch her staring intensely at my face. She looks sad for me, or maybe for herself? I can't tell.

"Don't feel sorry for me," I quickly say.

"I won't. Not yet."

Her hand is suddenly in mine. She's actually, with no purpose, holding my hand as we sit here. She's not dragging me around the airport, forcing me into shops or bars. She's just ... holding my hand. The warmth of her fingers pressing down on my own makes my entire body go completely stiff.

"You have really pretty eyes," she unexpectedly says. Her voice once again is making me swoon. "They're like the color of the ocean on the brightest day of the year."

I look up from our hands and directly at her, and say exactly what has been floating through my mind each time I've looked into her eyes today. "And yours remind me of the color of the ocean after a summer storm."

Her porcelain skin quickly turns pink in color and I swear she almost starts crying. That wasn't the reaction I was thinking I'd get.

*Say something else, you idiot.*

"Hazel, what's in Ohio for you?" I quickly ask her.

"My parents. They're good people."

"I'm glad you have that."

She lifts the armrest between the two of us and her head finds its way onto my shoulder.

*God, that feels nice.*

"Maybe you'll get that, with your dad," she softly says. "And with the little sister whose age you don't know."

Why do I find pleasure in the simple fact that she feels comfortable enough to rest her head against my shoulder? Why do I feel like she and I have this unspoken relationship brewing after hanging out in an airport together for a measly four hours? Why do I feel panicked that after this ninety-minute flight, my time with her is up, possibly forever?

Her head suddenly lifts from my shoulder. "Does this

make you uncomfortable? Me, this close to you?"

*Jesus, Killian. Don't say what you're thinking. Don't make a fool out of yourself. Just. Don't.*

"Hazel. Nothing about that question could be further from the truth."

*I said it. Shit.*

She lets out a loud sigh, but then puts her head back on my shoulder. "Don't, Killian. Don't do it."

My heart races. "Don't do what?"

She gives my hand a firm squeeze. "Don't let your emotions overpower rationality."

I push down on her knuckles. "English, please."

Her thumbnail digs into my skin. "Don't fall in love with someone you just met. This isn't a script. We aren't in a movie. It's not going to end the way the audience wants it to. Trust me, you don't want to fall in love with someone like me."

# Hazel

## -before-

The only seat left in first class is the one next to me. I know by looking around at the other passengers on this plane that *his* seat will be the empty one my bookbag is currently resting in. How did we even end up on this flight together? It makes absolutely no sense. Maybe I could get someone to switch with me? Maybe someone will take pity that the youngest girl in first class has to sit next to someone with that type of reputation?

Who am I kidding? I won't get pity from anyone here. People would literally sell an organ on the black market to sit next to him. I actually wouldn't have any issues getting someone to switch with me. Maybe that's what I should do. The girl in the next row over looks like she'd be the perfect obsessed fan.

Suddenly, he walks on the plane. His eyes go right to me and a huge grin appears on his repulsive face. "Birdie!" he cries out. "Looks like it's you and me for the next few hours!"

Wonderful. I'll just pretend to be asleep the whole time. Maybe he'll get the hint that I want to be left alone. But then again, he didn't get the hint when I never responded to his constant flow of text messages. Hundreds. For days, after he realized I auditioned for this role.

He picks up my bookbag and tosses it onto the floor in front of me. "You just might be my most favorite actress that I'm doing a chemistry read with for this movie. But don't tell the others."

I roll my eyes and tuck my bookbag under my seat. "Your secret is safe with me."

"If you get this role, we really need to work on our relationship. I mean, we'll be playing lovers. Shouldn't we have some personal experience to back it up with?"

Gross. I hide my gag by looking out the window at the baggage getting thrown onto the conveyor belt. It's carelessly being tossed. No one gives a damn what might be hidden inside. No one gives a damn what might get destroyed as these suitcases crash hard onto one another.

Mangled luggage suddenly reminds me of myself.

"You really should answer your text messages every once in a while," he continues. "Let me take you out. Trust me, I'd make sure you had a good time. Let the press see us together before we announce our roles."

I quickly turn to him. "How do you know I'll get the part?"

He smiles and pushes my hair off my neck, keeping his fingers on my skin for far too long. "Because *I've* already gotten the part, and you're my favorite actress I'm doing a chemistry read with."

Super. Just fucking super.

"What is this, a three-hour flight?" I ask him, already knowing the answer. "I think I'm going to catch up on some sleep while I'm stuck sitting here."

He laughs, like I might just be joking. "Look at you, being all responsible."

I give him a small smile and then rest my head up against the cold window. Crisis adverted. I sleep, he leaves me alone. I'll purposely bomb this chemistry read, and my heart can officially stop beating in weird rhythms in my chest.

But I should have known better. I should have known it wouldn't be that easy. Not with him. Not with someone with his reputation. Not with someone who obviously has never been told no in his entire privileged life.

Three minutes after the plane takes off ... his fingers find their way up my thigh.

# chapter seven

I watch her as she sleeps on my shoulder. Her eyelashes are so long, they look fake, but something tells me Hazel would never be caught dead wearing fake eyelashes in her normal life. They fan out over her eyes like a protective shield from visions of the outside world. She has these tiny freckles that line just her forehead and nose, too. God must have decided those were the only two spots on her delicate face worthy of those little marks.

Her lips rapidly start to tremble and small whimpering sounds are coming from her mouth, like the noise you hear just before a baby starts wailing. Suddenly, her whole body jumps in the seat and her arms flail protectively over herself. She quickly moves as far away from me as possible while still being buckled in, forcefully slamming her side and head into the window.

I reach for her and she flinches. "Are you okay?"

Her face spins to mine, relief. Instant relief. Her eyes look calm. Her whole body relaxes. "I—I thought you were—I thought you were someone else. I'm sorry."

Whoever this someone else is, they sure did damage her. She was scared to death to wake up with the seat next to her occupied. Scared to death was whoever she was remembering in her dreams.

"This someone else," I cautiously say, "are they the reason the seat next to you is usually empty?"

Her shoulders slouch down and she brings her knees up to her chest. "That was Birdie," she simply says. Like I should understand what she's implying.

"And what about Hazel?" is what I question her.

Her eyes immediately light up. "Hazel is glad to have you in the seat next to her."

If my heart would stop the frantic race that's going on inside the walls of my chest right now, that would be wonderful. "Hazel—"

"No questions?" she pleads with me. Her face is literally begging me with unspoken words.

I nod my head and gradually rest my body against the seat again, staring straight in front of me at the screen on the wall. The little plane bobbing around on the map is slowly approaching Cleveland. Thirty minutes. I only have thirty minutes left of being a part of what Hazel calls her after.

She's too quiet, and I can tell her thoughts are lost in the place she calls her before.

*Help her, Killian.*

Let her know you're here for her even though you barely know each other. Let her know you aren't like them, like the people that she's running from in her memories. Let her know she's safe sitting next to you. Don't end this day together with her being afraid.

I slowly turn my head. Her knees are still tightly tucked up to her chest, her forehead is resting on them now. She looks like a contortionist in her small seat as she tries to find some relief within her own body. I cautiously tap her shoulder and her head gradually lifts. Her eyes are wet with tears that she refuses to let drop.

I lift my arm and point to my shoulder, welcoming her back into the comfort she had found next to me just moments ago. "I'm not like them," I carefully say. "I'm not like the people you're scared of."

She wipes at her eyes and gives me a faint smile. "I know you're not." Then she scoots herself in right next to me, resting her head back on my shoulder, where she stays in complete silence for the remainder of the flight.

Walking through the Cleveland airport together feels nothing like it did as we lived our adventure in JFK. It's almost like a black and white movie. The color is gone, the joy is gone. We both realize an end is coming to whatever it is we had created when we were abruptly thrown together today, and this feeling is dreadful. I'm honestly terrified at the thought of this day ending.

Baggage claim is packed. We're like caged animals as we wait for the conveyor belt to start spitting out our belongings. Yet, even with the hundred other people we shared our flight with, both of our suitcases come out one right after another. Hers is resting comfortably on mine, exactly like her head was for most of our flight.

Fuck it. That's a sign, and I don't even believe in signs. I don't believe in fate. I don't believe in love at first sight.

I didn't believe in any of that ... until today.

We start walking to the automatic doors. It's too quiet. All the noise is replaced with my own loud conscience, which frankly is being extremely rude. Hazel's too quiet. I'm too quiet. I don't know how to process what's going on around me, and I don't know how I'm going to fix this never-ending feeling of emptiness I know awaits me once our rides get here and we go our separate ways.

I'm Killian Lewis. I can have any girl in the world with one phone call, but my heart is pounding in my chest over the thought of never seeing this American actress again. Birdie ... Hazel ... who ran away from the life I live, the life I question sometimes if *I* even want to live anymore.

She's almost through the door.

Do something you *fucking* fool. I grab her hand and pull her back into the baggage claim area with me.

"What are you doing?!" she hisses under her breath.

I drag her into an empty hallway across from the doors, filled with vending machines, a lone water fountain, and chewed gum that's disgustingly pressed along the wall. "Are you really just going to get in a car and drive away, pretending this day never happened?!" I exclaim.

"Are you?" she folds her arms and questions me.

"No! Hence the reason I pulled you over here!"

She starts laughing. "I've never actually heard someone use the word *hence* in a sentence before, on purpose."

"*Hazel*," I sigh in frustration. "I had no plans on even speaking to anyone over the last twenty some hours, but then I sat down next to you and my entire world was suddenly flipped. Being with you today might have just been the best day I've ever had."

She makes a weird noise under her breath. "Our six hours together was the best day you've ever had? At nineteen? Damn, you need to raise the bar a bit. Aim a little higher—"

"I want to see you again," I interrupt her. I know we're running out of time and I don't care how desperate I sound. "Talk to you again? Relive this day again? Anything is better than just forgetting about you."

Her face looks pained and she moves a few steps closer to me. "You *should* forget about me. I'm not good for you."

"I'm not asking you to marry me, Hazel—"

"I thought we were already married?" she raises her eyes and taps my ridiculous NYC hat.

*Why is it that everything she does seems so goddamn adorable all the time?*

"I'm just asking you to not erase this day from your memories," I explain to her. "Because I know it meant something to you, too. Don't leave this airport right now and immediately forget about me, *please.*"

She moves in even closer. "You're a part of my after now. I can't forget about you even if I wanted to. Just like you'll never forget about *me* now."

*Jesus.* I've never wanted to kiss someone as badly as I want to kiss her right this second. "Can I call you?" I hear myself ask, though my eyes are focused solely on her wet pink lips that she's currently pulled sideways.

She leans in, her breath hitting the side of my cheek like a puff of hypnotic air. "I normally don't give my cell number out to strange actors I meet in airports," she whispers into my ear. "They're usually psychopaths. But your English accent might have won me over today." I feel her hand grab my phone out of my back pocket. She holds it in front of my face, unlocking it. "One condition," she seriously says as she looks down, her fingers quickly tapping away on the screen. "You have to promise me something."

"Anything."

She holds my phone out to me but doesn't release it when I try to take it back. "Promise you won't fall in love with me."

*What the hell?*

I feel the heat rise on my face. I give my phone a firm tug until it's fully in my hand. "I promise," I then say.

She looks toward the doors at a BMW that's just pulled up outside. She points to it then leans in once more. "Your acting skills could use some work, London." Then she plants the smallest of kisses on my cheek, purposely brushing her fingers against mine as she walks away.

I stand there, looking down at my phone, looking at the new contact that she's created. Hazel, with a small bird emoji next to her name.

I'm Killian Lewis. I've been in over thirty commercials and movies. I'm wanted by numerous directors and producers. I can act out parts better than actors twice my age, but Hazel is right. My acting skills *do* need some work. Because no matter how many times I tell myself I haven't and I won't ... in just six hours, I've fallen madly in love with Birdie ... Hazel ... the American actress who wants nothing more than to be left alone.

# chapter eight

Killian, I can't tell you how happy I am that you're spending the summer with us," my dad says in his perfect English pitch as he pulls his truck away from the airport. His fingers brush his salt and pepper hair away from his face as he casually inspects my own.

I've only seen my dad a handful of times since he left London when I was seven. Little events threw us back together over the years, his wedding being the main one, a quick visit to Ohio when my sister was born being another. We have somehow managed to keep in touch and I give the credit all to him. I just don't have the time to try to bond with a father I might only see once a year, if that. Our relationship is what I would call permanently fragile. One little tap and it will shatter into a million unrepairable pieces.

"Thanks for having me," I say to him. "To be completely honest, I knew by coming here Mum wouldn't follow me. And Ohio seems like the best place to be invisible for a while."

He glances over at me while merging onto the highway. "Why do you want to be invisible, Killian?"

I don't answer him. I just keep watching the green scenery pass by out the window.

"Well, whatever the reason," he continues once he realizes I'm not going to reply. "I'm glad you're here. What's with the NYC getup?" he points to my shirt and hat.

I smile because I'm suddenly thinking about Hazel. "Just trying to blend in," I then say.

It's about thirty minutes of awkward forced conversation before he exits the highway and passes a white wooden sign on the side of the road that reads, "Sharon Center, Ohio, founded 1816." After this, we almost immediately turn into a tree-lined subdivision. The houses are all spaced at least an acre or two away from one another.

"Did you guys move?" I look out the window and ask, trying to recall the house I visited back when I was younger.

"We did," my dad nods. "A few years ago. Still getting to know all the town folks. Crystal wanted to be in a better school district for Maisy."

Maisy, my half-sister, whose age I'm not one hundred percent sure of. "Is Crystal still a counselor?"

"She is," my dad agrees, turning down a cul-de-sac. "Her office is still in our old city. Thirty minutes away. And Maisy's last day of school is today. Summer break for her is officially starting. She's really excited you're coming to visit. She helped Crystal get your room all put together."

"They didn't have to do that."

"They wanted to, Killian," he smiles, pulling down an egg white cement driveway that's lined with flowering bushes. A modern-looking house is waiting at the end.

This house is nothing like what I lived in as a child in London. This house is massive, with more windows than wall, which almost makes it look like an art institute. The front door is bigger in size than most garage doors, and you can see the impressive chandelier from the gaping window above it. This house would easily go for four or five million in California, wouldn't even exist in New York City, and is unheard of in London unless you're somehow related to the Queen. But here in rural Ohio, it looks normal. It looks like a picture-perfect family lives within its walls.

My dad pulls the truck into the garage. An Audi and a rather large SUV take up the other stalls. I sit here, not exactly sure what I should be doing next. A nap sounds glorious right about now.

His hand is suddenly on my shoulder. "Are you in some sort of trouble?" he nervously asks me.

I look down at the veiny hand that is now uncomfortably squeezing my skin. "It's funny that you think because I'm here, I must be in some sort of trouble. Don't worry, Dad, I don't need your legal advice. I think we're past the point in our relationship where I run to my daddy for help."

I open the truck door, slamming it as I walk to the back so I can grab the suitcase that holds my entire life for the next few months. Suddenly, the door that leads into the house flings open and my half-sister Maisy runs out.

"*Killian!*" she lets out a bloodcurdling scream. I shove a finger in my ear to try to get the loud ringing to stop. "I can't believe you're here! I can't believe you're spending the summer here!" She's now right in front of me, jumping up and down like an excited poodle. "My friends won't believe me! I saw your last movie! Well, not the last one because Mom and Dad said it was too mature—"

"Maisy," Crystal, my stepmum, exhaustedly sighs her name. "Let him at least come inside before you attack him. You're being a little overwhelming right now, honey."

Maisy's face turns bright red and she looks up at me, embarrassed. Her eyes lock on mine, the color of the ocean on the brightest day of the year. We have the same eyes. Our dad's eyes. I've never noticed this before.

"I'm sorry," she quietly says.

I ruffle her long dark hair, because isn't that what big brothers do to their little sisters? Ruffle their hair? "It's alright, kid," I tell her, and I actually mean it. "I can't wait to meet your friends."

Her eyes grow large and she grabs my hand, pulling me in through the door. "They're going to *love* you!"

The inside of the house is even more impressive than the outside, yet it sparks this weird feeling of *home* deep in my soul. Everything is high-tech, everything is touch screen and voice activated, but at the same time, Maisy's artwork lines empty wall space. Family pictures are placed in no particular order along shelves. The side of the refrigerator, which has its own TV, is plastered with postcards and magnets of foreign cities. This house screams, "We have money, but we are also a normal, typical family."

I find myself stopping in front of the two-storied stone fireplace in the gathering room. The mantel has colorful framed photos lining every inch. A cluster that would have an interior designer cringing in their shoes. I don't expect to see any of myself, but there I am, at all stages of my life. A toddler with my dad. A child at their wedding. Holding Maisy when she was born. A family picture when they came to London a few winters ago. My dad and I last fall, when he unexpectedly showed up at one of my movie premieres in New York. I'm not in their life on a constant basis, but it's apparent I *am* a part of their life.

*Shit.* My jetlagged self is suddenly feeling emotions I've ignored for the last ten years.

"He's so proud of you," I hear Crystal's voice behind me. "We all are."

I turn to her, quickly wiping my wet eyes. "Yeah?"

She warmly smiles and places her hand on my back. "Of course, honey. Life has a funny way of going by too fast. You just have to grab onto those good moments, the ones that matter. Like those," she points to the pictures. "Those moments matter to us, and we're really happy to get some more good moments with you for the next couple months. New pictures to add up there."

*Jesus Christ. Keep the emotions inside, Killian.*
"Thanks, Crystal," I manage to spit out with a shaky voice. Her arms suddenly wrap me into a hug. A hug. I can't remember the last time I was hugged without it being written in a script. I can't remember the last time someone I can call a mother figure hugged me without some sort of ulterior motive attached to it. I let the warmth of her hug overpower every inch of me, holding on as long as I can. She doesn't let go. As a mum, she knows this is exactly what my troubled nineteen-year-old soul needs right now.

"Can I show you my room?" Maisy's voice suddenly calls out as she tugs on my shirt.

Crystal gives me a couple pats on my back and then releases me from her hug. "Why don't you show him *his* room first?" she suggests to my sister.

Maisy looks disappointed. Surprisingly, this makes me upset. I don't want my little sister to be sad.

"How about you show me yours really quick, and then you can show me mine?" I say to her.

She doesn't hesitate. She grabs my hand and starts yanking me toward the stairs. Her room is the first door as we approach the top, and she pulls me inside to the light purple space and points right to a wall covered entirely with magazine clippings of myself.

I'm plastered all over a wall in my little sister's room. Shirtless pictures, movie stills, press photos, pictures I remember taking with the cast of my films yet they are strategically cut out and I'm the only man left standing.

"What in the—"

"It's you!" she cries out, like I didn't know. "I cut out every picture of you I can find and put it in my room so I can see you even when I can't see you! It's like you're here all the time! I don't have to be with you to see you every day!"

I sit down on the edge of her canopy bed and take a deep

breath. This is too much. My little sister has created an imaginary relationship with her big brother through magazine clippings.

"How old are you now, Maisy?" I struggle to get these words out of my mouth because I'm suddenly embarrassed over not knowing.

"I'm eight," she immediately answers, looking proud of her young age.

"Do you know when I was nine, I flew to America for the first time by myself?"

"Really?" her eyes grow wide. "Were you scared?"

"No," I truthfully answer. "I was actually coming here, to see Dad, and to meet your mum for the first time."

"What about me?"

"You weren't born yet. This was before they even got married. But maybe in a year or two if you're not scared, you can come visit me in London over the summer."

"Just me?!" she starts jumping up and down.

"Just you. We don't need Dad and your mum to ruin our fun, right?"

She pretends to lock our secret away on her lips. "Do you think maybe you can visit us more, before I fly by myself?"

Her eager face looks so innocent. Why did I never attempt to have a relationship with her? Even just a weekly phone call would have meant so much. *Why*? Because I'm Killian Lewis, and I don't have time for little sisters.

"I think I can do that," I say back to her. "Want to show me my room now?"

My room is the entire walkout basement of the house. There's an actual bedroom, a full bathroom, a workout room, a movie theater in which every single movie poster hung on the walls is of a movie *I* have been in, and there's a bar. An actual bar, with barstools, a counter, and an entire floor length cabinet of alcohol.

"Mom said you would need privacy," Maisy tells me as I stand in shock at this spread I now get to call my own. It's bigger than my apartment in London. It's *better* than my apartment in London.

"This is … this is great," is all I'm able to say.

"Can I come down here and hang out with you?" she quietly asks. She looks nervous, like I'm going to say no.

"Of course," I instantly reply. "But if the door to my bedroom or bathroom is closed, just knock. I might be naked."

She starts laughing. "I will definitely knock."

The rest of the evening is a blur. I'm jetlagged, overwhelmed, and emotionally a mess as I find myself fitting right in with this family I've always had, but never wanted anything to do with. We spend dinner outside, as my dad grills up steaks and Maisy shows me her impressive gymnastic moves on her trampoline. When I realize I can't keep my eyes open anymore, I excuse myself to my new basement apartment that I can simply walk into from their backyard.

I quickly shower and throw my exhausted body onto my memory foam bed, grabbing my phone for the first time all night. The message alerts are insane. I scroll through them all, looking for two specific names and ignoring everyone else.

Theo or Hazel.

They're the only two people I care about right now. I don't expect any from her, as I'm not even sure she put my phone number into her phone. But I do expect to see Theo's name. It's one thing I can count on in my life, my big brother checking in on me regardless of what he's up to. And he has.

"Yo little bro!" his familiar voice says as he picks up my call. "You made it to Ohio I take it?"

"I did," I reply. "Been one hell of a day."

"Yeah? How's the family?"

Theo has no relation to my dad, Maisy, or Crystal. My parents never married, just lived together in this weird relationship until my dad got tired of my mum's bullshit and left her for good. By the time I came around, Theo was already living in California with *his* dad. He would randomly come visit London when he wasn't busy with his child actor life, but by no means would I call *my* dad a father figure to him. I can't remember the last time Theo has even seen my dad, maybe a decade ago? Maybe more?

"They're all good," I tell him. "This house is huge, and I pretty much have an entire apartment to myself in their massive basement."

"Damn. Daddy Steve bringing in the big lawyer bucks?"

"I think he and Crystal are doing really well for themselves. Crystal, she's such the opposite of Mum. It's almost too much. Like I'm not sure how to behave around an actual mother."

"Act the part," Theo responds. "Best part about being an actor, no one knows when you're being *you*, or if you just slipped into a new role you're trying out. Crystal won't know the difference."

*I'll* know the difference. And for some reason I don't want to pretend to be someone I'm not while I'm here. Time to change the subject.

"Hey, Theo?"

"Yeah, Killian?"

"I met this girl today—"

"*Already?*" he interrupts me. "In Ohio? Is she a farmer?"

I start to laugh because I could never imagine Hazel being a farmer. "No, she's actually an actress. I met her in the airport in New York."

"Stay away from the actresses," he says in a drawn-out tone. "They are nothing but trouble. Actors don't have time for relationships, anyway. Just have fun. Screw as many girls as you can before that adorable face of yours loses its appeal. Does she live in New York?" he keeps going. "Or did you luck out and she was heading to Ohio like you? If she's in Ohio, have some fun with that. She'll give you something to pursue while you're there."

Theo has no shame in telling me about each and every single hookup he's had with random actresses and fans. The list is long, and honestly rather embarrassing. Even with just a day of knowing Hazel, I could never imagine just adding her to a list of conquests and then forgetting she even existed like Theo does with all his women.

"She was heading to Ohio, but she's different. I can tell."

"Man, Killian," his voice actually sounds annoyed. "You're falling hard in just one day?"

"Maybe?" I sit up in my bed. Now that I'm thinking about Hazel, I'm no longer tired. Instead, I feel like I just downed a few shots of straight caffeine.

"You have her contact info?" Theo asks.

"I do."

"Why the hell are you on the phone with me then?! Text her a few times. Or better yet, give her a call. The worst she can do is not pick up. At least you can drift off tonight knowing your name will show up on her phone even if she *has* already moved on since seeing you today. Booty call. Definitely. See if she's up for a—"

"*Goodnight, Theo*," I groan into my phone.

"Night, Killian. Let me know how it goes!"

I hit end on our call and give myself a few moments before swiping through my contact list. And even though my heart is racing and my fingers are bouncing around on my screen, I tightly close my eyes and hit her name.

Hazel, with the bird emoji.

# Hazel

## -before-

L ayovers are stupid. Why am I flying from California, to New York, just so I can get back home to Ohio? Could they not find me a nonstop flight into Cleveland from Los Angeles? I want to be home. I want to be away from this life for a little while. I just want to curl up on my bed with my dog, and pretend to be normal for a few days.

I've been in the JFK airport before, but today I've got a couple hours to kill and my mind is all over the place. My body actually hurts, I feel so messed up right now. He won't leave me alone. Ever since our flight together into California. The texts, the phone calls, the emails. It's only been three days, but it's becoming obsessive. It only got worse after our chemistry read and no matter who I talk to, no one takes me seriously. At this rate, even if I get offered the role, I'm not sure I'm going to take it.

The sad fact of this entire matter ... he is so well known in this industry; he knows he can do whatever he wants with absolutely no consequences, and that's fucking scary.

*I'm* scared.

I walk down to the food court, hoping that some coffee will help my body relax a little. Who am I kidding? I don't need coffee. I need hard liquor.

My phone suddenly vibrates in my hand. I look down and my heart literally falls out from my chest as his name stares back at me.

*I see you.*

His text message simply reads, *I see you.*

I spin in a slow circle, my eyes scanning my surroundings. There he is, standing next to the bathrooms, casually watching me. All the flights in the world and we both end up with JFK as a layover? How is that even possible? He doesn't live on the east coast. Hell, I don't even know where he lives, but I'm starting to think this wasn't a coincidence. I'm starting to think he planned this, somehow knowing where I would be for the next few hours, even if there was absolutely no reason for him to be here, too.

He flew to JFK with one simple task in mind. He flew to JFK to find *me.*

*Think Hazel. Think. You're in a packed airport with a potential stalker. A potential celebrity stalker.*

My mind filters out all noises, my heartbeat is the only thing I can hear, but then a loud honking pierces my thoughts.

"Move to the left please!" someone shouts at me.

I blink hard and see a man, dark skinned, mustache, older than my dad, driving an empty electric cart. I step right in front of it.

"*Please,*" I beg the stunned driver as he slams on his brakes. I know my stalker is watching this. "Please, I need your help."

"What's wrong, ma'am?" he worriedly asks.

"I need you to get me away from this area. There's a man, he's by the bathrooms—don't look! He's famous, and I just need you to get me away from him." The stunned tears start pouring down my face. "Can you help me?"

"Of course I can. Hop in and hang on. We're gonna move

64

quick." I jump into the cart and he starts flooring it in the opposite direction. "What's your name, sweetheart?"

I can feel my phone buzzing in my lap. I know it's him. I know I've pissed him off. I'm scared to death of what he'd do if he ends up finding me again.

"Hazel," I tell the driver. "My name is Hazel."

"Hazel, nice to meet you. You can call me Sammy."

# chapter nine

K illian Lewis," her familiar voice enters my ear after the second ring. "I thought *maybe* I'd get a few text messages, but did I think you'd be calling me already ... tonight? Nope."

"Hazel," I smile into my phone. Just hearing her voice makes my heart jump hurdles. I literally have a track meet going on inside my chest right now. "I hate texting. It's not personal, and I like to be able to hear my recipient's voice, so I know what they're really thinking."

"That's what emojis are for," she bluntly replies.

"You include emojis in all your text messages?" I ask her.

"I don't text," she makes known. "I'm like you. I'll read them, but I'm never going to respond to them. If you're worthy of my time, I want to hear your voice."

"Good to know, Hazel."

"How's Ohio life treating you so far?"

I roll over in my bed, staring out the window at the moon that's shining through. "Can't complain. Though I think my little sister is mildly obsessed with me. She has a shrine devoted to my work, on the walls of her room."

"Yikes," Hazel starts laughing. "You need me to come rescue you?"

The thought of Hazel sneaking in through the basement

door suddenly has me speechless. I swallow hard and answer with, "No, but you *could* spend the day with me tomorrow, if we don't live too far apart—"

"Don't you have family to keep you busy? Blood relatives you should be bonding with? A little sister whose age you should find out?"

"She's eight," I grin. "My dad's a lawyer," I then tell her. "My stepmum has patients she needs to see, and Maisy apparently is a budding gymnast who spends most of her day doing flips at the gym. I was told tonight that my weekdays will be pretty boring."

"We can't let that happen," Hazel slyly announces. "I refuse to let you go back to London with a bad taste of Ohio in your mouth. Do you have a car?"

"Uh, I'm actually not sure." The topic of driving never came up tonight.

She starts laughing again. "I have a car. I *guess* I can squeeze you into my schedule tomorrow. Might have to rearrange a few things ..."

I can't help the pathetic smile that appears on my face. I'm just happy she can't see it.

"What's your address?" she asks.

*Shit.* "I honestly don't know," I admit.

"Well, you'll need to figure that out at some point so we can plan our day accordingly. It's not going to be as exciting as JFK was—"

"I have a feeling any moment spent with you will be exciting and worth my time."

She pauses for a second. "You've known me all of one day, Killian. Don't have high expectations already."

"I don't have any expectations. I just want to see you, outside of airport walls and a stuffy airplane."

I can hear her sigh into her phone. "I can do that. I promised my dog I'd take him for a walk in the morning—"

"You promised your dog?" I start laughing.

"I can't break a promise to my dog!" she exclaims. "He'd never let me forget it. Call me when you're up? Once you memorize your address, little Killian?"

"I can do that."

"Okay," she replies. Then there's silence. "This is where we hang up now, after a long, dramatic, awkward pause."

Am I drooling into my phone? Yes, I am.

"Hazel?"

"Yes, Killian?"

"Thanks for picking up."

"You're welcome. Thanks for being persistent in a non-creepy sort of way."

I SLEEP THROUGH breakfast and by the time I'm fully awake, morning is sneaking into lunch already. I frantically change into some clothes and run upstairs to find a note from my dad on the counter.

*Didn't want to wake you. We should all be back home by four. Keys to the Audi are on the hook if you want to go out. Garage door code is your birthdate. Don't get lost.*

Typical dad note that for some reason makes me smile. I dig through their mail sitting in a neat stack on the table, snapping a picture of their address on my phone. I then grab an apple from the fruit basket and walk out onto their deck. It's raised, as their house is technically three stories high, and from this height I can see things I didn't notice last night from the ground level. There are walking trails everywhere behind their yard, hilly walking trails of which I have no idea where they lead. It almost looks like a painting, and I find myself staring at them questioning if it's just some fake backdrop placed there to make this neighborhood look extra appealing.

I sit down on the railing of the deck and call Hazel at the same time.

"Morning!" she greets me, sounding wide awake and a little out of breath.

"Morning," I respond. "What are you doing?"

"Walking my dog," she reminds me. "I don't think he's been walked in days, and he's pissed and taking it out on me."

"What kind of dog is he?"

"Husky," she responds. "Though I think the breeder might have lied to us and he's actually a hybrid or something. He's currently pulling my arm out of socket. You ready for our epic day of adventures in Ohio?"

"I am—"

"Shit!" she suddenly yells. "Aspen! No!"

I hear loud thumps and the distinct sound of a dog barking like crazy. "Hazel? Is everything okay?"

A few moments pass and staticky noise buzzes in my phone before her voice comes through again. "Killian! He got loose chasing a helpless rabbit! He's going to kill it and bring it back to me, and then I'm going to have to pull a dead, mangled, bleeding bunny from his mouth—I'm going to have to call you back, okay?"

My attention is suddenly diverted to movement on the hilly trails, as I see a dog running my way. At first, it's just a gray blob, but as it gets closer it's unmistakably a Husky, or a werewolf on all fours.

"Hazel, I see a dog. A Husky, running right to my yard?"

"What?!" she cries out.

"I think I see your dog!"

"Food!" she screams. "Get him in your yard with food! Save the poor rabbit!"

I run down the deck steps, waving my apple into his vision

as a rabbit darts past me, taking shelter in the closest bush. This dog is huge, like a bloody wolf, and as soon as the smell of my half-eaten apple hits his nose, he starts running right at me. I toss it to my side and make a frantic dash for his leash as he gets distracted and starts chowing down on the rolling fruit. I firmly loop the leash around my wrist a few times and cautiously sit down in the grass next to him to brace myself in case he takes off running again. I'm fully aware he will probably rip my arm right off my body if that happens. I'm not exactly sure how I feel about that, but I'm also not sure what else to currently do.

I can sense Hazel approaching from the trail, but I'm too afraid to look away from this beastlike dog that's just about done destroying my apple. She's suddenly in my vision and I glance up at her. Her wild hair is in a messy bun, a sports-bra type tank top is firmly clinging to her sweaty skin, showing off her chest in a way I didn't notice yesterday. And she has on these amazing bright pink yoga pants that look like they were actually painted onto her legs. I can't stop staring at how they cling so perfectly to her body.

I point to them. "I knew pink was your color."

She lets out a small laugh and then throws herself down into the grass next to me. She lies back, draping her arm protectively around her dog, who starts licking the sweat off her neck.

"Well, Killian," she breathlessly says. "This just made things a lot more interesting."

# chapter ten

S he keeps looking over at me as we walk along the trail. I keep looking over at her, too. We're both stealing looks at each other, which is making this stroll slightly awkward each time we catch the other one staring. Her dog is oblivious and has slowed down his pace thankfully. He started panting the moment we began sauntering our way back to her house, and I'm afraid if we don't get there soon, I'm going to have to carry him the rest of the way.

"Did you know yesterday that we lived within minutes of each other?" I ask her.

"How could I?" she replies. "You never told me your address. I mean, at JFK, I figured we weren't too far apart location wise. There aren't very many places you can go to once you fly into Cleveland. But connecting neighborhoods by walking trails? Definitely no."

We keep walking. The trails start to flatten out and I see a new neighborhood up ahead through the trees.

"This used to be a golf course," she tells me. "All these trails and such, they were the golf cart paths. And all the green mounds you see, they were part of the course, too. They just look like hills now, but fifteen years ago golfers were everywhere on them."

"What happened to the course?" I find myself asking.

She shrugs her shoulders. "No money? It's a nature preserve now, protected land that will never get built on. But if you stray off the trails, walk along the hills a little, go deep into the woods, you'll find lost golf balls. Kids around here collect them like they're discovering an artifact from colonial days."

I laugh at the thought. A little kid running home with their prized golf ball.

"Killian?" Hazel suddenly says my name. "You feel like we're in some weird rom-com movie?"

I snicker under my breath. I've been in quite a few of those and they usually all start like this. "It *is* the perfect setup." She guides me into a tunnel with a railroad track directly above it. The warm sunlight disappears and the air quickly becomes much cooler. "Well, now I feel like we switched from rom-com to horror. Are there clowns in this tunnel, by any chance?"

Her laughter echoes around us. "You're safe with me." And then I feel her hand take mine in reassurance. This is the second time she's done this now. My heart starts skipping like a little school girl.

A full twenty-four hours since knowing Birdie ... Hazel ... and I'm still one hundred percent certain that I'm madly in love with her. But she made me promise I wouldn't let that happen. I guess I'll keep those thoughts to myself until I convince her it's okay to let me show her what it's like to be loved by Killian Lewis, even if I don't know what that actually looks like myself.

"So, my parents," she says as we walk out of the tunnel, "they own a café in town. When I'm home, I tend to hang out there a lot. Want to go there after I change?" she points to a house that we're quickly approaching. "This one's mine."

Her house is nowhere near as elaborate as my dad's, but it's still pretty decent in size, and it's surrounded by trees. She lives in her own tree house, it seems like, which to me is pretty damn cool.

"That sounds like fun," I say in response to her question. "Do you get recognized a lot there?"

She pushes a few numbers into the code box on the side of her house and the garage door slowly starts to lift. "It's a small town, Killian. People care about each other here. I get recognized every second, but they don't make a scene. You'll see." She opens the door leading into her house and lets Aspen off the leash. "Go, you crazy dog." He barely makes it up the steps and she gives his butt a firm push to help him along.

I follow her in, taking in my surroundings as she grabs two water bottles from the fridge. She tosses me one. Just by glancing around her kitchen, it's so obvious how much her parents love her. So many pictures, so many awards, so many moments of her life I suddenly find myself a part of, by the displays her parents have put together and placed around their house.

"It's a bit much," her voice says from behind me.

I turn around and watch as she releases her hair from its messy bun. It falls below her shoulders in soft waves that once again look perfectly planned. I find myself pulling on the end of a curl that rests on her chest, once again touching her when I have no right to do so. Her eyes watch mine, and I can't help but feel as if she's fully aware I'm drowning in the storm of hers ... in the storm of Hazel.

"Why'd you run away from London, Killian?" she softly asks, her eyes eagerly waiting for my response.

I release her curl. "Why'd you stop acting, Hazel?"

She grins a little. "I can't tell you that," she then seriously responds. "Not yet, at least."

"When can you?" my fingers brush against her wrist, where I know her bird tattoo is.

"When I feel like you're ready to be a part of my before. When you're ready to hear about Birdie."

"When will I be ready? I want to be ready."

"We met twenty-four hours ago. You're not ready."

I step closer to her. "Will you ever let me be?"

Her finger suddenly appears on my lips. I get the feeling she's keeping it there to make sure our lips stay apart. "Yes, I will. Just not now."

I bring her finger away from my mouth and hold it with my hand. "That's okay. I can wait. I've got all summer and nothing but time on my hands."

Her thumb rubs on my wrist bone. "Why did the famous Killian Lewis disappear from London to hide out in Ohio, when every single director would bow to his knees to work with him right now?"

My fingers go back to her hair. I tuck the loose waves behind her ear. "Because he thought he needed a break. Which he does. He thought he was questioning if living his life as an actor was worth it anymore. Which it might not be. He thought his life was spiraling down the wrong path. Which it probably was. But I think I've realized fate had a bigger reason when I decided *this* was the place I needed to hide, and I just didn't know what that was a few days ago."

Her eyes narrow, like she knows what I'm going to say next. "Do you know now?"

I nod my head, my fingers run along the outside of her ear. "It was so I could meet you, Hazel."

# Hazel

## -before-

Sometimes when I'm home, I like to pretend I'm someone else. I imagine I actually live here permanently. I have a life, friends I keep in touch with who went all throughout school with me. We meet up once a month for dinner and talk about our time spent together as kids. We share stories that no one else will know about, laughing at memories that are an eternal part of our friendship.

I have a routine, too. A routine that involves a morning walk with my dog, a late breakfast with my parents at their café, and then an entire day of doing normal things around my town. Everyone knows who I am. We wave to each other as we pass, we help shovel each other's driveways when the snow is too deep, we attend neighborly events together and share recipes for pies and cakes.

I like to think five or six years have passed, because at eighteen, which is what I am right now, I should either still be in high school or maybe in college for my first year. Twenty-four. Twenty-four is that magical number I see in my head when I'm pretending I'm someone else.

It's easy to pretend to be someone I'm not, since I've actually been doing exactly that since I was a little kid. The

Hazel I am at home ... twenty-four, in an amazing relationship with the perfect, loving man, maybe engaged, maybe married. Maybe we live close to my parents. Maybe we have a beautiful farm house and have horses that run along in a pasture, because horses are the only animal I would ever consider owning on a farm. Maybe I'm happy.

Even if it's all just pretend, it's nice to imagine myself as being happy.

When I'm not home in this bubble of my perfect made-up life, I turn into Birdie. What's Birdie like? Sad, lost, alone, even when she's surrounded by people. She's controlled, a mere puppet to everyone in this industry, and she doesn't have the voice to speak up. She's weak, and I actually prefer her this way because if she were strong, she would have run away from this life a long time ago and people would have been pissed. Birdie doesn't like to disappoint. Birdie is a people pleaser.

Maybe the Hazel I imagine at twenty-four is the Birdie that finally had enough. Maybe Birdie was finally able to speak up. Maybe Birdie finally left that cage in which she was trapped. Maybe she's happy now, in love, surrounded by the normal life she always craved, the twenty-four-year-old Hazel I wish I could be.

Or maybe she's dead. That's always an option, too.

Don't get me wrong, I'm not wishing I were dead. I haven't reached that point in my life yet. But as horrible as it is to say, a dead Birdie sounds a lot more free than the trapped one I currently am.

# chapter eleven

O ver there is where the old elementary school used to be," Hazel points out her window at a vacant piece of land as she drives. A deserted playground can be seen in the distance, giving this area an eerie feeling. "I went there as a kid when I wasn't needed on set. They built a new one a few years ago, it's massive. Your little sister probably goes there." She then points right in front of her. "And straight up ahead is what we consider town."

I look forward and see a white gazebo placed intentionally in the middle of this roundabout of a road. On the outside of the circle sits numerous white buildings, local shops and restaurants, a hair salon, a hunting store. Then there's a massive white church, a town hall that *looks* like a church, as well as a small brick post office that seems as if it were plucked down in this exact spot by some sort of passing traveling giant who had it tucked away in his knapsack.

But that's it, there's nothing more.

"*This* is your town?" I ask her, shocked at what little there is here.

She parks her BMW X7 in front of one of the white buildings. "This is it. You should see it when it snows. It's magical and I never realized how small and quaint it was, until I was constantly thrown into big cities. When I'm away, I always feel lost. I always feel like I need to run and hide, and be by myself instead of surrounded by tall buildings and people I don't know or care about. Here, everyone knows everyone, and it's nice to just feel normal, and not so ..."

"Big?"

"Exactly," she smiles. She then places her hand on my shoulder and points to the sign out the window. *Coffee and Stuff.* "I'm very loved here. Very protected. So when you walk in with me ... duck. They might throw pitchforks at you." She then steps out of her BMW and waits for me to follow.

Her parents' café is filled with customers and the door jingles as she opens it. She wasn't lying. The second she steps foot inside her name is being shouted in recognition. It's a little overwhelming, watching a crowd of people greet her, loudly acknowledge who she is, two things I usually run from when I'm in public. But what's even more distressing are the looks that follow when they see she's not alone. Their sudden joy over seeing her is replaced with anger and worry. A few even stand up from their seats as if they're really going to throw pitchforks at me.

"Okay, you guys!" she suddenly shouts, pulling out a chair and standing directly on it. She then points to me. What the *hell* is she doing? She's throwing me to the wolves.

"Hazel—"

"You guys!" she shouts again, ignoring my panicked self. "Quiet down!" Her parents, people I recognize from pictures I just saw in her house moments ago, appear from behind the counter. "This fellow here," she says to the crowd of onlookers. "This is Killian Lewis." I hear a few murmurs from people who recognize my name. "I need you to pay him the same respect and privacy that you pay me, got it?" There's a bunch of yeses and nods from her loyal posse. "He's visiting his family for the summer and they're also members of our community, so you'll be seeing him around, probably with me. If the paparazzi show up in our town, I'm kicking all your asses. You've been warned." She then hops down and grabs my hand, pulling me to the counter. "Mom, Dad, Killian Lewis."

I can't tell if their shocked faces are because of my celebrity status, or because their celebrity daughter brought me into their café with her. *I'm* not even sure how to react right now. Hazel is just ... Hazel. I'm starting to realize just how eccentric she truly is.

Her parents' eyes are looking down at her hand that's still holding my own. They stare at it for an uncomfortably long time, but she doesn't let go even though she's fully aware they're questioning what they're seeing.

Then her mom's face finds mine.

"Pleasure, Killian! Tim!" she turns to her husband and punches him hard in his arm, snapping him out of his curious daze. "Go cook them something!"

Tim rubs at his shoulder. "Nice to meet you, Killian," he grins at me. "I have quite a few questions, but I guess I'll go cook some food first?"

"Nice to meet you both," I quickly say.

"Questions," Hazel grumbles as she waves her hand at her dad, finally releasing mine to do so. "We met in JFK yesterday. Killian's staying the summer here, running from life as an actor. Sounds familiar, right? I haven't scared him off—yet, which is actually really surprising. Yes, you'll probably see him with me when I'm home. I don't think he's crazy, but time will tell. We're both legal adults, so I actually don't have to be telling you guys any of this. But I respect you both and still live with you, so ... here we are."

"Thank you, Hazel," her mom smiles, not at all taken aback from the blunt and honest truth that just flew out of her daughter's mouth. "Killian, you're welcomed in our house anytime you want. And our café, too. Sharon Center is a safe zone for runaway actors. Hazel would know this. You're in good hands."

*What the hell type of twilight zone town have I found myself in?*

Hazel grabs my arm. "Taking my booth!" she calls out to her parents as she pulls me to the far corner of the café. "Oh, and by the way," she quickly turns back to them. "Aspen just about ripped my arm clear off my body chasing a rabbit this morning. He needs obedience school, or at least one of you can take him for a walk every once in a while, when I'm not here." She then sits herself down and stares up at my face. "He's not just *my* dog," she says to me. Then she points to all the customers. "Everyone here will keep your secret. Trust me. Sit," she points to the empty seat.

I do as she says. "Your parents seem ..."

"Protective," she finishes my sentence. "They're protective of me. And probably very surprised to see me walk in with you. Not because of who you are, though. They've met people like us loads of times."

"Then because of ...?"

She lets out a small laugh. "Because of the fact that I've never brought anyone in here with me before."

I can't help the smile that immediately forms on my face.

"Jesus, Killian!" she shakes her head and rolls her eyes. "You can stop smiling now."

I nod my head at the customers behind me. "How long have they all been—"

"Watching out for me? Forever," she says. "But definitely more so over the last year. I think the world knows what state I call home, but I don't think the world knows that this is where I am. I'm guessing everyone pretty much thinks I'm dead or in rehab. Either way I don't care, as long as no one shows up here and tarnishes this town with their accusations and personal questions. I don't owe anyone an explanation, at least not until I'm ready."

*Damn.*

My phone suddenly starts vibrating in my pocket. I pull it out to see it's Blake calling and I know if I don't pick up, he'll just repeatedly call me until I do. "Unfortunately, this is my agent calling," I wave my phone in front of her. "And if I don't pick up, he won't stop."

"Persistent little shit," she smirks.

I nod in agreement. "Blake?" I rudely answer. "It's only been a few days—"

"Killian!" he shouts robustly on the other end, like I can't hear him from where I am. "I've got your mum conferenced in on this call—"

"Killian!" she theatrically calls out my name. It's like nails on a chalkboard. I actually think I cringe. "We miss you! When are you coming back home?"

"I just got here," I roll my eyes.

"You can't be enjoying yourself there," she snidely remarks. "Come on, Killian."

"Actually, I am—"

"You need to be back by next week," Blake cuts me off. "Is that enough time to clear your head?"

"No," I can't help but laugh. "It's not enough time to clear my head. I told you both I was taking the summer off, not just a week."

"If you aren't back in seven days," Blake's furious voice booms into my ear so loudly, I hold the phone away from my head to protect my eardrum from bursting, "the director of your next film is recasting your role! *Recasting* it, Killian," he repeats powerfully.

"Don't do this, Killian!" my mum tearfully yells. "Don't do this to us!"

*Damn.* How is that for dramatic?

Hazel's reassuring hand is suddenly on my arm. She doesn't say anything, but her soft fingers and steady gaze are exactly what I need right now.

I put the phone back to my ear. "Blake, Mum, I am not flying back in seven days," I tell them as I watch for Hazel's reaction at the same time. "I'm also completely fine with my role in my next project being re-cast, because if I remember correctly, I never wanted to be attached to that role to begin with. I'm sure they can find someone else to fill the lead. Someone who actually cares about that film."

I can hear my mum gasp. "Don't say that! Don't let anyone hear you say that!"

"I'm staying here for the summer," I continue. "I'll touch base with you all once a week if you'd like, but please stop calling me. As of right this second, I'm not taking your phone calls anymore no matter how often you blow up my cell or send me desperate texts." I then quickly hit end before they can say anything back, and place my phone in my pocket knowing they'll both try calling me again within a matter of seconds. Surprisingly, I then drop my forehead onto the wooden table in an overwhelming shock at what I just did.

I feel fingers massaging my head. The steady pressure is amazing, and is taking away some of the panic currently floating in rapid waves along my veins. I've never given up a role that I was cast in. I've never gone more than a day or two without talking to my team, making plans, doing interviews and photoshoots, heading to a set. This is all new for me, and as much as I believe I'm going to enjoy the freedom, I'm also suddenly terrified.

I slowly raise my head from the table, the blood rushing back into my face instantly. Hazel leans forward, resting her chin on the tops of her hands. I can't help but tuck her hair behind her ear again, like this simple embrace is something we've already shared hundreds of times before and I can claim it for myself.

"How that'd feel, Killian?" she delicately asks.

I'm not sure if she's talking about my fallout with Blake and my mum, or the way her fingers felt running through my hair. But I hope she understands that as I tug gently on her brown waves that hang over the table and say, "Absolutely wonderful," I'm indeed talking about both.

# Hazel

## -after-

Y ou've come such a long way, Hazel," my counselor says to me from the familiar chair in which she's sat at every appointment I've attended this last year. "I'm so proud of you."

"Thank you," I sincerely say. "I really don't think I would have made any progress if it weren't for you, my parents, and the town I call home. Especially you. I know I wasn't exactly your easiest client."

"Cut yourself some slack, honey. All of your success is because *you* wanted it to happen. You were determined."

"I was," I agree. "I definitely needed a change, and you really opened my eyes to who I actually am. The Hazel I deserve to be. I think I see my life in three different ways now."

"How so?"

"Before, during, and after?" I reply in a questioning way. "*Before* was my life as an actress, up until those awful moments happened. *During* were those two days and the few weeks that followed them, when I hit rock bottom. Then *after*, after started the moment you took me on as your client. It was that very second I started climbing my way back out."

"I think that's a perfect representation," she agrees. "Your *during*, if you were to simply file it away for good and not give it its own title, where would you put it? Before, or after?"

"Before, definitely before. Before is Birdie, after is Hazel. Hazel's not Birdie. Hazel's happy and ready to live; to make new memories, good ones."

"Sometimes you just need to grab onto those good moments, the ones that matter," she tells me. "I have a feeling you're going to be making a lot of new good moments as time goes on."

"I hope so."

"Just remember that it's okay to let people in," she smiles. "I know it's not easy to trust after everything that's gone on, but there *are* good people in this world."

"I know the difference," I nod my head. "The difference between obsession and actual love. I think if the time ever comes, I'll know when it's right."

"You will. You'll feel it right here," she points to her heart. "We haven't discussed your screenplay since you finished it. What's going on with that? Did you meet with those producers in New York already?"

"I did," I smile.

"And ...?"

"And one of them is interested. I have to head back to the city next week for the *big* meeting."

"Hazel!" she cries out. "That's amazing! You should feel extremely proud of yourself!"

"It's huge," I tell her. "And if they want to work with me, it will be a lot of going back and forth between here and New York for a while, but I think I'm ready for it. JFK doesn't scare me anymore like it used to."

"You *are* ready for it," she nods her head. "And when that time comes, when it's out there for the world to see, we'll figure out where to go from there if we have to. But I'm here anytime you need a little maintenance, or just a friendly person to talk to. Just because we won't be seeing each other on a regular basis anymore does not mean I'm not here for you if you need me."

We both stand up and I find myself throwing my arms around her. I haven't hugged anyone like this in over a year. Not even my own parents, but I owe her a lot. She helped pull me out of one of the darkest times of my life. She gave me the hope I needed to see that I can have an after ... that I don't need to live the rest of my life in the shadows of my before.

In the shadows of Birdie.

I give her a tight squeeze and say, "I know you'll always be here for me, Crystal."

# chapter twelve

How was your first full day in Ohio?" Crystal asks me as she places dinner on the table.

I dive into the grilled chicken and salad, famished even though Hazel's parents fed me a rotating lunch of every single item on their café menu just a few hours before. "Can't complain," I declare. "How was work? You still working with crazy people?"

"Killian!" my dad shakes his head. "They're not crazy."

Crystal gently taps me on the back. "They just need a little professional guidance."

"Mom says sometimes it's nice to have a stranger listen to your problems," Maisy announces in between bites. "Hey! I got my back tuck on the low beam today!"

"Your back *tuck*?" Crystal gasps. "I need to come see that."

"Killian," my dad says my name in a swooning tone, pouring some wine in my glass at the same time. "Who dropped you off this evening?"

I take a sip and let the robust flavor sit in my mouth for a minute. "A friend," I finally answer.

"A friend?" Crystal smirks. "Twenty-four hours in Ohio and you already have friends here?"

I glance at my dad and Crystal as they both stare at me, knowing they most likely won't back down. Don't parents just keep prying for more information until you finally crack and give it to them? That's how it works, right?

"If you must know," I say between bites, "it's actually someone I met yesterday in the JFK airport. She lives here, in this town, and we have a lot in common."

Crystal slowly sits, picking up her wine glass but never taking her eyes off of me. "Does this girl have a name?"

"She does, but she sort of doesn't like the attention."

"Tell us, Killian!" Maisy cries out. "Maybe we know her! Everyone knows everyone here!"

"Yeah, Killian," Crystal hesitantly smiles. "Everyone knows everyone here. Except for us. We're too busy all the time for the community to know who we actually are."

"Yeah?" I question, taking another sip from my glass. "I sort of gathered that today, actually. Fine. She's an actress, or she was an actress but I'm not sure she's done much—"

"*Hazel Hemingway*?!" Maisy shouts out. "You're hanging out with *the* Hazel Hemingway?! She's actually letting you go places with her? Be seen with her? You were in her *car*?!" she grabs at her chest. "Why does my heart feel so funny?! Mom, is this what a panic attack feels like?!"

While Maisy has her meltdown, I'm busy watching Crystal, whose face has lost most of its color. "You guys know who she is?" I ask them all, but really I'm asking her.

"We do," my dad replies. "We don't actually know her, but we know *of* her. This town loves her. They protect her like she's an endangered species, almost."

"Crystal?" I question her specifically. "Do you know who she is?"

She regains her composure. "She's a sweetheart, and you're right. I think you two have a lot in common. Will we have the honor of seeing her in the house?"

Maisy gasps loudly. "She might come inside my *house*?!"

I almost choke on my wine at the thought. "Uh, maybe? I

literally just met her, and haven't really given it that much thought. Is it okay—if she comes over here? I mean, we totally skipped my teenage years and at nineteen I've been living on my own—"

"She's welcomed in the house, Killian," my dad starts laughing as he dishes himself some salad.

My head swivels to Crystal. She takes a massive sip from her glass and says, "She's welcomed here anytime. You're both adults, and I would love for you two to feel like you can trust each other with parts of your lives that you might be questioning—"

"Okay, honey," my dad pats her on her shoulder. "Leave counselor Crystal at work if you can."

"No," I shake my head. "She's right. I'm literally questioning every single thing about my life right now, and Hazel just *gets* it. Even though I've only known her since yesterday, she understands everything that's going on in my mind." I forcefully tap the side of my head, and then take a sip of my wine. "I backed out on a movie today that I had a lead role for. The *lead*," I stress. "And then I told Mum pretty much to fuck off—"

"Cover your ears, Maisy," my dad quickly declares. Her hands fly to the side of her head.

"I told Mum and Blake I wasn't going to answer their phone calls anymore," I continue. "And when I hung up on them and almost had a panic attack sitting in a booth at this small-town café that Hazel's parents own, she just sat there and made me feel like everything I had just done was totally okay and the world would keep spinning regardless of whether I ever took another movie role for the rest of my entire life. I could give up acting forever, and she makes me feel like that's completely fine to do."

I look between my dad and Crystal, waiting for one of them to say something in return.

Crystal smiles a genuine smile. "It sounds like you have a lot to think about while you're here—"

"You ever talk to Theo about how you're feeling?" my dad interrupts her as he asks.

Crystal makes a weird grunting noise, like she's choking on her dinner.

"Theo wouldn't understand," I tell him. "When's the last time you've actually seen him? He's not the same ten-year-old you met a few times when he'd fly back to visit in London."

"That's a shame," my dad takes a bite of his chicken. "He was a cute kid."

I laugh at the thought of anyone calling Theo a kid when I know he'll be thirty soon.

"Want to elaborate a little?" Crystal asks me.

"On Theo?" I question. "No. Not really. We just aren't the same person, and although he might pretend to understand what I'm saying, nine times out of ten he's drunk or high when I'm on the phone with him."

"When's the last time you've seen him?" she sadly asks.

"A while ago," I answer her. "Over a year at least. And you know what's really sad? I barely remember my time with him. It was so short, and just ... not memorable, I guess," I shrug my shoulders. "I mean, I still talk to him once a week or so, but our lives are by no means comparable."

Crystal gives me a sympathetic smile and then changes the subject of Theo. "It's absolutely okay to be thinking these thoughts. You've been doing this for a really long time, Killian. And if you ever wanted to stop and try something different, you're allowed to do that. No one has the right to control you."

"Yeah?" I question.

"This is *your* life, Killian," my dad raises his wine glass up at me. "Don't let other people tell you how to live it, including Theo and your mum."

I suddenly feel a tug on my shirt sleeve. I look over to see

Maisy's wide eyes staring up at me. "Can I hang out with you and Hazel?" she quickly asks.

I pat her head. "Sure thing, kid."

After dinner, I find myself helping Crystal clean up the kitchen while my dad and Maisy start a loud match of Monopoly at the table in the gathering room.

"Are they always this loud when they play board games?" I ask her as I rinse off the dishes in the sink.

"Always," she sighs, taking them from my hand and placing them in the dishwasher. "Especially Monopoly. They don't always end happy, either. Monopoly games last days, and usually one of them walks away in tears."

For some reason I find that hilarious. My lawyer father crying over a board game.

"Hey, Crystal?"

"Hmm?"

"Do you know Hazel *more* than her being a part of this town? I got this really weird feeling when we were talking about her."

She turns the water faucet off and slowly turns to face me. "Hazel is very special to me, here," she points to my heart. "I do know her a little bit more than most people in this town do. And I know when she's ready, she'll tell you more about her story. I can't do that. But I trust that she will if you two keep seeing each other."

"When do you think that will happen?"

"You haven't known her that long, Killian. She'll tell you when she feels like she trusts you completely."

"She trusts *you* completely?"

"I like to think I earned her trust somehow, but Killian?"

"Yeah?"

"Hazel is never seen with anyone," she tells me with a small smile. "*Never.* Just her parents. I think she already trusts you. She's just scared to let you in fully. I mean, you two *did* just meet, right?"

Why does that question sound like a loaded question? Like the correct answer isn't the one I think it is. "Yeah. Does she have a reason to be scared?" I carefully ask.

She nods, a sad nod, like she feels bad for confirming what I asked. "She does. Just be the good guy, okay? She needs to see that good guys actually do exist in this world, and I think you could definitely be that person for her. If you decide that you want to be."

# chapter thirteen

Give me two fucking minutes!" Theo shouts loudly in an annoyed voice. "My baby brother is on the goddamn phone! Sorry about that," he says to me. "I'm on set, so you've seriously only got two minutes."

"Just called to check in," I say, sipping my coffee as I stare out the patio door.

Everyone ran out of the house promptly at nine o'clock this morning for their typical summer weekday of work and gymnastics. After a few days of settling in, I'm used to this routine already.

Maisy will run down to my room before she leaves, just to say good morning and to remind me of what time she'll be back. You would think I'd be annoyed with the regular wake up calls from my eight-year-old sister, but I find myself actually loving them. She plops herself down on the edge of my bed, asking what my plans are for the day, then tells me what trick she's hoping to land at the gym. She'll inform me what Crystal is planning for dinner, then taps me lovingly on the head and runs back out of my room all in a matter of three minutes. The house is delightfully quiet the rest of the day.

"Everything good?" Theo questions. "Family? Life? Mom? That girl?"

"Family's good," I tell him. "Dad's so bloody normal,

Crystal is like the perfect mum and wife, and Maisy is surprisingly ... cool."

"Oh yeah?" he actually sounds confused. "I didn't know little kids could be cool."

"Maisy is. But then again, I don't really have another kid to compare her to. You should see her do these tumbling passes; she flies—"

"How's Ohio life?" he interrupts me.

"Boring, but in this interesting way? Like every day I'm finding the lamest shit fascinating?"

Theo laughs. "You buy yourself a tractor yet?"

"Fuck off, Theo," I joke.

"I'm just saying, you might look good wearing a straw hat driving a John Deere down the street. How's Mom?"

"Annoying. Angry. Sends me texts twenty times a day on shit she thinks I'm missing out on. Apparently because I'm taking the summer off, my career is now officially over."

Theo sighs loudly into the phone. "Don't listen to her. She'll back down after a couple weeks. She's just not used to not controlling you."

"How pissed do you think she'd be if I decided to look for a new manager?"

I can almost see the shock on Theo's face in my head. "Honest to god truth?"

"Yes."

"She'll disown you, *but* ... is that necessarily a bad thing? One minute left, Killian. How's the girl?"

I swallow my coffee down hard. "I can't seem to stop thinking about her. Like even if I spend the entire day with her, it's not enough?"

"Shit, Killian. Sounds like Ohio is turning you into a sap. Curious, does *she* drive a tractor?"

"Fuck off, Theo," I laugh. "Go do your acting shit. I'll talk to you later."

94

I put my phone on the counter and open the patio door, stepping outside onto the deck. There's something calming about living in a rural subdivision in Ohio. The air is always still. The noises are simply that of birds chirping and lawnmowers starting, the occasional kid shouting as they ride their bike along the sidewalk. There's no rushing, everything moves in slow motion.

I see her walking on the trail before she's even clearly visible in my eyesight. She does this every morning, her and Aspen, walking along the trail as if there's nothing better in life to do at that moment in time. A walk, a simple walk with your dog. The most important part of your day.

I sit out here every morning now, watching her, knowing exactly what time she usually makes her way over in my direction. I'm not an obsessed fan, not someone she needs to worry about, just a curious bystander who questions how something so simple in life can so easily be overlooked by those who don't realize its importance.

She's never noticed me before, sitting out here, because the trails are a good length away from my deck. I usually give her an hour after I see her before I call her, before we make our plans for the day together.

But today she looks over in my direction, and today ... she spots me.

*Shit. Act normal.*

I give her a small wave, and instead of veering to the left and looping back in the direction of her own house, she heads this way. To me. Where I'm sitting here with my coffee, pretending I wasn't watching her. Pretending I haven't done this every single day since Aspen came running into my yard last week.

She doesn't say anything at first as she strolls through the dewy grass. She's wearing another pair of tight yoga pants. Today they're black with little planned holes trailing up the

95

sides. A snug, gray tank top covers only half of her stomach and I'm quickly aware of the fact Hazel has amazing, chiseled abs and muscular arms.

She lets Aspen vigorously pull her up onto my deck, and then she plops herself down right next to me. Her knees are hitting my knees as she sits there, and the loose strands of her hair, which is pulled into another messy bun, are moving with the gentle morning breeze.

"You know," she suddenly announces, "you can join me every morning instead of just standing there watching me like some weirdo."

*Shit. Be cool, Killian.*

I take the leash from her as Aspen starts to forcefully wander over to my patio door. "To be quite honest with you Hazel, watching you so gracefully walk this beast every morning is the highlight of my day."

She narrows her eyes at me, then takes my coffee out of my hand and helps herself to a few sips. "Maybe I *want* you to join me."

*Slow down heart. You've made your point. No need to scare her away with your loud thumping drum beat.*

"Then I *will* join you."

Her eyes wander nonchalantly to the patio door. "Everyone gone already?"

I nod my head. "Work and gymnastics," I confirm.

She takes one more sip of my coffee and then hands it back to me. She then reaches for the leash. "I'm picking you up in an hour, okay? I want to take you somewhere."

"Yes ma'am," I smile at her demanding announcement.

Then she tugs Aspen back to the steps, walking off the deck and straight to the trails, like this quick moment never even happened.

One hour later, after a cold shower and another cup of coffee, I'm sitting in the front seat of her BMW.

"Wolf Creek?" I point to the name attached to the open gate she just drove through. "Are there actual wolves here?"

She looks over at me and rolls her eyes. "No. Well, actually, just because I've never seen any doesn't mean there might *not* be wolves here, right?"

"Hazel, you're taking us to a nature preserve, to be eaten by wolves?"

"Calm down, city boy," she stresses as she parks in the treelined lot. "The coyotes will get to us way before the wolves ever do."

She first leads me into a brick building, hidden deep in the woods, a learning center for everything you might spot as you stroll along this secret habitat. The walls and ledges are lined with dead animals that have been stuffed and mounted for our benefit. Birds, squirrels, beavers, foxes, deer, bears. I look around in wonder at all the wildlife that has been found in the woods of Ohio. You'd never see this parade walking along the streets of London, that's for sure.

"As a kid," she tells me, "we used to come here for field trips. A park ranger would gather us into one of the rooms in the back and talk about all the different types of animal scat we could come across. Then we'd spend a few hours in the woods trying to find some. Can you imagine?" she looks up at me and grins. "Being excited to find piles of animal poop?"

"Is that what we're doing today?" I laugh at her. "Searching for shit?"

"No. No shit searching today. This way, Killian," she pulls me to a wide, springy door that leads us outside again.

We are deep in the forest now, and the wooden deck we're standing on eventually trails off into a dirt path, guiding us through the trees. And just as Hazel starts leading us along this path, a flock of wild turkeys saunter out right in front of us. There has to be at least ten of them, but my brain won't allow me to count because it's currently wondering if this is real, or just some robotic welcome show that happens every time you walk into Wolf Creek.

"What the hell?!" I finally cry out, as more keep coming out of the woods.

She grabs my arm. "Quiet!" she hushes me. "Don't scare them. We're in *their* home and they're harmless."

We wait a few moments in silence, letting them all cross in front of us, making their obnoxious turkey calls as they completely disappear into the woods. She then takes my hand and starts walking again, like seeing a flock of wild turkeys a few inches from our feet meant absolutely nothing.

"Are we going to discuss what just happened in front of us?" I ask her.

She looks up at me with confusion. "You've never seen wild turkeys in the woods?"

"No, Hazel ... I haven't."

She squeezes my hand. "Welcome to Ohio, Killian."

We go further into the woods when the rustling of leaves and twigs catches our attention. We both stop at the same time, and Hazel immediately starts scanning the tree line for a possible predator.

"I swear to God," my voice quivers, "if a wolf walks out in front of me—"

Her hand is on my face, turning my head so that I'm staring into the trees. "Look carefully," she points beyond the stumps and branches. "Do you see them?"

I do. I see a deer and two fawns, elegantly snacking on the greenery that mixes in with the trees. The fawns are barely old enough to stand up. Their fur is covered with the untouched white spots of a newborn animal.

"You don't have to be scared of the unknown," her voice whispers into my ear. "Usually the nightmare you're imagining ends up being rather beautiful once you take the time to actually look."

She starts walking again, so I follow, and I suddenly see a body of water with a wooden bridge that snakes its way around this still pond. Beaver dams are everywhere, and the bridge allows you to get up and close to each one, so you can practically see every little detail of their hard work.

She stops along the bridge as a beaver swims effortlessly in front of us. "Can you imagine having to rebuild your home constantly?" she asks. "Think about it. One heavy gush of water, one twig that falls out of place, one bad storm and everything falls apart. Yet they just pick up each and every branch and start over. It's like life almost, right? Always starting over when shit falls apart? Because if you don't, what are your other options? A slow, drawn-out death."

She keeps going, stepping off the bridge and now walking us into an open field. The field is beautiful just as it is, since it's filled with colorful wildflowers, but in this field there are also hundreds of birdhouses. They line the greenery and flowers in no particular pattern, and each little opening has the remnants of grass, straw, petals, and little twigs poking out as if to say, fly away ... this place is already occupied.

"This is why I brought you here," she turns to me and says. "This is what I wanted you to see."

"Birdhouses?" I question with a raised eyebrow.

"Not just birdhouses," she smiles, and then she plops down on a bench, patting for me to join her. I sit, waiting to see if she's going to explain herself a bit more. "Just watch for a few minutes," is all she says.

I do. I watch as birds fly in from unknown places, perching themselves along the roofs of these little houses. I watch as they float down, looking inside the open hole, sometimes flying fully in, sometimes flying over to the next one. I watch as they leave their houses, abandoning their little town, only to land on a nearby tree and return moments later. I watch as the baby birds poke their heads out and get fed by their protective parents, whose only mission right now is to fatten up their offspring so that at some point, they can all fly happily together. I listen as the air erupts into a chirping musical melody, everyone joining in as if this were planned out ahead of time just for me and Hazel.

Such a simple, wonderful life.

And although these preplanned houses sit in front of us, these wooden boxes that were built specifically to draw in these birds and keep them here so we can see them on display, the birds are not caged. They're meant to be here; this is their life, their everyday purpose, but they're not trapped.

I get it now. I understand why she wanted me to see this.

I look over at her, her eyes are staring at mine like she knows I just made the connection to the thoughts that float along in her beautiful mind. She rests her head on my shoulder and asks, "Do you understand why I wanted you to see this now?"

"I do," I say, gently placing my arm around her back and pulling her in a little closer. "They're like you, like you were. They're caged ... but they always have the ability to let themselves fly free."

Her hand suddenly finds its way into mine and her fingers weave in between the empty spaces. "They're not just like *me*, Killian," her voice sings out exactly like the birds chirping in front of me. "They're like *us*."

# Hazel

## -during-

I think it's been a few weeks. I honestly don't know. I've lost track of time. I thought the hardest thing ever would be reliving those days in my head. But the hardest thing ever was when my mom and dad picked me up at the airport. The looks on their faces and the fear in their eyes. Not only do I relive those days over and over again, but I relive that moment over and over again. That moment in which they realized something horrible had happened while I was away.

As a child actor, you grow up too fast. You spend your days on sets, in rehearsals, table reads, makeup chairs, fittings ... it's really no place for a child. Yet there I was, a child actor, with either my mom or dad by my side for most of it.

I want to say it was when I was around fifteen that they stopped showing up with me for every little thing. I was mature, wise beyond my years, and didn't need a babysitter to hold my hand through this thing I called life. By the time I was eighteen, I was on my own completely. That was fine, I was ready for it ... my parents had done their job, for the most part.

It was normal for them to drop me off at the airport. It was normal for them to pick me up a few days later ... maybe a week, maybe a few weeks, maybe a month. It all depended on where I had been and what I was doing there. This was our routine. Drop off, pick up, go home, do it all again at another time. What *wasn't* normal? Picking me up at the airport after I had hit rock bottom while I was gone. This was a first for sure, and they were scared.

I hated that I made them scared.

They tried to talk to me. They tried to get me to tell them what, if anything, had happened. I think I might have spoken just a couple words on that drive back home. I was relieved to be in the safety and comfort of my parents' hands, but I was still falling apart and there was nothing they could have said or done to prevent that from happening.

Here I am now, a few weeks later. I'm not falling apart anymore, but I also haven't been able to pick myself back up, either. The days all blend together, rolling into one dust cloud of nothing. I don't shower, I barely eat, I don't answer phone calls, I don't leave my room ... I cease to exist. I actually think I'll just stay like this, trapped in this cage of memories and regrets, until I die.

There's a knock on my door and I lift my head from my pillow to see who it is. It can only be one of two people.

"Hazel," my mom quietly says from the hallway. "We're coming in, okay?"

Great. Both of them.

They walk in and my dad goes straight to my curtains, letting in the daylight for the first time in weeks. How sad is it that I didn't even know if it was the middle of the day, or the middle of the night? They both stand at the side of my bed. They know not to sit next to me. They know not to touch me right now.

"Sweetie," my mom carefully says. "You need to get up, you need to get out of this room. Your agent won't stop calling the home phone—"

"Fire her," I bluntly say. "Fire all of them. I want nothing to do with them anymore."

"Are you being serious?" my dad questions.

"Dead serious," is what I say. "I will not be answering to any of them from here on out."

"Okay," my dad nods. "I'll pass on the message."

"Change my phone number," I quickly add. Now he'll never find me again. My cell has been off this whole time. I can't imagine how many horrible messages are waiting for me. "I need a new phone number. One no one knows, one no one can give out. It's just mine, and only *I* will give it to people. People who deserve to know it."

"Consider it done, Hazel," my dad confirms.

My mom quickly wipes at her eyes. I know she's not crying because I pretty much just told them I quit acting, she's crying because she's worried about me. I push my face into my pillow so that I don't have to watch her.

"Please, Hazel," she says through her tears. "Please let us help you?"

"How?!" I look up at her and shout. "Look at me!" I wave my hands at my disgusting self. "No one's going to want to help this! No one is ever going to want to help me!"

"*We* do, and we need to get you up," my dad declares. "Get some food in you, get you outside—"

"You think food and some fresh air are just going to magically fix everything?!" I cry out at him.

"Why don't you let me help you get in the shower?" my mom asks. She reaches down for my arm and I flinch, scooting further back on my bed.

Her poor face. I hate what I've done to her. My mom and dad are the only people in this world that will always care about me, and I'm literally killing them right now.

"I can get in the shower myself," I simply reply.

She nods her head hard, thinking I just agreed to take one. "I'll sit in there," she offers. "Just in case you need anything?"

She then points to my bathroom door, like I didn't know where it was.

It's funny, but also not funny. When you're in the deep stages of depression and you don't even want to leave your bed, you find that you fight with yourself over very simple tasks. I've actually questioned how long it would take my parents to notice the smell if I just peed in my bed. If I seriously just laid here and peed myself instead of getting up to use the toilet, how much time would I have before they forced me up to inspect the bitter smell that was seeping out from under my covers? An hour? A couple hours? Maybe the whole day? I haven't done it yet but I've questioned it, and I guess that's pretty damn dark.

The last thing I want to do is get up. I'd rather just stay in my bed until I wither away into nothing. But I *do* have to pee, and I'm at that point where I either get up and do it, or piss myself right in front of my worried parents. I don't want to hurt them anymore. I don't want to do anything else that would make them question my sanity, so I push myself up in my bed, feeling lightheaded as the lack of food has suddenly hit me hard.

"Fine," I reply. "I'll take a shower." And then I cautiously make my way into my bathroom, using the wall to support my weak body.

It takes me a few minutes, once I'm in there, to actually get anything accomplished. I have to coax myself with each movement as I'm on the verge of passing out.

Tattered pajama pants ... off.

Panties I should just throw away at this point ... off.

Sit down and pee ... done.

Stand back up and grab the wall ... done.

Pull off the London Underground t-shirt ... freeze.

This shirt. I don't think I've taken it off once since it was washed after I got home. It magically appeared in a perfect pile of clean laundry that I saw stacked on my dresser when I woke up from one of my many slumbers I've had over these last few weeks. I immediately jumped out of my bed, having forgotten about it and actually feeling this flutter in my chest over seeing it again. I slipped it on over my head and it brought instant comfort.

You would think it would have the opposite effect. You would think I would want to burn it, light it on fire and watch it disappear into oblivion, but no. It's the only thing right now that makes me feel remotely better, and I actually hear myself gasp as I peel it off my body for the first time in probably a week or so.

Pull off the London Underground t-shirt ... done.

My mom really does sit in my bathroom with me. She waits until the shower starts running, until she hears me finally get in, and then her soothing voice mixes in with the water falling like acid on my body. It hurts, this pressure of hot water that I've denied my body of because being tainted and dirty was what I figured I deserved.

"Hazel, honey. It's okay if you don't want to talk to us, I understand. But your dad and I, we really think you should talk to *someone*." She rests the side of her head up against my shower door. "Please, Hazel, will you talk to someone for us?"

I place my head against the shower door, too. Just the frosted glass is separating us. "Who?" I quietly ask. "Who am I going to talk to?"

"I'll find you someone," she assures me. "Someone who's not in our town. Someone who doesn't know you. Someone who will help bring you back, I promise. You just need to trust me, okay?"

I've heard those words before. *You just need to trust me.* It takes me back to him. It takes me back to our moment, and with just those simple memories, I can't keep my damaged self hidden any longer.

I slide down against the shower door. My back leans up against it as I bring my knees up to my naked body. The hot water forms a cocoon of steam around me and my breathing becomes heavy through the quick and emotional tears. A panic attack—not my first, sadly—suddenly makes me feel as if I'm indeed dying. I can't breathe in here, but I can't leave this space right now. I can't move. I'm paralyzed with these memories and thoughts.

"Hazel?" my mom's worried voice seems to break through the shower door.

"Don't open the door!" I manage to wail. "*Please* don't! Just let me—just don't open it!"

"I won't, honey. I won't." Her voice carries down as she sits herself on my bathroom floor.

"I just feel so *empty!*" I cry into my knees. "Just gone! I just want to disappear! I'm so sorry, Mom! I'm sorry—"

"I'm right here, okay?" I hear her hand hit the door. "I'm not leaving. Deep breaths, Hazel. In and out. We'll get through this, I promise." Her voice is strong yet worried, confident yet alarmed. "You're still here, you're just trapped right now," she attempts to reassure me. It's not working, but I don't have the strength to tell her to stop talking. "But I promise," she goes on, "we're going to find you. We won't give up until we get Hazel back. I promise."

# chapter fourteen

O kay, so more than two weeks in Ohio now. Spill little bro," Theo's voice carries through my phone. "No tractor, no farm buying. You still seeing that girl?"

I throw on my t-shirt and pick up my phone from the bed, turning Theo off speaker. "I am," I say to him, resting my cell between my shoulder and ear as I put on deodorant. "Actually, Maisy and I are leaving soon to pick her up for some craft fair in the circle."

"Craft fair in the *circle*? God, Killian," he laughs. "Please tell me that's code for some overall wearing cult that smokes weed all day?"

"No cult," I make known. "No weed smoking, either. Just a legit craft fair in the circle."

"I'm having a hard time buying this day of yours," his voice sounds alarmed. "Last time we were together, I watched you down a fifth of Jack and smoke some—"

"That's because I was with *you*," I point out. "I don't need to keep up with *you* here in Ohio. And what the hell did I smoke? I don't remember smoking—"

"Alright, brother. I'll keep that in mind tonight while I'm out in LA drinking away the weekend, and you're singing campfire songs while knitting throw blankets for the local nursing home."

"You're seriously an asshole."

"And you're seriously a country boy now. I'm actually slightly jealous. Let me know when you start making moonshine, okay? So ... when are you going to tell me this girl's name?"

"I'm not," I say for the hundredth time. Hazel has asked that I not tell anyone outside of Sharon Center about her. And although I trust Theo ... or maybe I don't actually trust Theo. Regardless, I don't trust that he wouldn't tell one of his celebrity friends. "There are some things about my life I need to keep private for a while. She's one of them."

"I don't understand that, but I respect that, I guess," he makes known. "How's the sex? I mean, over two weeks now, and you *are* Killian Lewis—"

"Theo. She's different."

"Different than all the other girls you've slept with? That list is impressive—"

"Yes, different than all the other girls I've slept with," I sigh, trying to fight back the memories of random girls that have suddenly taken over my thoughts.

"Are you telling me you haven't slept with her yet?" his voice is shocked as he asks.

"I haven't even kissed her yet."

There are deliberate choking noises through my phone. "I'm sorry," Theo dramatically coughs. "I'm drowning on my Bloody Mary here, on purpose. Kiss her, you stupid idiot! Kiss her today and then tell me about it tonight. I've got to go. My Uber is here and I've got a meeting I can't miss. Call me tonight!" Then the phone goes dead.

"Maisy!" I shout from my open door. "Let's go!"

Sharon Center has an annual Herb and Craft Fair every summer, called the Sharon Showcase, held right around the gazebo in the circle. Hazel said it's required in this town to support the local arts. She easily drops thousands of dollars buying from every single vendor that sets up a booth on this day; not because she needs anything that they're selling, but because she has the money to do it, so she does.

"I seriously can buy anything I want, all day long?" Maisy questions us as we walk our way into the circle from where we parked at the church.

"All day long, Maisy," Hazel smiles down at her. "I have enough cash in my pockets to buy everything here if we wanted. You be the buyer today, okay? Stop at every single booth and choose one thing from each one. I don't care how much it costs. You're the buyer, your brother and I pay."

Maisy looks up at me for approval. "You heard her," I nod my head. "One thing from each vendor."

She starts jumping up and down. "You guys are the coolest!" Then she takes off running to the nearest booth.

"She's adorable," Hazel says to me. "And she absolutely loves that you're her big brother."

I look down at Hazel's free hand and slowly bring it into my own. She lets me do this. She lets me hold her hand whenever I want, and apparently from the shocked looks of everyone who sees this whenever we're in public in this postcard of a town, it's a huge deal.

I'm Killian Lewis. I stupidly have slept with a rather large list of my fans, and all I ever had to do was look at them to seal the deal. Yet here I am, in Sharon Center, Ohio, holding the hand of Hazel the American actress, and I literally feel like every time her fingers simply weave in between mine, my heart forgets how to beat on its own.

"Killian?" my name rolls smoothly from her mouth with a little uncertainty. "I have to go to New York for a couple days this week."

"Yeah?"

*Shit.* She hasn't gone anywhere since we both magically arrived in Cleveland together a couple weeks ago. I've seen her every single day since then, and I feel absolutely gutted at the thought of her leaving me here.

"Yeah. It's only two days. I was thinking of asking you to go with me, but I have back-to-back meetings and you'd just be alone—"

"You were going to ask me to go with you?" I stop walking and turn to face her.

Her cheeks are bright red and she looks embarrassed at me asking this question. "Yes. But it's such a quick trip and I don't have any down time—"

"Next time," I say. "I'll go next time, okay? You don't even have to ask. And add a couple free days to whatever it is you're doing there, so we can walk around like honeymooners exploring the city."

"Can we wear our NYC t-shirts and hats?" she laughs as she asks.

"Of course."

She doesn't say anything for a moment, just watches my face. She does this a lot, stares at me, almost as if she's trying to read my thoughts, or dare me to back down from whatever it is I just said. Every time she does this, I find myself eagerly staring at her lips. Theo might not be right about a lot of things, but he is right about one. I need to kiss her.

"Killian," she finally says my name. "My parents are wondering if you want to come over for dinner tonight."

"Your parents? What about you? Do *you* want me to come over for dinner tonight?"

"I do."

"Then I'll be there. You ever going to tell me what you're doing in New York?"

We start walking again. "Yes," she confidentially says. "Just not right now."

This mysterious side of Hazel has officially started to make my head spin.

110

"I found our first purchase!" Maisy suddenly runs up to us and cries out in excitement. "It's a goat!"

"A goat?!" Hazel stutters.

"Yes! A goat!" Maisy repeats. "There's a family of fair kids here, raising money for their new barn because the old one burned down this winter, and they're selling their baby goats to help pay for a new one!"

"Uh, Maisy," I try not to laugh at her. "I'm not sure if Dad and Crystal—"

"We'll get the goat," Hazel says as she grabs my arm. "Because I know a farmer who would love a baby goat, but then we're going to surprise these kids and their family. Maisy, *you* are going to have the honor of telling them that you're paying for their new barn."

Maisy gasps. "All I have is a twenty-dollar bill."

"Save your money," Hazel says as she squats down in front of her. "Your brother and I will pay for it."

"You and Killian?!" she cries out. "You're going to pay for their entire barn? But that's like, a *ton* of money probably."

"We are, Maisy," Hazel runs her fingers through Maisy's thick dark hair and then stands back up. "Because when you're fortunate enough to have a lot of money, you share it with the people who need it. Show me where they are. I want to meet my new goat."

Maisy grabs her hand and starts pulling her away from me. Hazel looks over her shoulder. "You coming, Killian? We've got a goat to pick out!"

In that one moment, I suddenly realize two very important things in my young, privileged life. First, I will never meet anyone more pure or beautiful than Hazel Hemingway. And second, although she might feel like this town has blessed *her* with the protectiveness that she needs to live her life out of the spotlight, it's actually this town that is blessed to have Hazel call it her home.

111

# Hazel

## -before-

When I was little, I liked to collect things. My parents would find the most random shit shoved under my bed, in my closet, and hidden in bookbags. I was a charismatic collector, they told me. I never gravitated toward the normal things girls my age would want. Dolls, hairbows, books, stickers ... I collected the odd stuff. Rocks, dead flowers, broken crayons. I think one time I even hid a jar of grasshoppers in my room that accidentally opened during the middle of the night.

I never thought anything of it. I never felt weird or different when my little girlfriends would show off their itty-bitty babies, and I would show off my shoebox filled with broken glass. It was just me. It was just who I was.

Thankfully, I outgrew my weirdness and stopped collecting things shortly after I started acting. I was one of those people who was *discovered*. On a family vacation to California, we were at a park eating ice cream when my big moment came. I was six, and bored, so I took my ice cream cone and climbed onto the very top of this tall jungle gym. And when I mean top, I mean the *very* top, like the roof. Everyone around me was panicked at this little girl who had climbed thirty feet up and was teetering on the top of this play structure with her ice cream.

Everyone except my parents, because I had done this before. Numerous times. I was a rather adventurous child.

So, just to paint the picture for you ... a crowd of anxious onlookers, my annoyed parents, and me, standing thirty feet in the air, watching everyone. You would think at six years old I would be petrified by my current state, but I wasn't. I stood up on this wooden beam, held my ice cream cone in the air like a torch, and starting singing.

What I didn't know was that there was a casting director in the crowd of people, and my performance would pique her interest in me. Had I known that, I might have stayed on the ground that day. But instead, I stood there and belted out a song from Annie, and when I was done everyone clapped. I loved the attention and I remember shouting down to my fans, "Do you guys want to see me fly like a bird?!"

This of course made everyone panic again, and I was softly coaxed to the ground by my now embarrassed parents. Once my feet were firmly in the grass, this casting director walked up to us and begged my parents to let me audition for the role of a little girl in a new feature film. Not thinking anything would come from it, they took me the next day.

I booked it. And this casting director officially gifted me my new stage name, Birdie.

Like I said before, had I known what was coming from my performance at that park in California, I probably would have just sat bored, eating my ice cream with my parents.

After that day, I started collecting something new. Starring roles. I booked pretty much everything I auditioned for. I was fearless and I was gifted. I didn't need to collect random shit anymore. I was now collecting characters. I was now collecting respect. I was now collecting fans.

Little did I know this would all lead me to my new

collection. Once again something odd, something normal people don't collect on purpose.

Text messages.

Thousands. I have thousands of text messages from him ever since that plane ride to California. Ever since I managed to sneak away from him in JFK. They just keep coming. A hundred or so a day. Some are innocent, most are not. He has no self-control, no respect for other people, and I'm almost embarrassed for him.

I don't respond anymore. Not since he showed up in the airport. That was when all my internal alarms went off. But that doesn't stop him. He keeps going. And even when I block his phone number, he just gets a new one. He's obsessed with me and all I can do is sit here and stare at my collection of text messages that rapidly grows higher every day.

Had I known at six what I'd be unintentionally collecting at eighteen, I would have absolutely stuck with rocks and dead flowers.

# chapter fifteen

H ow do you like your burgers?" Tim asks me as he throws the meat on the grill.

"Medium is good," I announce. "But honestly, I'm so hungry right now, you can burn the shit out of it and I'll probably still eat it."

He laughs as he closes the grill lid. "Lori likes hers burnt to a crisp," he points to his wife. "And Hazel is somewhere between burnt to crisp and the dust of Satan."

Hazel promptly sits herself down on my lap, something new, which catches me by surprise. I'm not sure where to put my hands. I settle them on her back and feel a sense of relief as she comfortably leans into them.

"If I'm going to eat a cow, I want to make sure it's fully dead," she says.

I can see her parents exchange a quick smile, and then her dad says, "Glad to have someone else finally join me on the medium side, Killian."

"My pleasure. Do you need any help?"

"No!" he quickly announces, holding out his hand as if to stop me from getting up. "No, that's okay. You two just sit ... relax. I've got it covered."

"How was the craft fair today?" Lori asks, handing both of us a beer.

One thing I've noticed between my family and Hazel's is that neither one of them care about the legal drinking age in America. I think because we've both grown up in the spotlight, we've both attended premieres and after-parties, we've both traveled the world, no one cares that at nineteen we actually shouldn't be drinking alcohol here. I think it also helps that neither Hazel nor I plan on getting plastered. We aren't careless drunks. Those days passed for me, at least, probably sometime last spring.

"Hazel bought a goat," I can't help but say with a laugh.

"A *goat?*" Lori raises her eyebrow.

"A goat," I repeat, twisting the top off my beer, then doing the same for Hazel's.

Tim looks around. "Did you bring it home?" he asks her.

"No," Hazel replies. "Loaded it in the back of Killian's Audi and took it to Brent's farm. His kids went nuts. They'll love on it until they leave for college in fifteen years."

"Why'd you buy a goat?" Lori asks.

"Because this family needed a new barn," she tells them. "Their barn burned down this winter and they didn't have insurance, and these small, sad kids were selling their goats to try to pay for a new one. Killian's little sister had us buy one of them ... and then ..." she takes a large sip of her beer and looks away from her parents.

"*Then?*" Tim questions, grinning like he knows exactly what she's going to say next.

"Then Killian and I paid for their new barn," she answers.

"That's my girl," Tim smiles. "Nice job, Killian. That family will never forget what you did. You've changed their lives."

"There's going to be a barn raising party," Hazel tells them. "We're invited. All of us. And I told them you guys would supply the food."

"Just put it on the family calendar, sweetie," Lori bluntly tells her.

Eating dinner with Hazel and her family is the most thrilling event of my two and a half weeks in Ohio thus far. I learn a lot about their family dynamic by just watching the three of them interact with each other. It's strong and comical, but I can almost see the cracks that once tore them apart. And I can tell by just the little snippets that get thrown my way as we eat this meal together, that the cracks, they're Hazel's past.

After dinner, Hazel and her dad go inside to grab supplies to make s'mores. Something so childish, but apparently, it's the staple dessert of a good grilled meal here in Ohio. This leaves me with her mum, gathering the dirty plates to bring into the house.

"Killian," she suddenly says as I stack our plates together. "Sit down for a minute."

Her voice sounds soothing, and not at all like she's about to tell me to stay away from her daughter, so I do as she asks, fully prepared for whatever is coming my way.

"I just wanted to say thank you," she reaches for my hand and says to me.

"Thank you?" I repeat.

She looks toward the house, where Hazel and Tim are clearly visible from one of the kitchen windows. "Do you know in the last year I've barely been able to touch my own daughter? I know there's a lot she hasn't told you, a lot she hasn't even told us, but for almost an entire year, she would flinch at even the smallest of touches."

"I didn't know that," I sadly say, watching Hazel move through the windows. I remember the airplane, when she flinched thinking I was someone else. "Why does she do that?"

She shakes her head. "I know bits and pieces," she tells me. "And she's gotten the help she's needed to overcome whatever it is that happened, but even after we saw her spark start to come back, she still refused to be touched. Tim and I, we thought there was never going to be a time where she felt comfortable enough to let someone touch her again. Someone other than what she allows from us. A hug, a kiss, just simply holding someone's hand. We thought she'd never get to experience those everyday embraces. And then two weeks and some odd days ago ... she walked into our café with you."

I look back at the window and Hazel catches my stare. She smiles, and then walks out of my view. "She lets me touch her," I turn to her mum and say. It sounds weird, this sentence coming from my nineteen-year-old mouth in front of Hazel's mum. But I feel like she's desperate to hear this, and I want her to know. "She's always let me touch her, actually."

"She lets you touch her," she nods her head in agreement. "I've seen it, Tim's seen it. This town has seen it. You're the only person we've ever seen her touch, or let touch her back. I don't know why that is, why she trusts you so quickly and suddenly, but don't stop trying. We were so close to losing her, and you're the one who seems to finally be bringing her back to all of us. Don't give up on her, okay? The Hazel we lost a year ago is absolutely worth bringing back."

AFTER S'MORES, WHICH are surprisingly a messy affair, Tim and Lori head inside, calling it a night and leaving Hazel and me alone by the firepit.

"You survived your first dinner with my parents," she jokingly says as she sits next to me on a wooden bench.

"I love your parents," I honestly tell her.

"Yeah?"

I nod my head. "Absolutely. I'll eat dinner with your family every night from here on out, if you let me."

"Be careful what you wish for." She then stands, throwing another log on the fire as she pokes the ashes with a stick.

Her back is to me, and the fire is illuminating her body as

she folds her arms over her chest. The heat from the flames is enough to bring warmth to this cool summer night, but I can tell she's trying to find comfort in her own body again. She's thinking about something that has her remembering her life before, her life as Birdie, and she doesn't like the way this is making her feel.

I know there's a lot about Hazel I still need to learn. I know I've barely scratched the surface. I know I'm never going to find out what's hidden below the calm character she tries to portray every day, until she trusts me completely. I know over our weeks spent together I've earned some of her trust. But I want her to know that it's okay to let me in further. It's okay to let me peel back some of the layers she refuses to let anyone else touch.

I stand, walking up behind her, carefully bringing my hands to her waist. She doesn't flinch, she's never flinched with me since that moment she thought I was someone else. She actually moves in closer to my body like she's craving this simple embrace.

"Hazel," I whisper into her ear. "Why are you so afraid to be loved?"

The back of her head leans into my face. "Don't fall in love with me, Killian. You promised."

"I'm an actor," I say in return. "We lie a lot."

I can see her lips form a grin. "You don't want to fall in love with me."

"Why not?"

"Because when you learn why I'm afraid to be loved, you won't want to love me anymore. I'm saving you the heartache. I'm only going to break your heart."

"You can't possibly break my heart, Hazel," I honestly say. I spin her around to face me, keeping my hands on her waist. "I think my heart has been broken for a really long time. I actually think you might be the only one who can fix it."

"Don't say that," she whispers, literally begging me with her eyes to stop talking.

I purposely run my fingers along her skin. Simultaneously on both sides of her body. I start at her cheeks, then down to her neck, her chest, her arms, touching her because I know she'll let me. "Why do you let me touch you, when you won't let anyone else?"

Her eyes close as I continue to move my fingers along her bare skin. "Because I trust you," she answers. "I've always trusted you."

"Look at me for a minute, Hazel."

She does. She opens her eyes and stares into mine.

"You trust me?"

Her head slowly nods.

"Then trust me when I say there's absolutely no way you can break my heart when it's already broken. You're healing it, Hazel. By being here with you, I think you're healing my heart that I didn't even know was shattered. You're not going to break it any further."

"I will," she says, her lips actually start to tremble. "I will."

"I'm going to kiss you—"

"You promised—"

I put my finger over her lips. "Tell me it's okay, *please*. Tell me it's okay to kiss you right now."

She shakes her head but I know she's only saying no because she's scared, not because she doesn't want me to.

I keep my finger on her lips. "There's a reason we met. There's a reason I decided Ohio was where I needed to escape to. There's a reason you trust me when you don't trust anyone else. And even if I don't know that reason, *you* do, and I really hope you clue me in on that someday. Most importantly Hazel, there's a reason why I've wanted to kiss you from the moment you looked up at me in that goddamn airport two weeks ago. I feel like we've known each other forever, so let me in, Hazel. *Please*, just let me in. Tell me it's okay to kiss you, because I won't, unless you tell me that I can."

She forcefully tugs my finger away from her lips. "It's okay to kiss me. But you're going to regret this. I know you will."

"Never." And then I place my hand to the back of her head and bring my lips to hers.

# Hazel

## -before-

Hazel? Can I give you a little bit of fatherly advice?"

"Sure, Sammy," I say, grabbing onto my seat as he makes a sharp turn with his electric cart.

"Throw the fucker in jail."

I smile at his bluntness and then frown because it's not that easy. "I've tried talking to the director of this new film I might be in. He pretty much laughed at me because apparently that's just his reputation. His reputation is known, and no one does anything about it."

"He's stalking you, Hazel. You're smart enough to realize that. Are you sure you want to be in a movie with him?"

"This is the biggest movie I've ever been considered for," I make known.

"Yeah, but you said you two would be playing lovers, right? Are you really going to be comfortable around him while filming those type of scenes?"

My mind goes back to the time we flew to California for the chemistry read. How his fingers were on my thigh for most of the flight. The way he touched my cheek and moved my hair, claiming those embraces for himself even though we barely knew each other. Then the way he found me here in

JFK as I was flying home. Not to mention all the text messages that flood my phone every day.

There's no way I could make it through even one take of a romantic scene with him, let alone numerous ones.

"No, Sammy, I won't be." I throw my head into my hands.

Sammy abruptly stops his cart outside of a dark airport bar. "You've got two hours, right?"

"Yes?"

"And you're sure his flight gets in at this terminal?"

"Yes. He texted me. He knows I'm here right now because my stupid agent blabbed it to him. He knows I'm flying to California today. But he's not. He's got shit to do here in New York, thank God."

"Follow me." Sammy guides me into the bar, walking right to the counter where a pierced and tattooed bartender is casually standing.

"Sammy!" the bartender kindly says his name. "That grandbaby arrive yet?"

"Last week. Nine pounds even."

"Congratulations!" he warmly smiles. "You off the clock? Want a celebratory drink?"

"Not for another few hours," he says. He then points to me. "This is Hazel, you recognize her?"

The bartender squints his eyes and brings his lip ring into his teeth. "I think I've seen you on my TV," he then declares. "My partner made me watch that last movie you were in. You made him cry. Shit, you made me cry. Talent, raw talent that you should be proud of."

I give him a small smile, not sure what to say back.

"Hazel here has some time to kill," Sammy goes on. "But she also needs to remain unseen until she boards her plane in a couple hours. She's got a creeper out there, another actor that won't leave her alone ..."

The bartender places the glass he's holding down onto the

counter. "You need to hide for a little bit?" he asks me. "That would be great," I respond. "I've got it from here, Sammy," the bartender says, walking around the counter. "Follow me, Hazel. I know the perfect booth. It's yours anytime you need to hide, all right? You here at JFK a lot?"

"Seems like it," I sigh, as he stops us next to a hidden booth in the back of his bar.

"No creeps allowed in here," he warmly smiles. "You need anything, just holler. My name is Fred."

# chapter sixteen

So you *finally* kissed her?" Theo slyly says in my phone. "I did. A few times, actually," I tell him, rolling over in my bed. "I kissed her and then she had to leave for New York for a couple days."

"What's she doing there?"

"No idea," I sigh. "She won't tell me."

"You making this shit up, Killian?" Theo laughs. "Secret actress, whose name you won't tell me, mysteriously goes to New York and won't tell you what she's doing there ... have you looked her up yet? All her social media accounts or anything like that?"

"I have," I admit. "She doesn't have any social media accounts besides a few made up fan ones, and there's nothing about her online that I didn't already know."

"Well, she obviously has you extremely whipped since you're going on week three of knowing her and you haven't sealed the deal yet."

I roll my eyes. "I don't need to rush and seal the deal, Theo. I actually like her."

"Like her, little bro? Like, *like* like her?"

"Yes. I *like* like her. What are we, ten?"

"You guys!" Theo shouts to whoever is in his house with him, which on a Saturday evening in Los Angeles, is probably half the goddamn city. "My little bro has his first real crush!"

"Jesus Christ, Theo," I groan.

He starts laughing. "I'm joking. Seal the deal, Killian. I'm excited to meet my future sister-in-law—"

"Would you stop already?"

"I can't!" he cries. "This just isn't *you*—"

"How do you know it's not me?" I ask him. "We never see each other anymore. You have no idea how I behave around women who I might actually want a relationship with—"

"That's it right there," Theo interrupts. "A relationship. You've never had a serious relationship."

"Neither have you," I point out.

"And I don't plan on it. Ever. Because I know how to have fun. The same girl every night, is not fun."

Disgust. I feel absolute disgust.

"You're telling me if I actually find myself in a stable relationship with someone of the opposite sex one day, I won't have any fun?" I question him.

"At first," Theo bluntly replies. "Until the sex gets boring."

"You're ridiculous, you know that? Like, I can't even—"

"Bring her to California this summer. Or maybe I'll find my way to Ohio ..."

My phone dings as another call is coming through. I pull it away from my ear and see it's Hazel. "I gotta go, Theo. I'll call you tomorrow," then I switch over to her. "Hazel, are you home?" I immediately ask, feeling this inexplicable sense of relief at the mere thought of us possibly being in the same state again.

"I am," she coolly replies. "I'm actually sitting in my driveway right now. I've been sitting here for a few minutes. Can't seem to get out and go inside."

"Why not?" I push the covers off my body as I suddenly feel like I'm on fire.

"Because it's after eleven, I'm exhausted, my mind is going

in a hundred directions, and I should just crawl into my bed and force myself to go to sleep—"

"But?"

She pauses for a second before blurting out really fast, "But I really just want to drive over to your house and see you."

Is it possible for your heart to actually jump into your throat? Because mine has.

"Come over, Hazel. I want to see you, too."

"Yeah? That's okay?" she nervously asks. "Your family ...?"

"We're adults, Hazel. They're sleeping. And I practically have my own apartment down here ... come over. I'll meet you in the driveway, okay?"

"Okay. I'm on my way."

I jump out of my bed, throwing on a t-shirt to wear with my pajama bottoms that are sagging off my hips. I give the basement a swift look and quickly clean up the random messes I've made these last couple days. I turn on a few lights so I don't bring her back into a dark dungeon, and then I head out through the door. Her BMW is driving up the driveway as I appear from the side of the yard, and I stand barefoot in the grass watching as she steps out.

She looks wrecked. I'm afraid to ask what happened in New York, because something obviously happened while she was there. She's wearing the same damn London Underground t-shirt she had on when I first met her, and I'm flashing back to JFK and how she was acting moments before she pulled that shirt off and crumpled it in her bookbag. I want to hug her, comfort her, hold her, but I'm afraid my quick embrace after not seeing each other for a few days would just frighten her.

She stands in front of her car, not moving, just staring at me and waiting to see which one of us will move first. It's almost as if both of our minds finally catch up to our emotions at the exact same time, and we clear the few steps together. I breathe in her scent as her arms wrap around my back. I run my fingers through her hair as she buries her face into my neck. I bring my lips to the side of her head as her palms press against my shirt.

"I missed you, Hazel," I whisper into her ear.

Her warm voice steams through the fabric on my chest. "I missed you too, Killian."

I give her a minute or so, the two of us just standing in my driveway locked in this embrace. Then I wrap my fingers around hers and lead her around the back of the house and into the basement.

"Damn, you weren't joking," she grins, looking around at the impressive place I get to claim as my own while here.

I close the door behind me, then lean my back up against it and watch as she moves further in. She stops at the bar, immediately pouring herself a shot of vodka and tossing it back. She grimaces as the raw alcohol burns down her throat, but then instantly does one more.

This is not the Hazel I'm used to seeing. I walk over, taking the shot glass away from her because I'm not about to let her get plastered tonight when it's obvious there's a reason she's knocking back vodka right now.

I stand in front of her and the bottle, waiting to see if she's going to attempt to pour some more.

"Going to be hard to leave this behind at the end of the summer," she waves her hand around the basement.

"This space isn't going to be what's hard to leave behind," I truthfully reply. Even in the barely lit walls of the basement, I can see her cheeks turn pink. "London seems like a different life now," I tell her. "All of that seems like it was lived by someone that isn't me anymore."

She doesn't say anything in response. She just looks down at her fingers as she runs them along my arm.

I reach at her hand and pull her body closer into mine.

"I'm not sure what I want to do anymore, Hazel," I say my thoughts out loud.

She places her arms around my neck and I can smell the vodka on her breath as she goes to speak. "You don't have to decide what to do right now. That's the good thing about being in control of your own life. You get to make your own choices when you're ready, not when someone forces you. You only answer to yourself."

Even though I've kissed her a handful of times since our first kiss in her backyard a few nights ago, I'm worried to do it again. Like she'll suddenly turn me away, make me feel like I'm not worthy of her trust anymore. She's let me in a little ... finally, but will she ever find a reason to force me back out? This feeling is new to me. I've never questioned if I'm overstepping boundaries before.

She doesn't wait for me to make the first move this time. She brings her perfect lips onto mine, pushing me back against the bar with the force from her own body. She's never done this. She's never kissed me first, and her lips are moving frantically as our tongues dance around the new familiarity of each other's mouths. I feel her hands under my shirt, trailing my bare skin and making me feel as if my body has suddenly turned into complete liquid. She pulls her lips from mine and lifts my shirt over my head, throwing it to the ground as I stand there in shock over her unexpected actions.

I don't wait to see if this is some sort of test, or if she's suddenly going to shut herself down. I pick her up, her legs wrap around my waist and I press my lips against hers as I carry her over to my bed. I place her down and her shirt comes off. I don't even know who took it off, but it's off, and she's lying back on my pillows with her breasts spilling out from her red lace bra. I start moving my lips around her body, kissing every bare spot of her skin as her fingers tug firmly on my hair.

My hands slide to her back. I unclasp her bra and pull it

from her chest. Her shorts are thrown and my pajama bottoms are being kicked from my feet. One quick slip from either one of us and there will be nothing keeping our bodies from doing what we both obviously want to do right now. My hand wanders to the outside of her thigh and she lifts both her legs to my sides, welcoming me to do whatever the hell I want to her. I eagerly wrap my fingers around her panties.

*Seal the deal.*

Theo. His loud American voice is shouting in my head.

*Seal the deal.*

This is Hazel I'm currently on top of. This is Hazel that has my heart racing. This is Hazel's body I want to so desperately enter—her body that just weeks ago she refused to let anyone touch. Her body that just moments ago felt so defeated she was trying to drown her thoughts away with vodka. And now her breasts are under my lips, her hand under my boxers, and I know we could easily have sex right this very second.

I want to, so badly.

But if I'm the one that she's somehow blessed with the honor of bringing back the old Hazel, she deserves so much more than just a s*eal the deal* type of moment from me.

I reluctantly pull my lips away from her chest, almost growling with my noble act as I do. "Hazel," I say her name. Her eyes instantly open. "Did you really come over here tonight to do *this?*"

Her face looks taken aback and she slowly pulls her hand out from my boxers. "Does *this* need to be something I plan ahead of time?" she quietly asks.

"No." I shake my head. "Of course not."

"You don't want to?" her eyes narrow.

I wave my hand to my boxers that are obviously tented out with my uncomfortable boner. She laughs under her breath. "Hazel, I would gladly have sex with you all fucking night long. I *want* to have sex with you all night long, a marathon, hours

130

of you and me."

"Hours?" she smiles. "Raising the bar?"

"Hours," I promise. "But tonight," I fall onto my forearms so our chests become one, because staring at her breasts is not helping me keep course with my honorable actions. "When you got out of your car ... the sudden need to slam down shots. Hazel, tell me what happened in New York. Tell me why you're always going there. Tell me why you looked so beaten down when you showed up here tonight."

She lets out a sigh, an obviously overwhelmed one, and then she places the most delicate kiss on my lips. Her hand cups my cheek and stays there even after her lips have moved off of mine. She then points to the pile of clothes on the floor. "Think maybe we can put on some clothes before I spill my New York secret to you?"

I give her forehead a firm kiss then climb off my bed, gathering every clothing article from the outside of my bedroom door and the floor of my room. I then toss it all onto her lap and watch with surprise as she reaches for my t-shirt. She doesn't ask, nor does she hesitate at all as she slips it on over her head.

I can't help but smile like a fool as I pull my pajama pants back on, staring at her as she sits on *my* bed, in *my* t-shirt, in *my* room, in just *her* panties. "It looks good on you," I say to her, pointing to my t-shirt.

Her eyes suddenly look sad, but she quickly blinks the emotions away. "You're probably not going to get it back," she honestly says as she makes herself comfortable against my pillows. "I have a feeling I'm going to end up with an entire drawer filled with t-shirts that I steal from you."

"And I'm totally okay with that," I truthfully reply, climbing in next to her.

She turns her body to face mine, her finger suddenly caressing under my eyebrow and down the side of my eye. She gives me another quick kiss before speaking. "Your eyes," she quietly says. "They were the very first thing I noticed about you when we first met."

"Oh yeah?"

She nods her head. "The color of the ocean on the brightest day of the year. Whenever I have a moment where my mind starts to wander to things I don't want to remember, your eyes have this weird way of pulling me back into the present. I absolutely love that."

"I love that, too."

"Killian, there's things I can't tell you yet ... certain things about me—"

"And that's okay," I make known. "I'm okay with not knowing everything right now."

"Good. About a year ago," she continues, "I started writing. It was therapeutic, almost. Writing, watching a story unfold from my thoughts, emptying that part of my mind. And before I knew it, I had written an entire screenplay."

"You did?!" the shock can be heard in my voice.

Her head nods. "A movie. And I had some connections— obviously, we both have those connections in our back pocket at all times. So I went to New York for a bit to meet with a few producers not knowing what, if anything, would happen, and one of them bought it—"

"Hazel!" I cry out. "That's amazing!"

"I know," she acknowledges her accomplishment. "I know it is. I think this is what I want to do. I don't think I ever loved acting. I was just really good at it. I was thrown into it at such a young age, it's all I knew. But screenplay writing, I'm good at it *and* I love doing it. I've been going back and forth to New York to work with the production company to get everything rolling along. They want me to be thoroughly involved, and they're hoping to start filming this fall."

I lean in and kiss her lips. I couldn't be more mesmerized

by this stunning human being lying in front of me right now. "Hazel—I just—you're bloody astonishing. You know that, right? To be nineteen and to have this type of success already in your life. You're incredible."

She gradually rubs her finger under my bottom lip. "Thank you. I really appreciate you saying that. It means a lot coming from you."

"It's the honest truth."

She casually nods her head. "So the casting director ... they're having a hard time finding the right people to cast as the two leads. Everyone else has been cast. And every time we think we've found the right leads, the chemistry read is awful," she groans. "There's absolutely no chemistry between these actors at all, and there needs to be. That's what I was doing these past two days. Sitting there, cringing as I watched actors try to read my lines together."

I slowly move her hair away from her face. I can tell this is really bothering her. "You'll find them," I assure her. "It just might take some time."

"Yeah," she gives me a knowing grin. "It might. But right before I left New York this evening, they actually told me they think the best person for the lead girl is me."

My eyes raise. I wasn't expecting that. "Oh, yeah? Well, that's a compliment, Hazel. You're an amazing actress. I have no doubt you could step into any role and make it your own."

"I don't know, Killian. I don't know if I want to do that again. Be that person again."

I can see the worry in her eyes even just thinking about it. "Maybe you should just give it some thought for a while. Tell them you need some time to make a decision. It's definitely different than blindly going into an audition and being cast for a film. I mean, you wrote the bloody script. Maybe you *are* the best person for the role."

She squeezes herself right up against me. Her head rests

on my chest. I know by her body language that this conversation is abruptly coming to an end. "I *am* the best person for the role," she confidently whispers against my skin. "But I don't want to be. I don't want to act out what I wrote."

"Why not, Hazel?"

She lifts her head. Her stormy gray eyes seek immediate comfort from my ocean blue ones. "Because I've lived it already. This screenplay, Killian, this screenplay is about me. It's everything that happened when I was Birdie ... everything that happened in my before."

# Hazel

## -before-

"Y ou got it, Birdie!" my agent screams into my ear from the speaker of my phone. "You got the role! They *loved* you! The director, the producer, the rest of the cast!"

My heart is in my throat. I got the lead. The biggest role of my life, beating out hundreds of other actresses, even though I purposely tried to bomb the chemistry read. I should feel ecstatic, yet I don't. I feel ... scared.

"This movie is already in talks for Oscar nominations!" my agent goes on. "And the cast list is remaining tight lipped until the movie awards in a couple weeks. They want you all to spend some time together, bonding, acting like a family—"

"I'm not sure if I want to accept it," I nervously whisper into my phone.

Silence, but I know the panic is coming.

Three.

Two.

One.

"Are you fucking insane, Birdie?!" she screams. "There better be a good goddamn reason! Like you're dying! Or pregnant! Or fuck that, get an abortion! You are *not* backing down on this role, you hear me?!"

"But I just—I don't trust—I have this bad feeling—"

"You just nothing!" she cuts me off. "I'm sorry, Birdie, but I'm not letting you ruin your entire career over some ridiculous childish bad feeling—"

"Fine!" I cry out, just to shut her up. "Fine! I'll take it! I'll go bond with the cast. I'll go to the movie awards and announce my role. Just ... fine."

"Good," she sighs in relief. "I'll send you more details later today. Cast is meeting up in California next week since that's where filming will take place. They rented you all a house for a week. Then back to New York for the movie awards, got it?"

"Got it."

"Good! You won't regret this, Birdie. This is huge!" Then the phone goes dead.

The car I'm in starts to slow down, pulling up to the warehouse where my photo shoot is today. "We're just about here, Hazel," my driver announces.

"Thanks, Neil," I smile at him. Neil is my personal driver whenever I'm in the city, which lately has been way too often.

"Hazel, new role I hear?" he looks through the rearview mirror and asks.

I slowly nod my head. "Yeah, a *big* one. One that will probably take my acting career to a whole new level."

The car pulls up to the curb and stops. "You would think with news like that, you wouldn't look like your dog just died."

I frown, thinking about Aspen. "I don't know, Neil," I sigh. "There's just something that feels off about this."

"You recently turned eighteen, right?" he asks in a protective fatherly way.

I nod my head as my phone beeps in my hand.

"Making all the big decisions on your own now," he continues. "Can I give you some advice from someone who has had his fair share of regrets?"

My eyes dart down to my phone, thinking it's my agent with more details. But it's not. It's a text from *him*.

*Heard you got the lead. Might have pulled a few strings to make that happen. I knew you were the one the moment I met you. You can thank me later.*

I look back up at Neil where his eyes meet mine. "Hazel, usually when your gut is screaming at you that something feels off, it's because you need to turn around and run away as fast as you can."

# chapter seventeen

One month.
One month of living in Ohio. One month of not acting. One month of not being controlled by anyone other than myself. And most importantly, one month of knowing Hazel Hemingway.

In this one month of my life, Hazel has taught me more about myself than anyone else ever could. For starters, I've discovered my love of ice cream. In London, and in all the other random cities to which I've traveled, I never thought to stop and find the best local ice cream shop. Hazel has taught me the importance of small things.

Like a good scoop of ice cream.

Sharon Center doesn't have an ice cream shop, but the next town over does. Chill, an Artisan Ice Cream Company, owns not only my heart but my money, as well. The owners also respect our privacy and never make a scene when we arrive, which makes this place even better. One month and one day ago, if you would have told me that Killian Lewis would be drooling over the display case at a local ice cream shop in northeast Ohio, I would have asked you what drugs you were on.

"Look at these flavors today!" I point in disbelief. "Pineapple Habanero? Maple Bacon Cornbread? My mind is blown! How do they come up with these?!"

"You'll have to excuse him," Hazel jokingly says to the person behind the counter. "He's not from around here."

I settle on Apricot Almond, Hazel on Lavender Queen Bee, and we head back outside to her waiting BMW. She turns the air on as we sit in our seats, attempting to keep the ice cream from melting out of our cups as the temperature today is brutal. Ohio is experiencing a heat wave right now, and the London boy in me is not used to dripping sweat by just walking five steps outside.

I turn my back to the window, trying to block the intense ray of sunlight from burning a hole in my arm. "When does your flight leave tomorrow?" I ask Hazel, trying to ignore this sudden feeling of emptiness in the pit of my stomach.

"Early," she groans.

"You sure I can't go with you this time?"

She looks up from her ice cream. "Next time. I promise. I just have a lot of meetings again, and as much as I would love to have you as my arm candy for the next couple days, you would also be a huge distraction."

"Your arm candy?" I ask, licking my spoon.

"Has no one ever told you how attractive you are?" Hazel sweetly smiles.

"Maybe my mum when she's had too much to drink?"

"Have you by any chance talked to her at all lately?" she hesitantly questions.

"Ugh! Way to ruin this delightful day," I grumble between bites. "No. I haven't talked to her."

She brings her hand to my neck, pushing her fingers firmly into my muscles. "You can run from your manager, but your mom might want to know you're alive."

"And if you ever met my mum, you would realize how much of a lie that statement truly is."

Later that day, Hazel and I end up at my house. She's

resting up against the headboard of my bed, her knees pulled up, her iPad propped against them as she scrolls through e-mails. I'm pretending to look through a script that I allowed Blake to send my way. It's a horror movie, a genre I typically don't gravitate toward, but the director specifically asked for me. I promised him I'd at least give it a chance.

Will I take it? It starts filming in New Zealand this fall. Such a beautiful country. The old Killian would have said yes without even questioning it just because of the location.

The new Killian? He's questioning it.

I look up from my stack of papers. Hazel is focused solely on her iPad, a disgruntled look on her face. I've noticed over this last month that when something is pissing her off, her nose turns up and she gets these three creases right above her eyebrows. I've never paid this great of attention to anyone else before, and the fact that I want to break down every little emotion that shows up on Hazel's face makes my stomach drop down to my toes.

My fingers start to trail up her leg. She's wearing jean shorts, tight ones, and with her legs pulled up as she sits here, I would be more than willing to make large bets that her body is ninety percent legs. They're so long, something I don't always notice as she simply stands next to me every day. Her disgruntled appearance flips, and a smile appears on her face as my fingers work their way up to the top of her thigh.

Her eyes dart to mine and she points at me. "A huge distraction," she smirks.

I gently take her iPad out of her lap, placing it on the nightstand with my script. I then pull her over so she straddles my body. I'm not scared to do this anymore. I don't question it anymore. In a month, I've broken down this piece of her, the piece where she didn't want anyone to love her. We haven't had sex yet, and the words "I love you" haven't left our mouths because to me, those words need to be spoken with extreme caution. But I can touch her, *all* of her, without the fear she's going to shut me out or back away.

I run my finger along the strap of the ridiculously tight halter top she's currently wearing. "Sometimes a huge distraction can be beneficial for both parties involved."

"Oh yeah?"

I nod my head, teasingly playing with the buttons that keep her halter top firm on her chest.

She looks over at my closed door, and then to the clock that sits on the bookcase against the wall. "What time does your family usually get home?"

"Four," I answer, already unbuttoning the first button.

"So we have an hour?"

The second button comes undone. "One hour."

She unbuttons the last two, shaking it off her arms so that her exposed breasts are now directly in front of my vision. I'd be lying if I said I'd never had a girl in this exact position on my body before. But as my mouth goes to Hazel's and I flip her over so I can kiss her naked chest, I realize just how little of those encounters with other girls I even remember now. I don't remember the details of their faces, any of them, but I always remember every single detail of Hazel.

Her hair, how the waves and curls have a mind of their own. They act like fingers as they constantly tickle my skin. Her lips, how the bottom one is almost double in width compared to the top one, and they look pink no matter if she's put anything on them or not. Her eyes, with the color of gray that changes throughout the day. Stormy gray one minute, then calm gray with hints of blue the next. How the freckles that line her forehead and nose also line her chest and a few random spots on her back.

I remember all the details of her because she actually matters to me.

My lips are softly moving along her toned stomach, down

to the top of her shorts. I haven't had sex in months, and jerking off in the shower isn't as glorious as it sounds. The old Killian would already have her shorts off, would already be reaching for a condom. This Killian though, I care about what she wants, what she's thinking. Having sex with her isn't just some pointless act to make us both feel good for the brief moment we're together, simply to forget about it the next day. To forget about *her* the next day.

I haven't had sex with her yet, because I want her to *know* she actually matters to me.

Her hands pull at my shoulders, bringing my face back up to hers. Her hips raise into mine as her mouth glides over the skin of my neck. "Killian," her voice floats into my ear. "Do you have a condom?"

I pull off my shirt. "I do," I answer.

"*Please*," she begs, her hips once again slamming into mine as she slips her fingers under my shorts.

*How the hell can I say no to that?*

"You sure?" I question. "Right now?"

"I'm sure. You?"

Not one girl has ever asked me that before. Not one girl has ever questioned if *I* wanted to, or if I was ready. They just assumed because I'm a guy, because I'm Killian Lewis, I'm always ready and willing to have sex. And because I am a guy, because I am Killian Lewis, I've been groomed to believe I should always be ready and willing, even when I'm not.

This one simple question that just drifted from her mouth has made me realize something right this very second. Yes, I'm in love with Hazel Hemingway, but I also *love* Hazel Hemingway. There's a difference between the two. There's a difference between being in love with someone and actually loving them. And if there's anything I know for sure, it's that if you're fortunate enough in this lifetime to find that one person who can claim both spots in your broken heart … never let them go.

"I am," I say to her, pulling a condom out from the nightstand drawer. "No one's ever asked me that before."

Her face looks pained as she says, "No one's really ever asked me that before either." She then crashes her lips back on mine, biting down on my bottom one as her fingers unbutton my shorts.

"Killian!" my name is suddenly screamed from somewhere upstairs. "Is Hazel here with you?! Her car is in the driveway!"

It's Maisy. "Fuck, fuck, fuck!" I cry out, rolling off Hazel and grabbing for our clothes.

"Are you down there?!" Maisy yells from the top of the basement steps.

I throw Hazel her halter top and she quickly starts buttoning it back onto her chest. Maisy's footsteps can be heard flying down the basement stairs. I slip my t-shirt back on, button my shorts that have started sliding off my hips, and toss Hazel her iPad as she fluffs out her hair and props herself back up against my headboard. I see the condom on the bed and make a mad dash to shove it back in the drawer just before my bedroom door flings open.

"She *is* here!" Maisy squeals in delight, standing outside my room in just her gymnastics leotard and sweatpants.

"Hi, Maisy," Hazel smiles.

I tap Maisy on the head. "Hey, kid. I thought we discussed knocking if my bedroom door was closed?"

"We did," she agrees as she walks further in and jumps on the bed next to Hazel. "But I knew if Hazel was here, you wouldn't be naked behind your door, right?"

Hazel stifles a laugh under her breath and literally has to look away from the two of us.

I know my face is bright red. "True, Maisy. True. Hey, you're home early—"

143

"Water leak at the gym. It was spraying everywhere. Will you stay for dinner tonight?" Maisy pulls on Hazel's arm and asks. "You never stay for dinner here. *Please*?"

It took Hazel until that night she flew home from New York to even step foot in my house, and since then she's only been here a few times. The one time she stayed over, she set her alarm and left before my family even woke up that morning. I have a feeling she's avoiding Crystal. I know she has a past with her, and I've made my own conclusion that Crystal was her counselor. But Hazel doesn't *know* that I know this, and the last thing I want is for her to feel uncomfortable around my family.

"Hazel has an early flight tomorrow," I say, giving her the excuse to say no.

"*Please*?" Maisy pleads with puppy dog eyes.

Hazel lets out a small sigh. "Sure, Maisy."

"Yes!" Maisy shouts. "I'm going to go tell Mom!" She jumps off the bed and runs out of my room.

Hazel slowly puts her iPad down on the nightstand and looks up at me. I point to my door. "I should probably start locking that." She grins and pats my bed for me to join her. I sit down, throwing my arm around her shoulder and pulling her in. Her head rests under my chin and I can tell by how quiet she suddenly is that she's wandering around in her memories again. "I have an idea," I say to her.

"Oh yeah?"

"Let's go away. You and me. Just us. Let's go somewhere different before the summer is over. Not Ohio, not New York, definitely not London. Somewhere neither one of us have ever been before."

"Where do you want to go?" she looks up and asks.

I give it some thought. "Somewhere no one knows who we are. Somewhere we won't be bothered. Somewhere we can disappear and just be Killian and Hazel, together."

She wraps her fingers around mine. "Can it be tropical? Can we pretend to be honeymooners? Can we sleep in wooden bungalows along the ocean blue water? And can there be little wild monkeys that run around stealing the fruit floating in our drinks with those tiny paper umbrellas?"

I let out a laugh. "That sounds perfect."

"End of the summer?"

"Okay."

She rests her head under my chin again. "Killian?"

"Yeah, Hazel?"

"I know your stepmom. I know Crystal."

I give her forehead a kiss. "I know you do." She doesn't move or react, but I know she's waiting for an explanation. "I mentioned your name when I first got here, a month ago. I could tell Crystal knew you on a personal level, more than just being the Hazel in this town. She didn't tell me anything, but I kind of gathered that she was your counselor, right?"

"She was," she agrees. "She met me at my lowest, at the very bottom. I owe her a lot. I wouldn't be the person I am right now if it wasn't for her."

"Well, then, Crystal just moved her way up to my favorite family member."

Hazel starts laughing. "This won't be awkward for you? Me, joining your family for dinner? All of us together?"

"No, Hazel. Not at all. Why would it be awkward?"

She wraps her fingers tighter around my own and says, "Because Crystal is the only person who knows everything. Crystal knows everything that happened in the past ... she knows what happened when I was Birdie."

# Hazel

## -during-

It's nice to meet you," my new counselor says as she closes the door behind her. She looks friendly, warm, like I actually might be able to trust her.

"You, too," I say back.

"You can make yourself comfortable," she points to an empty couch.

I haven't actually been in a real counselor's office before. I've been in a few movies where my character desperately needed the guidance of a professional, but up until a few months ago, I never thought of myself as needing mental help.

This room, though, looks exactly like those sets I walked out on as a happy, thriving teenager. A chair, pulled out in front of a desk, where the counselor will sit and ask me how I'm feeling. A couch, where I can lie back on the overly cushioned pillows and tell this lady my deepest, darkest secrets. The box of tissues on the side table, looking untouched even though I know hundreds of shaking fingers have, at one point or another, reached for one.

"Hazel," my name is softly said. I slowly turn to face her. "You can sit," she's still pointing to the couch.

I do, leaning back on the soft fabric, wondering how the

hell I got to this point in my life.

"My name is Crystal," she says, like I didn't already know this. "Do you want to tell me a little bit about yourself? What brings you in here today?"

My parents, my parents begged that I come in here today. My mom made a list of all the counselors in the neighboring towns, all at least twenty miles away from my own house. Crystal's name jumped out at me.

"I sort of hit rock bottom," is what I find myself saying. "Stopped eating. Didn't leave my room. Thought about death a couple times." The truth. The honest, blunt truth.

She doesn't falter, which makes me feel like she already knew all of this. "I'm sorry that you got to a point in your life where you felt like that was the only way out."

That's not what I was expecting her to say. "I'm sorry, too."

"Do you feel the same way right now?"

I shake my head. "No. I'm actually pissed at myself for thinking those thoughts. For allowing myself to feel that low." The truth. The honest, blunt truth.

She smiles. "Regret is actually progress, even if it doesn't feel like it. Are you comfortable telling me some events that have happened over this year? Things that led up to hitting your rock bottom?"

I look past her shoulder, to the bookcase behind her desk. You can gather a lot of personal information from looking at someone's bookcase. Favorite reading material, professional awards, family life. I stand from the couch and walk closer to the shelves, scanning the contents as if they're going to share a secret with me. She has a daughter, a gymnast.

"You have kids?" I turn and ask her.

"Two," she answers, standing to join me. She points to the picture I'm currently looking at. "My daughter is seven, she's extremely gifted in gymnastics. Definitely didn't get that from me." Then she points to another picture, one of a man I can only assume is her husband, with his arms thrown around someone I know.

Someone I recognize.

Someone from my before, from when I was Birdie.

"And I have a stepson," she then says. "He lives in London. You both have something in common; he's an actor, like you."

I pick up the picture with trembling fingers and hold it under my face, remembering everything about him.

Every.

Little.

Thing.

My body suddenly feels warm, like hot liquid was injected right into my veins. "I'm not an actress anymore," I tell her.

"Would you like to tell me why?"

I put the picture on the shelf, going back over to the couch I just decided I'll claim for the next year of my life, or however long it takes me to feel normal again. "I would, Crystal," I finally say. "But that all depends. If I tell you things, are you going to tell other people?"

"Doctor-patient confidentiality," she gives me a reassuring smile. "You're safe to tell me anything you want, and it stays right here, in this room. As long as there are no threats made to harm any individuals, you are safe to talk to me about anything."

"Good. That's good." And then I swiftly blurt out, before I can change my mind, "Am I safe to talk to you about Killian?"

# chapter eighteen

D ad! This is Hazel!" Maisy excitedly introduces her when she and I walk up from the basement an hour or so later. "Isn't she beautiful?"

Hazel starts to blush and smiles down at Maisy. "Nice to meet you," she says to my dad. "I can see where Killian gets his good looks from."

He holds his hand out to her and she cautiously shakes it. "Pleasure is mine. You can call me Steve, and yes Maisy, she is beautiful."

Hazel lets out a nervous laugh just as Crystal enters the kitchen. There's a brief moment where they both exchange a look, a look that a normal bystander wouldn't pick up on, but *I* pick up on it.

Crystal then walks right over to us, not hesitating at all as she places her hand on Hazel's shoulder. "We are so happy that you're joining us for dinner."

"Thanks for having me," Hazel replies. "My parents are at a wedding in Columbus tonight, so I was just going to force Killian to order pizza with me."

"Can *we* order pizza?!" Maisy looks between my dad and Crystal and asks.

"Is pizza good with everyone else?" Crystal questions.

We all nod our heads.

"Pizza it is," she smiles.

"Let's go outside!" Maisy suddenly declares, grabbing Hazel's hand and pulling her to the patio door. "I want to show you and Killian what I can do on the trampoline!"

"Maisy," I shake my head. "Hazel doesn't have to—"

"Of course I'll go watch," Hazel turns to me and says. "You coming, too?"

"I'll be there in a minute." I wait until they're both out of the house before turning to Crystal. "She thinks this is going to be awkward for me. Does this have to be awkward? Why does this feel so awkward?"

"Of course she thinks that," Crystal responds. "Hazel's a sweetheart. Naturally, she'd be concerned for you."

My dad clears his throat. "Someone want to tell me what's going on? Why is dinner with us awkward?"

I wave my hand at Crystal because I'm sure as hell not going to say anything.

"Steve," she sighs. "Hazel was a patient of mine for the last year. She and I had a professional relationship in the past. We no longer do, though, and that's all that matters right now."

"You don't say," he nods his head. I can tell by the look on his face that he honestly didn't know this. "Is there some sort of breach of doctor-patient confidentiality we should be worried about here?"

"Would you stop with the lawyer shit?!" I cry out, slightly shocked over my sudden outburst.

Crystal reassuringly places her hand on my shoulder and says to both of us, "Hazel is *not* my patient anymore. She hasn't been for a few months now. There is nothing legal at this very moment that anyone needs to be worried about, okay? Go out there, Killian," she nods to the door. "This will only be awkward for you if you make this awkward. Don't make it awkward."

My dad walks over to the fridge and grabs two beers. He

then places them in my hands. "She *is* really beautiful," he then smirks. "Don't embarrass us all by being awkward and flustered around her."

I purposely nudge him in the shoulder as I head outside. Hazel's sitting in the grass, directly in front of the trampoline that Maisy's flipping around in. "You don't want to get in there with her?" I ask as I approach. "Don't tell me you don't have gymnast listed under your special talents on your headshot."

The sun hits her eyes as she looks up at me. Blue swirls are now floating along with the gray. "I broke my ankle on a trampoline when I was ten," she tells me, taking one of the beers from my hand. "I tend to stay out of them now."

I sit down next to her and watch as she leans back on her elbows and closes her eyes. The rays from the sun make her porcelain skin glisten, and creates a rainbow of different shades of brown that erupt throughout the strands of her wild hair. Her cleavage leaves little room for my imagination as her halter top dips low on her chest. But I don't need to try to imagine what's under there, as just a little while ago I had a clear visual.

Maisy and my dad are right, she *is* beautiful, every bit of her, which I already knew. I wonder if she's ever been told that before, though? I wonder if any other guy has ever had the luxury of confessing her beauty out loud for her to hear?

"Hazel?"

"Hmm?" she replies, keeping her eyes closed.

"Has anyone ever told you how beautiful you are?"

Her eyes open and she slowly turns her head to face me. She casually takes a sip of her beer before responding. "You don't have to throw compliments my way to get me to sleep with you, you know," she smirks.

I take a sip of my own beer. "And you don't have to use humor to hide the fact that you feel uncomfortable with something I just said."

Her smirk grows wider and her eyes get large. She taps her beer against mine. "Uncovering the layers of Hazel at only one month in? Impressive."

I tug on her hair. "You're beautiful, Hazel. No one has ever told you that before?"

"Are we counting every love interest that's played opposite me in the last five movies I've been in?"

"No, we're not."

"Then no. No one ever has."

"That's a shame," I honestly say.

She sits up fully. "No, it's not. Because now whenever I think about the first person who *really* told me I was beautiful, I'll think about you. You'll always claim that memory now, and you owning that moment of my life is not a shame to me."

*Did time just freeze? Did her words literally cause time to stand still?*

I don't know what to say in response, and she knows this. I lean in, cradling the back of her head as I place my lips on hers. And as they brush so thoughtfully along her tender mouth, I realize I *do* have words for this, three of them actually, and right now is the perfect time to say them.

"Hazel, I—"

"Killian! Can you help me for a minute?!" my dad shouts from the deck.

*Goddammit.*

"I need helping bringing in the new desk from my truck! Meet me in the driveway, okay?!"

Hazel runs her thumb over my lips, almost as if asking me to not let those words leave my thoughts now. The moment has passed and whatever was getting ready to float out of my mouth, won't have the same meaning it would have had three seconds ago. She leans in, giving me a soft kiss, and then rests herself back on her elbows again and closes her eyes.

She's beautiful. Every single bit of her.

I walk to the driveway, where my dad is standing at the back of his truck. "What the hell did you buy another desk for?" I ask him.

"My office," he bluntly replies. "This beauty was on sale and I couldn't pass it up," he points to the box sitting in the bed of his truck.

"Please don't tell me we have to put this together tonight?"

"Nah, maybe tomorrow. Help me get it inside?"

I grab an end and tug it toward me. "*Jesus*," I groan as I lift my side out of the truck. "This is heavy as fuck."

"That's why I enlisted the help of my rugged son," my dad grumbles as we carry it into the garage. "So ... Hazel—"

"We really going to talk about Hazel as we're carrying five hundred pounds of wood shoved in a box into the house?"

"Yes, because you can't walk away from me right now."

"I could, but I'd break all the bones in your feet," I growl, walking backward up the three garage steps.

"I'll sue you," he jokes. "You serious about her? I mean, extremely handsome actor, visiting just for the summer—"

"I think I love her."

My dad stops moving, resting his back against the wall of the mudroom. "You think you love her?"

"Can we get this in your goddamn office please?!"

He shuffles with me down the hall. "Love is a very strong word. One that shouldn't be said without some deep thought."

"No shit," I agree.

"And you think—"

"I do," I grimace, my arms getting ready to collapse. "I love her. And this isn't crazy actor Killian *thinking* he loves her because this is what happens in all the movies he's been in since he was thirteen. Real life here, and I love her. I know I do. I've never felt like this before."

He grins, or he could just be suffering from a ruptured blood clot. "Well, okay then. What are you going to do at the end of the summer?"

I push open the French doors of his office with my back. "No fucking idea. I don't want to think about it."

He slowly lowers his end of the box, allowing me to rest my portion up against the wall. He sits next to it, wiping the sweat off his forehead with his arm. "That son of a bitch was heavy. Sit, Killian."

I throw myself down against a bookshelf.

"You don't have to go back to London, you know," he points out.

"Easy for you to say. You don't have to answer to Mum."

He laughs uncomfortably. "No, I don't. I stopped answering to her a while ago."

"She'd kill me," I confide in him. "I honestly think she'd come to Ohio just to murder me, and then fly back to London like nothing happened."

"Sadly, I can see that. But I'm a lawyer, we could slap her with a restraining order."

I let out a grunt. "You think *that* would stop her?"

He raises his eyes at me. "No. But what's really keeping you from just calling it quits? It's not just your mum."

I shake my head. "It's her, Theo—"

"Theo?"

"Without acting, Theo and I have nothing in common," I tell him. "It's just sort of been our thing all these years. Without it, I'd probably lose him forever—"

"Killian," he interrupts me. "If *you* making a choice for your own life cuts the ties between you and brother forever, what does that say about Theo?"

I narrow my eyes at him. "Crystal is rubbing off on you."

His hands raise. "All I'm saying is to stop putting other peoples' opinions and thoughts first. If Theo and your mum abandon you, you've always got us ... and Hazel."

I know he's right. But I won't tell him that. "Why'd you

leave me with her? Why'd you leave me with Mum when you left London? When you got the job here?"

His face looks surprised and wounded all at once. He wipes at his forehead again. "Because you didn't want to go with me. We gave you the choice—"

"I was seven! Younger than Maisy!" I kick the box with my foot. "Why the fuck did you leave that decision up to a seven-year-old?! Do you realize how different my life would have been if you had just taken me with you?!"

My dad places his hand on my shoulder. "I'm sorry."

"You're a goddamn bloody lawyer! You should have fought for me! You didn't even try!"

"I should have," he immediately agrees. "I absolutely should have."

I wasn't expecting him to admit he was wrong so quickly. I was thinking we'd have a few more rounds of fuming conversation to get through before I heard him say that.

"Yeah, well, it's too late now," I kick the box again, instantly regretting it as my foot is now throbbing in pain. "I don't need you anymore."

He grabs my shoulders, firmly pushing his hands onto them. "It might be too late for us, but it's not too late for you. I should have fought for you, Killian. You should have seen me fight for you. I'm sorry I didn't. But learn from the mistake *I* made. Fight for her, okay? Fight for the life you want, not for the life you *think* you have to live. If that means you have to change your entire future to fight for her, then do it. Fuck everyone else and what they think."

He then stands and walks away. I give myself a second, sitting there in his office, staring at the life he's created here. A life away from me, away from the spotlight. A life of family dinners and nightly board games. A life I was never a part of except for brief moments here and there.

I don't want a life of brief moments anymore.

I head down to the basement, slamming down a shot of vodka as I rip my sweaty shirt off. I throw on another one, pacing the floor of my bedroom, questioning every single second of my future. A future that has always been so planned out. A future in which I now know I don't want stardom or fame ... I just want her. Hazel. But am I allowed to think like that? Am I allowed to believe that after knowing her for just a month, I'm ready to change my entire life to be with her?

I open the basement door, walking outside. She's no longer lying in the grass where I had left her. I hear her voice from the side of the house, and I pause. She's talking to Crystal. I can see her reflection in the window of my bedroom. She's sitting at the patio table, her head resting in her arms. I should probably turn around, walk the other way and give them some privacy.

But I can't.

"You haven't told him anything?" I hear Crystal ask.

Hazel's head raises. "Just a little, but not what he needs to hear. I don't want to hurt him."

"Not telling him is what's going to hurt him. Especially if this is serious, you two ... the two of you together. What are you hoping for with this?"

"I don't know!" she cries out. "I mean I *do* know, but it can't, right? It won't, not after he finds out. Did you know the last time I saw you, that last appointment? Did you know he was coming here for the summer?"

Crystal shakes her head. "I didn't know until a few days before he arrived. It was all very quick and sudden."

"Did you know all this time we lived in the same town?!"

"I did," she answers. "I realized after our first appointment and I had a feeling at some point we'd run into each other—"

"You should have told me," Hazel quietly says in return. "It wouldn't have changed anything, but you should have told me. It would have been nice to of known this before ... before something like *this* happened."

"Yes, but I typically don't give my personal address out to my clients—"

"I'm not your typical client. I never have been."

There's a moment of uncomfortable silence. "You're right," Crystal finally says. "You aren't my typical client and I should have given you a heads up. But it's irrelevant in the present. What's important now is that you know it's okay to let yourself fall in love. It's okay to *be* loved. It's obvious that there's something special going on between you two and that's okay, no matter what the past circumstances are. Why don't you come to my office—"

"No!" Hazel shouts out. "We definitely have a conflict of interest now."

"Then how about I set you up with someone else?" Crystal calmly suggests. "Someone I trust? Someone you can talk to if you think you need to again."

"Maybe," Hazel whispers.

"It's okay to want something more, honey. Something bigger. If you and Killian—"

"But I have to tell him," she quietly says. "I have to tell him everything, and it's going to destroy him. How do I do that? How do I destroy him like that?"

"Killian has to hear it, Hazel. And then you have to let him make that decision on what he does from there. You made your decision. Now it's his turn."

"I know," she sighs. "I'm just afraid."

"What are you afraid of?"

She starts crying, like actual tears rolling down her face. "I'm afraid that once I tell him everything, once he decides what he wants to do, he's not going to choose me. I'm afraid I'm going to lose him."

# Hazel

## -during-

I've shocked her. That's extremely apparent. I bet she never thought when she showed up for work today that she would find out all this.

She's not sure what to say or what to do, so I just sit there and wait for her to speak. She's the only person in the world who knows my story now. I haven't even told my parents, because how can I look them in the eyes and tell them what I just told her? But I knew. I knew the moment I saw his picture on her bookshelf that she was the one who needed to hear what happened to me.

She gets up from her chair and moves over to where I am on the couch. She reaches for a tissue from the box next to me on the side table, and dabs at her eyes before sitting down. I don't scoot over. I don't flinch. I trust her. Even though I don't even know her.

"Hazel," she calmly says my name. "Would you like to report this all to the police? I can go with you. I can sit with you as you tell them everything you just told me. Would you like to press charges?"

"I would not," I simply answer. I've already thought long and hard about that option. "Doing that would only bring more attention onto myself, and him ... and I can't handle that right now. Plus, no one would really believe me."

"Okay," she nods her head, though I can tell she doesn't agree with my choice. "Okay," she says again. "Honey, I don't think I'm the right counselor for you—"

"You are," I confirm.

"No, I'm not. We have a conflict of interest—"

"No, we don't," I remind her. "How often do you see him? If *ever*?"

I can tell she's thinking this over in her head. She knows I'm right.

"There's a reason why I'm here today," I say. "Why I chose your name out of all the other counselors available." I then point to his picture on the bookcase. "I think he's the reason. It's fate almost."

I watch her eyes as she turns to look at him. She then spins back to me. "You're going to feel comfortable with me as your counselor? With everything that happened?"

"I am comfortable. And to be completely honest, Crystal, I don't plan on needing you for the rest of my life. I'm at my very lowest right now, rock bottom, but I know someday I'll be back to the real Hazel and I won't need to come here anymore. But you are the only person in the last few weeks that I've said more than five words to, except for my breakdown with my parents yesterday. I wasn't planning on that happening at all—talking to you—I was just going to sit here ... until I saw his picture over there." I suddenly have memories of him, and I can't help the tears that fill my tired eyes.

She turns back to look at his picture again.

"Please," I beg her. "Please don't turn me away for a conflict of interest that doesn't even really exist. Just give me one year. I *need* you to help me bring back Hazel. I trust you already, and I know it's because of him."

The room is suddenly so quiet, I can hear myself

breathing. I can hear her breathing, too. I can hear the tick of a clock. I can hear the hum from her computer. I can hear a sound machine of ocean waves going off in the hallway behind the closed door. And then I hear her take a deep breath. She stands and I'm assuming this is it, that she's going to ask me to leave, direct me to another counselor's office who I won't trust, who won't be able to bring me back like she can.

But then she takes a firm seat in her waiting chair and sits straight up. Her eyes look into mine and they're calm, reassuring, and I know she'll get it done. She'll find Hazel and bring her back.

My soul might actually smile as her confident voice fills the air. "Let's get to work, Hazel."

# chapter nineteen

Hazel's quiet the rest of the night. Quiet, withdrawn, not how she normally is with me. And because my mind is desperately trying to process everything I overheard her say to Crystal, *I'm* quiet the rest of the night. Quiet, withdrawn, not how I normally am with her. We're both our own ticking time bomb, with no simple way to be extinguished.

I walk her to her BMW after dinner, feeling exactly how I felt in the Cleveland airport when I thought I'd never see her again. But what am I supposed to say? That I heard the conversation she had with Crystal? That I'm fucking confused as hell? That I want her to stay with me tonight so we can figure this shit out together?

Yes, that's exactly what I should say, but I stupidly don't say any of that.

"Do you want me to take you to the airport in the morning?" is what I end up asking.

She shakes her head. "It's so early, Killian. You don't have to do that."

I *want* to do that. I *want* to be the one that takes her to the airport before the sun is even up. I *want* to be the one she kisses goodbye as we stand under the departure sign outside, wishing she didn't have to leave.

"Fine," is what I end up saying. "I guess I'll see you when you get home?"

She sadly nods her head, leaning in and giving me a small kiss before walking around to her BMW. I watch her get in. I watch her avoid my stare. I watch her start the engine. And then I watch her slowly pull down my driveway.

I hear footsteps and suddenly feel a hand on my shoulder. "Killian," my dad's voice bellows out from next to me. "What the fuck are you doing standing here?" I turn my head to look at him, shocked over his blunt words. He nods to the trails and raises his eyes, "*Fight* for her, you bloody idiot."

He's right. I need to fight for her. She needs to *see* me fight for her. But I'm not going to stand there and tell him that. I'm just going to hastily take his advice and ignore the fact that he's the one who gave it to me.

I take off running through the yard, past the patio table, past the trampoline, and straight to the trails. If I run fast enough, I can make it to her house before she even does. I move quickly, my feet pounding on the pavement as I run up and down the hills, knowing exactly where to go thanks to my daily walks with Hazel and Aspen. I veer to the right, out of breath as I approach the tunnel of terror. My eyes shut tight and the loud thumps of my determined footsteps echo and sound like a herd of elephants as I make my way through the darkness. My eyes open, and the soft evening sunlight hits me in my face as it streams in through the branches of the trees. Almost there, just another minute or so.

I can see her pulling up the driveway at the same time I approach it, out of breath and feeling as if I'll never be able to breathe normally again.

"Killian?!" she exclaims, her car door slams behind her.

I can't look up at her. I'm too busy trying to catch my breath and staring down at my feet gasping for air seems to be the only thing helping.

"What are you doing—did you *run* here?!"

"Yes!" I cry out. "And I swear to God I'm having a heart attack!" I gasp. "I'm so fucking out of shape—"

"Why?" she asks. I can sense her moving closer. "Why did you run here? You could have just called—"

"*Why*?!" I shout out, finally looking up at her. "Because I wanted to tell you this to your face!"

"Tell me what?"

"That I love you!" I wheeze, clutching the cramp in my side. "I love you, Hazel! I'm in love with you and I don't care that there's shit you're not telling me!" I wave my hands in the air for dramatic measure. "I know you're scared for some reason, but you shouldn't be scared that I'll love you any less once I know what it is you're keeping from me! Because I won't—there's no way that's possible!"

"You don't know that," she sadly declares.

I move a few steps closer to her, finally feeling my lungs start to inflate again. "No. You're right. I don't know that. But do you know what else I don't know? What the weather is going to be like in ten days. What will happen at the end of the summer. If Maisy will ever become an Olympic gymnast. If I'll ever buy a goddamn tractor and raise my own goats, or if a bloody wolf will walk out of those woods right this second and rip us both to pieces. But I *do* know two things for sure." I hold my fingers out to her. "One, my life is better with you in it. I have an actual purpose for waking up every morning now. *You* are my purpose and I know there's a reason why we met. And two, that I love you. I *know* that I love you. It's the only thing in my life I have ever been one hundred percent certain about. And I don't want you to think you have to tell me everything tonight, because I don't want to hear it tonight. I can wait until you're ready. Tonight, I just wanted you to know that I love you. And I wanted to say that to your face, before you went to bed, before you fly off to New York in the morning, so I ran over here—"

Her body slams into mine, almost knocking my weakened self to the ground. Her lips press hard against my lips, forcing my words to an abrupt stop. Her hands wrap around my neck and she makes this beautiful sound of contentment as she presses herself harder against me. I sigh into her mouth, relief flooding every inch of my exhausted body as she melts into my arms. This feeling right here is far better than scoring some movie role that only gives you satisfaction for a brief moment of time in life. This feeling right here is *everything*.

I slowly pull my lips away, resting my forehead on hers. "I love you, Hazel. I absolutely know that for certain. Thank you for letting me love you."

"I love you, Killian," she finally says, her voice is confident, yet anxious at the same time. "I know that for sure."

If my heart had the ability to burst right out of my chest and flap away into the humid summer night, now would be the time that would happen.

"Thank you for showing me what love should look like," she then says.

"My pleasure," I give her a single kiss on her soft lips. Mission accomplished. I can go home and pass out now. "I'll head home," I then say, pointing at the trail through the trees. "Let you get to sleep—"

She throws her head back and laughs, then grabs me by my t-shirt and starts pulling me into her garage. "You think I'm letting you go home, after that?"

Thank God. I would have never made it. "I wasn't too sure what would happen," I tell her. "I was just hoping you'd actually see me and not run me over."

Aspen greets us as we walk into the kitchen, searching my hands with his nose as if I brought him home some dinner.

"He wants a treat," Hazel says, pointing to a cookie jar on the counter filled with dog biscuits. I open the lid, tossing one right into his waiting mouth. "You know," she says, sitting down on the barstool at the counter, "he hates most people."

"Aspen? He hates people?"

She nods her head. "Everyone except his family, and you. Haven't you noticed me warning people to keep their distance on our walks?"

"I just thought that's because he'd jump on them and slobber all over their face."

"Eat their face is more like it," she grins.

Aspen rubs his wet nose on my leg and I give his head a scratch. "Sure did fool me."

"Killian?" Hazel's voice is unsure as she says my name. I abandon Aspen and walk over to her. "When I'm ready, will you read my screenplay?" she looks up at me and asks.

*Yes.* Fucking *yes.* "Absolutely, Hazel."

She gives me a small smile. "I think I need to make a couple changes—things have changed. I'm going to bring it up while I'm there tomorrow, see what they all think."

"Something about your *before* has changed?" I ask, curious as to what she means.

"No ... but I think there might be a better ending. I think I can write a better ending."

I find myself stifling a cough as my heart flutters erratically in my chest. "You can *write* a better ending?"

"I can *have* a better ending," she corrects herself. She then stands up and places her arms around my back. Her face hovers right in front of mine so close, I can see myself in her eyes. "Will you stay here with me tonight? All night?"

"Hazel, I'll stay with you all night, every night. You don't have to ask."

She leans in, her lips softly brushing on mine before she pulls me toward the staircase and declares, "You might just be my better ending, Killian."

165

# chapter twenty

Hazel's room, a fortress of her life that I've had no part of. Its light blue walls, framed photos of people I don't know, a bookcase filled with books I never saw her read, a bed with blankets I've never slept on. A bed on which I'm now lying her back as my mouth moves along her neck.

"Dresser," she mumbles, pointing to it across the room. "Top drawer. There's condoms."

"Why does it piss me off that you have condoms in your dresser drawer?" I groan as I pull my shirt off my body.

"Are we really going to sit here and discuss our past sexual history, right *now*?"

"Hell no," I reply, quickly walking over to her dresser and grabbing one from a pile mixed in with her bras. "In fact," I say as I walk back over, "I don't want to hear about it at all."

"Noted," she responds, pulling at my arm to bring me back down on top of her.

She takes the condom from my hand, placing it on the nightstand next to her bed as if telling me we aren't just jumping right to that. I'm totally fine with this. I could spend the entire night just exploring every inch of her body with my lips, but that's not what Killian Lewis usually does. Killian usually just *seals the deal* and then falls asleep and forgets about who he's even with by the time morning rolls around.

But this is Hazel.

*Make it count, Killian. Make it matter.*

My fingers start to unbutton her halter top for the second time today, blindly as my mouth is currently moving like ocean waves against hers. When I get to the last button, it opens, and I bring my eager lips right to her breasts. She lies there, her fingers pulling firmly on my hair as my mouth possessively claims each one.

Her body quivers under my tongue, like she's forcing herself to not release whatever it is that's building up inside of her right now. I question why I never noticed this in other girls before. How their bodies reacted to my touch and embrace. Or is it simply that I just didn't care?

She suddenly flips us and now I'm lying under her, her half naked body moving in the perfect rhythm against my own. I didn't think I could possibly get any more aroused than I am right now, but then her mouth is back on mine with her hips still moving and I realize that yes, I can.

I feel her fingers on my shorts, unbuttoning them at the same time her body rocks against me. She pushes them down and my legs kick them firmly off my feet and to the end of the bed. I work on her shorts next, guiding them past her hips, off her legs, and to the floor all while our lips are still joined perfectly together as one.

Boxers, panties, that's all that's left between the two of us now. Yet we still wait, not rushing straight into the main event, and instead treating each other as if we're dangerous volcanos getting ready to erupt as we explore each other's bodies. We push each other, her hand moving on me, my fingers moving on her ... it's like a game almost, a game in which we both excel. And then suddenly, I can tell by the way her face changes as she's moving against me, feeling me firmly through the little fabric that's left, she's right there, right at the cusp of letting go.

I flip her off me, pulling her panties down as she yanks my boxers to my feet. And now here we are, both of us more than ready to find out what our bodies feel like together. She grabs the condom and rips the wrapper open with her teeth, and then *she* slips it on me, quite possibly the sexiest fucking thing that's ever been done to my body before.

"*Now*, Killian," she begs me, her fingernails digging roughly into my shoulders.

I lower my head down to hers because I'm desperate to hear her enjoying this, and then I guide myself in, listening to her gasp into my ear as I fully enter her.

"*Fuck*, Killian," her eyes roll into the back of her head while I move my hips slowly into hers. "We should have done this a long time ago."

"Does it feel good?" I start to move faster, raising one arm in order to grab the headboard to brace myself. I selfishly need her to tell me that I'm making her feel good.

She groans with my movements. "Yes, Killian!" she then screams my name. "God, it feels good ..."

I move even faster, knowing every amazing sensation she's keeping locked up inside of her body is about to finally reach the surface.

"Killian!" my name is screamed again. She arches into me and she claws at my back. "I'm so close," she suddenly whines into my ear.

I bring my lips to hers. The passion from our mouths moving in the same pace as our rocking bodies literally makes the air feel thick around me.

"I'll get you there," I confidentially declare into her ear. I thrust myself harder and her fingers suddenly pull at the hair on the top of my head. Her moans echo around me and her body becomes rigid for just a split second, before collapsing completely. My name mixes repeatedly with the sounds of pure ecstasy coming from her mouth, as she rides this intense wave of pleasure I've just given her.

My turn.

Both hands hit the headboard and I push against them. Her high becomes even more apparent as I am now so close to my own. She's still riding it out, still withering in bliss underneath me as I squeeze the wood of her bed and roll my hips one more time, allowing her to hear from *me* just how incredible she has made me feel. And then I join her in this perfect state of paradise that I can honestly say I've never experienced before, knowing that tomorrow, I'm going to remember *every* single second of what we just did together tonight.

MORNING COMES TOO soon. The sound of Hazel's phone alarm going off is what wakes me. I reach for it on the nightstand, leaning over a sleeping Hazel and brushing away the numerous condom wrappers we went through last night. My fingers hit her phone hard, forcing the loud buzzing to an abrupt stop. Hazel hasn't moved. Apparently, she sleeps through alarms. Good to know.

I lie back down, gently placing my arm around her warm, naked waist. "Hazel," I whisper into her ear. I kiss the side of her head and she smiles with her eyes still closed. "Hazel, baby ... you need to get up."

"No," she growls. She turns to face me and her breasts are clearly visible as she scooches her body into mine. *Fuck.* I wasn't sure after how many times we had sex last night, if I would be able to get an erection again anytime soon. But here I am, hard, and right up against her. She smirks as she obviously can feel me, then snuggles in deeper.

"You have a plane to get on," I remind her.

"*No!*" she growls again.

Okay. So Hazel is *not* a morning person. "I think you're going to be really pissed at yourself if you go back to sleep."

"But I *want* to go back to sleep," she groans into my skin. "And *you* won't stop talking."

I laugh under my breath. "How about I go make us some coffee, and bring it to you while you get in the shower?"

Her eyes pop open and she looks up at me. "Why is it that everything that comes out of your British mouth sounds so perfect and beautiful all the time? Stop that! Stop hypnotizing me with your English accent!"

I give her forehead a kiss in response. "I love how grouchy you are in the morning."

"This isn't morning!" she grabs her phone to look at the time. "This is still middle of the night! Didn't we just go to bed like an hour ago?"

"Maybe," I grin. "But that doesn't change the fact that your plane is leaving at seven o'clock sharp, with or without you."

She buries her head back into my chest. "Damnit, Killian!" she moans. "Fine, I'll get up. And I guess I'll drop you back off at your house on my way out?"

"No you won't," I laugh at the thought. "I'm driving you to the airport."

"What?" her eyes find mine and she looks confused.

"I'm driving you to the airport, Hazel. I'm also picking you up when you fly back home in a couple days."

"Why?"

"Because I want to. Do you not want me to?"

Her eyes squint and she places a quick kiss on my lips. "I want you to."

"Good," I say, brushing her hair away from her eyes.

She lets out an overly dramatic sigh and then says, "I think I love this."

"Us waking up naked next to each other?"

She places one single finger on my lips. "Obviously that,

but I was actually talking about how what we did last night, it's just *our* moment. No one else will ever know about it. Well, except Aspen maybe, because we *were* pretty loud ..."

I remove her finger from my lips. "What do you mean?"

She stares at me for a second before responding. "Growing up in the spotlight, everything I did was always documented. Who I went out with, who I took to premieres and award shows. People knew whose apartment I was sneaking out of in the morning, or who was leaving my hotel room, before I could even drink a cup of coffee. You can't tell me it hasn't been the same for you? I know it has. I've seen pictures, Killian."

It's rather sad how right she is, and it pisses me off that she's thinking about me with other girls right now. "It's been the same. It *is* the same."

She nods her head in agreement. "You and me, last night, no one else can claim that or make money off of the damn walk of shame pictures they decide to plaster all over the internet. It was just us, Killian and Hazel, invisible to the outside world. Free. And together."

Jesus Christ. Moments when she speaks so honestly and truthfully hit me the hardest in my heart. "Sometimes I don't know what to say after you throw these meaningful words in my direction."

She starts to laugh. "I have that effect on people." She then leans forward and kisses me, cradling my chin in her fingers. "Guess we should get moving, right?"

"You get in the shower; I'll go make some coffee."

"Oh no you won't," she kicks the covers off our naked bodies and pulls me up by my hand. "*We* go get in the shower, then you make some coffee."

It's quite comical how much time I've wasted in the arms of strangers. Hours, days, weeks, time that I'll never get back. In the moment, that time seemed worthwhile, but in the long run, those moments meant nothing. Being with Hazel all night, sleeping with her in my arms, watching as she moved her stunning body on top of mine as I sat on the ceramic bench in her shower, giving us both one more perfect moment together before she leaves ... *those* moments are worthwhile. Everything before was just ridiculous.

I used to look at my life as a before and an after. I used to not know where to put the split, where the before ended and where the after started. I used to think my before was by far the better of the two. But as I stand under the departure sign at the Cleveland airport with Hazel, holding her in my arms as we attempt our first emotionally draining goodbye, I realize I know exactly where to put that split. The before was every moment without Hazel. And the after, well it's definitely better than the before.

# Hazel

## -during-

"A re you fucking kidding me right now, Birdie?!" my agent
screams at me through my phone. "You *left* the house?
You just left? Got in an Uber and left?!"

"I had to," my voice comes out in a whisper.

"No, you didn't!" she screams at me. "Once again, you
were just being overly dramatic! When are you going to learn
that you can't behave like that in this industry?!"

I don't say anything in return. I don't know what to say.

"And what about the cast?! What are they going to think
when they wake up tomorrow and realize you're gone?!"

"I don't know!" I cry out, my emotions getting the best of
me as I bury my head into my knees.

"We're going to pretend you're sick. We're going to
pretend that *I* told you to leave so that you didn't get the rest
of the cast ill. *I* called you the Uber to protect everyone else.
Put the blame on me so you don't look like an idiot. I'll call the
director right now and send texts to everyone else, okay? Do
you understand?!"

"I don't want to do this film!" I sob into the phone.

I literally hear her gasp in shock. "You are doing this film,
Birdie! You are not backing out on the role of a lifetime! That
is career suicide!"

I should just tell her. I should tell her what happened. I should let her know everything I've gone through these last two days. Hell, these last couple months. I should tell her what he did. But do you know what? Even if I did, she would blame it on me. *His* actions wouldn't matter, it's how I responded that would.

"Where are you right now?" she hastily asks.

"At a hotel, right by LAX," I quietly answer. "I want to fly back home—"

"You are not going back to fucking Ohio right now, Birdie!" she screams at me.

I start crying harder but she doesn't care.

"Here is what you're going to do. You are going to get on a plane to JFK in the morning. I will book you a flight when we hang up. First class, sitting alone, so that if paparazzi see this, they will buy into the sick story. Then you're going to check yourself into the Ritz for the next three days, pretending to ride out whatever illness you want to make up. I don't give a damn what you actually do, but you are not to leave that room. Are you listening to me?"

"Yes," I whimper.

"And then you're doing the movie awards with them all on Saturday. I don't care what happened in that house, you *will* show up. You will show your pretty face and you'll announce your role in this new film with everyone that you just walked out on. Do I make myself clear?"

Locked. Caged. Trapped. Put on display. No control over my own body. No control over my own life. No control over my own choices. But if I don't surrender to them all, if I don't do exactly what they tell me to do ... I hate to think how much lower I could possibly get.

"Yes," I whisper quietly, staring down at my London Underground t-shirt. "Perfectly clear."

# chapter twenty-one

"Your voice sounds different," Theo says when I call him after waking up from a much-needed nap. "Almost like you're doing some voiceover for a cartoon fairytale movie—wait! You slept with her, didn't you?! You finally had sex with the mysterious actress whose name I still don't know, and by the sound of your dreamy voice, it was recent."

"Jesus, Theo—"

"It's a gift, little bro. I know the blissful tone of someone who just got laid. You going to share any of the details with me or just leave me guessing—"

"Nah," I stretch my arms over my head, suddenly realizing that I'm famished for food. I have no desire to share any of the details about my night with Hazel with anyone, including Theo. Especially Theo.

"That bad?"

I stifle a laugh. Sex with Hazel was by far the best sex I've ever had. "No, Theo. It was bloody amazing. I just don't think I need to share details about my sex life with you anymore."

There's a pause. I'm sure Theo's trying to think of something witty and comical to say like he always does.

"Theo?"

"Hang on, Killian. I'm trying to wrap my head around this new you all of a sudden. You love this girl? Because you never had issues in the past spilling all your under the sheets moments with me."

"You going to erupt into a fit of laughter if I say yes?"

"Jesus, Killian. One month and you think you *love* her?" he questions.

I get out of my bed, searching my room for clean clothes. "Is that wrong?"

"Not if you're in a dramatic love story film. I think you're just being a tad bit over the top here. Why would you want to tie yourself down to one girl when you could have them all? I mean, it's not like you're thinking of leaving London and moving to America to be with her, right?"

I don't say anything in return because my mind is now imagining Hazel and I living together. Our own apartment, somewhere we can just be us, regardless of if I keep acting or if she decides to star in the film she wrote.

"Killian!" Theo shouts my name. "Please don't tell me you're going to give up everything you've worked so hard for, to settle down in fucking America with a girl whose name you won't even tell me!"

"I'm not giving up anything," I finally say. "I'm just not sure if I want to go back to London after summer. I can still be an actor here. I can be an actor anywhere. Look at you!"

"Mom is going to *kill* you. Like chop up your body into little tiny pieces, and feed you to the fish in the pond at Kensington Gardens."

Yes, I know this. "Dramatic much?"

"I'm coming to Ohio—"

"Bullshit."

"I'm serious. You need some big brother time. If you can't find the time in your busy farm life in Ohio to come visit me in California, I'm going to squeeze in a trip to come see you."

"Uh huh," I mutter as I pull on some shorts. Theo always promises to come visit but he never does. If I want to see Theo,

I have to go to him, and I actually have no desire to see him right now. "You let me know when that's going to happen."

"Soon, few weeks, okay?"

"Sure, Theo. I got to go. I need to eat something."

"Killian?"

"Yeah?" I question, somewhat aggravated and just wanting this phone call to come to an end.

"I'm looking forward to meeting her, whoever she is."

I actually feel my stomach drop at the thought of Theo meeting Hazel. Why do I not want Theo to meet Hazel? Why do I want to keep my relationship with her separate from my relationship with him? Why do I feel disgusted over the simple idea of Theo being in the same room with her?

The odds of him actually coming to Ohio, though, are slim to none, so I reply with, "I'm sure you are."

Food. I need food. I hang up with Theo and finish getting dressed. It's almost lunch time and I think I must have burned off enough calories last night that my body is craving the richest comfort food I can get in my mouth. I need to be replenished. I know exactly where to get my fix, and because my dad and Crystal took Maisy and her friends to the zoo today, I'm yet again on my own.

I get in my dad's Audi and pull out of the garage. I'm barely out of the neighborhood when my phone starts ringing in the seat next to me.

Hazel.

"Everything okay?" I greet her as I pick up. I didn't expect to hear from her until later tonight.

"I'm starving, Neil!" I can hear her exclaim. "Can we stop and grab a few bagels or something before my next meeting? Killian? Hi!" her voice softens.

"Hi, Hazel."

"I'm so hungry," she groans. "And I didn't have time to get something when I first got here—right there, Neil! Bagels! I can run in and get one—"

"No, Hazel," I can hear a man's voice say in return. "You stay in the car and make sure we don't get a parking ticket. I'll grab the bagels. An everything with light cream cheese?"

Why does he know her bagel order? Why does this make bile rise up from my empty stomach? *I* don't even know her bagel order.

"Yes! Thank you, Neil! Okay—Killian—hi," she says again.

"Hi, Hazel," I say for the second time.

"Neil's my driver," she tells me, like she knew I needed to hear who he was. "He's been my driver for a while now, whenever I'm in the city. He has triplets—high schoolers. Talks about them a lot. I think I'll get an invite to their grad parties next summer," she rambles.

"Is he part of your family of trustworthy people?"

She laughs. "He is. Speaking of my family of trustworthy people, Sammy says hi. He carted me over to baggage claim because my plane was twenty minutes late arriving and I was going to miss my first meeting."

"How *was* your first meeting?"

"Productive," is all she says.

I wanted more, but I'll settle with productive. "Hazel ...?"

"Yeah, Killian?"

"I want to be there with you."

God, I'm a lovestruck loser. The old Killian would never have said that. Theo would be gagging right now if he had heard what I just said.

Hazel makes a small, yearning noise through the phone. "I know you do. I'm just not used to sharing this part of my life with people, with anyone actually. This New York part of my life, but I want you here, too—"

"You do?" I can hop on a plane right now and be there before dinner.

"I do, Killian. Of course I do."

I pull the Audi into a parking spot and lean back into the leather seat.

*Say the right thing, Killian. Don't scare her away.*

"Well, Hazel ... what should we do about that?"

I can sense her smiling through the phone. "We should talk about it all when I get back."

I know that's all I'm going to get right now, and I'm totally okay with that. "Yes, Hazel, we *should* talk about it all when you get back."

"Good ... what are you doing today?"

I look up at the *Coffee and Stuff* sign swaying in the slight breeze. "Currently, I'm sitting outside of your parents' café."

She starts laughing. "You're going to go sit across from my parents and have them cook you lunch after we had very loud sex all night long in their house, repeatedly?"

My cheeks flame red and I'm not sure if it's because I'm suddenly riddled with anxiety over seeing her parents, or because I'm currently remembering Hazel's naked body under my own. "Uh, well ... now I might not be."

"Go inside, Killian," her calm voice hits my ear. "They'll be happy to see you. I unfortunately need to go. Neil is heading back out and I have to inhale this bagel in under five minutes."

"I miss you, Hazel," I quickly blurt out. I never realized it was possible to miss someone as much as I currently miss her.

"I miss you, too, Killian. I'll call you tonight." Then the phone goes silent.

I walk inside her parents' café, and the smell of fried food and coffee hits my nose the second the door opens. Comfort food. It's almost like the smell alone has the ability to wrap me up in a warm hug.

"Killian!" Lori warmly calls out my name from behind the counter. "Come sit!"

I walk over, taking a seat on the swiveling bar stool, forcing myself to push back the memories of Hazel and I last night into a secret lockbox in my head. "How was the wedding?" I ask her.

"Really good!" she answers. "College friend—her daughter, it was beautiful. Hazel said you took her to the airport this morning?"

"I did," I reply. I also had sex with her in her shower this morning, and now have a very clear visual in my head of the way her body looked as it moved up and down on top of mine. *Shit*. This was not a good idea.

"Tim!" Lori shouts into the kitchen. "Bring Killian out some fried chicken!"

Fried chicken. Yes. Comfort food. Think about fried chicken, not about a naked Hazel as you're standing in front of her mother.

"These trips to New York are becoming quite frequent," Lori says as she pours me some coffee. "I told Hazel she should just lease an apartment there for a while."

"Yeah?" I reach down for my coffee. It's brutally hot as I allow the first small sip to painfully swirl around my mouth. "What did she say?"

"She's thinking about it, at least that's what she said the last time we talked." She leans into the counter on her elbows. "You know about her screenplay, right?"

I nod my head. "She's bloody amazing, to write something like that—"

"You've read it?!" she stands straight up and asks.

"No, I haven't. Not yet. You?"

"No. No one has read it except those people in New York."

I add some creamer to my coffee, hoping to cool it down a little. "Why do you think that is?"

Lori leans back into the counter. "Because it's about her. I think she's protecting the people who love her. She doesn't want to upset us with whatever happened in the past."

I take a sip. Still steaming, creamer didn't do shit. "She

asked me if I would read it at some point."

Lori's eyes go huge, but then she pats me a few times on my shoulder. "That's wonderful," she sincerely says.

"Yeah? I almost feel scared to read it," I confide in her. "This top-secret screenplay that she's only allowed a handful of strangers in New York to read."

"She obviously trusts you."

"Yeah." My mouth is numb now from scalding off my tastebuds, so the coffee goes down quicker as I bring the mug back to my mouth. "You ever get nervous over what you're eventually going to find out?"

"All the time, Killian. Because I know at some point, I'm going to discover that someone hurt my baby enough to damage her almost beyond repair."

"Do you think that's why she stopped acting?"

"I *know* that's why she stopped acting." Lori turns to grab my fried chicken that's appeared in the kitchen window.

"Did Hazel tell you they want her to play the lead?" I ask her as she places my plate down in front of me.

She smiles. "She did. I'm hoping she considers it, because it's the perfect form of revenge."

"Revenge?" I question, spooning some mashed potatoes into my mouth.

"Yes. Revenge," she repeats. "When her screenplay actually becomes a movie and the entire world can view it, it's going to expose a lot of people in the industry that you both work for. They're not going to be able to hide anymore, or get away with the awful things they've done to other people. And who better to expose the truth than my Hazel, the person who had to suffer through it all." She refills my coffee cup and places her hand on my arm. "You're one of the good guys, Killian, but the list of good guys is much smaller than the list of bad ones. And I would hate to be on the wrong list when our Hazel finally storms through."

# Hazel

## -during-

I'm walking aimlessly around the JFK airport hoping not to be seen, hoping to be invisible. I can't live like this anymore. I don't want to be like this anymore. I just want to go home.

I walked out on the movie awards. I knew there was no way I could do it. There was no way I could pretend nothing had happened in California. I have finally reached the point where I can't do this anymore, and because of my actions last night, there's no way I'll work a day in the entertainment field ever again.

I can't be around him. I can't be in the same room with him. I can't even be in the same city with him without feeling as if I'm suffocating. When I was told he wanted to talk to me and was on his way to my dressing room, I immediately threw up. Everywhere. All over myself, all over the floor, all over the poor assistant named Evelyn, with the slick ponytail and loud stiletto heels.

She stood there not knowing how to properly react. She tried to help me, tried to ask me what was wrong, but I couldn't respond. I couldn't speak. And then she said his name again, and my entire body started shaking. And she knew. She knew something wasn't right.

I went into shock over the simple thought of having to look at him. I went into shock just thinking that he would be standing in front of me, with no shame for what he did. I went into shock over hearing his fucking name.

I can't pretend that what he's done is okay. I can't pretend that *I'm* okay.

Evelyn. This stranger who saw the fear in my eyes. I owe her a lot. She locked my dressing room door, squatted down on the floor with me, wiped the vomit from my face and then said the exact words I needed someone to finally say. "Let me get you out of here."

Evelyn. Snuck me out through a back door.

Evelyn. Already had a car waiting.

Evelyn. Booked me a hotel right by the airport, and told me not to worry about anything else but getting myself home in the morning.

I'm done.

I'm done being Birdie.

I just want to be Hazel.

Forever.

I find an empty gate and curl myself into a chair like a cat would in the comfort of its own home. My body hurts, like it's been in a car crash only it hasn't. Will it ever not hurt again? Or will I always feel like this? Tainted, bruised, dirty, not worthy of a simple touch. Not worthy of anything.

I only have an hour before my flight leaves, but my gate is packed with morning travelers. Sammy's not here today. Fred's bar doesn't open this early. I just need to stay right here, at this empty gate. Not being seen.

One hour.

Sixty minutes.

"Honey," a soothing voice is in my ear and a hand suddenly touches my arm.

I flinch hard. I don't want people touching me anymore. People shouldn't touch me anymore. You shouldn't touch something as repulsive as me.

"Sweetie," this voice calmly says. "You're okay. Can I sit down with you?"

I glance up to see a motherly-looking gate attendant standing in front of me. She holds her hands out in assurance that she won't try to touch me again. I nod my head.

She takes a seat across from me, watching as I stare at her from my curled position in the chair. "I know you," she softly says, her voice sounds concerned. "You're the actress, Birdie?"

"Please don't tell anyone!" I quickly cry out. Tears start pouring down my face. I don't want to be recognized anymore. I don't want anyone looking at me like I'm a bird trapped in a cage that they can just watch and judge.

Her head shakes fast. "No, sweetie. I won't. I won't tell anyone. Birdie—"

"It's Hazel. My name is Hazel."

"Hazel, whatever happened honey, you're safe right here with me, okay? I promise."

I start sobbing into my seat. Tears are collecting on the worn leather and pooling under my cheeks. She gets out of her chair and squats on the floor in front of me, kneeling on the thick, coarse carpet.

"Can I try to comfort you?" she asks with a choked voice. "I won't hurt you. I have babies at home. I'm a mom and I just want to comfort you. Can I try?"

I nod my face into my own puddle of tears.

Her fingers suddenly start running through my hair, delicately but with purpose. She's slow with her movements, like she knows if she moves too fast, it will alarm me and make everything worse.

"I see you in here a lot," she softly says. "Will you be back after today?"

"I don't know!" I wail into my arm. "I don't know what's going to happen now!"

She brings her eyes right in front of mine. Her face instantly imprints into my memory. "You're safe right now. You're safe with me," she says for the second time. "And if you come back after today, anytime you need to feel safe while you're here, you come find me. Right here at this gate. My name is Meredith."

# chapter twenty-two

God, I missed you," I say, a little out of breath as my face buries into her warm, sticky neck. I place my hands under her head, repeatedly kissing her salty skin as her fingernails drag gracefully across my bare back.

After four days of her being in New York, I picked up Hazel from the airport tonight and brought her back to my house. We didn't last more than five minutes before I was pulling that goddamn London Underground t-shirt off of her body and laying her back on my bed. And now we're both comatose, enjoying those blissful moments after sex where time doesn't seem to exist.

She squeezes her fingers into my sides. "I missed you, too. A lot, actually."

I look down at her flushed face. "A lot?" I grin.

She gives me a small nod. "It was nice, actually missing you and wishing you were with me. I've never missed anyone like that before."

I keep my eyes on hers. "I haven't either, Hazel. I've never cared about anyone enough to actually miss them when they aren't with me."

She lets out a sigh and raises her head so our lips can connect. "I care about you, too," she simply says.

I give her one final kiss and then roll off of her, grabbing a tissue from the nightstand to conceal the evidence of what we just did.

"I think I'm going to get on birth control," she announces as she flips onto her side. "The pill."

I look over at her, the sheet is barely covering her perfect naked body. The dip that's created from her hourglass figure is dangerous to stare at, and all I'm able to say back is, "Yeah?"

She nods her head. "Although I'm very appreciative for the reasons condoms exist, I hate them. Nor do I want to always have to remember to have one. I mean, what if the moment strikes in a location where a drawer filled with condoms isn't readily available?"

I've never had sex without a condom on. One simple rule in my life. Always wear a condom. I pull up my boxers and hand Hazel my t-shirt as I climb back into my bed with her. "You ever have sex without one?" I curiously ask.

*Please say no. Please say no.*

"No. Never. I've never been with anyone I would even consider it with."

Relief. I gently kiss her lips. "Neither have I. But it's your body, and if you don't want to go on the pill, I'm fine with using condoms."

"I don't like them," she repeats as she tugs my t-shirt down over her naked chest. "I'll get a prescription for birth control this week." She pulls her hair out from under the collar. "Why are you smiling like that?"

I know I have a ridiculous grin on my face. "No real reason," I reply. "Except for the fact that I'm the first guy you've ever considered having sex with without a condom. And because you're thinking about going on the pill, which means you plan on having more sex with me."

Her lips pull up sideways. "Would you like a gold star sticker? A special prize?"

"You're my special prize, Hazel."

"Stop!" she hits my arm as she laughs. "Your dreamy English accent is making me want to break out into a musical number or something!"

I pull her over so that she's resting on my chest. "Did you get everything accomplished in New York that you wanted?" I carefully ask.

I can feel a puff of hot air on my skin. "I guess so."

"You guess so?"

"I think I'm going to do it, Killian. I think I'm going to take the lead role."

*Be supportive. Let her talk. This is her decision, not yours.*

"You're okay with that? Reliving whatever those moments are, in front of all the cameras and people?"

Her gray eyes look up at mine. "Yes. I will be."

"Then okay. You're going to be fucking brilliant," I give her forehead a kiss. "What about the other lead?"

Her fingers move in a circular pattern around my stomach. "They're giving me one month to write a different ending. I'll go back then, present it to them, and then tell them who *I* think should play the part opposite me. They want to hear my thoughts now that I took the role."

"Do you have any ideas?"

"On the ending? Or the other lead?"

"Both."

Her fingers creep up to my neck, and then back down to that small patch of hair that rests above the top of my boxers. It's a hypnotizing feeling, the sensation of her fingernails moving along my bare skin so slowly and elegantly.

"I do. On both," is all she says.

"So, one month?" I ask. "You go back in one month?"

We're already halfway through the summer. I don't want to think about one month from now, when we'll be so close to summer ending. One month from now, I'll be having to make the decision if I'm heading back to London or not.

"Yes." She looks up at me again. "Will you go with me this time? Listen to everything? Calm me down when I feel like I'm drowning because I know I'll have moments where I question my sanity. Be my arm candy, too?" she grins.

One month. This means that sometime in the next month Hazel will clue me in about her past. This also means Hazel still sees us together, as close as we are right now, in one month.

"Absolutely, Hazel. To be honest with you, I thought you'd never ask."

She leans in and our lips connect for the hundredth time this summer. "This is going to change things," she breathlessly says against my mouth.

"Nothing has to change, Hazel."

"Everything will change," she whispers back. "But this bubble in which you and I have found ourselves, this *amazing* bubble, there's a thousand reasons out there for it to pop, and I don't want to be one of those reasons anymore."

She lies back down on my chest, silent, lost in her own thoughts. "I turned down the film in New Zealand," I tell her. "I think I killed my mum with my choice, and apparently Blake now smokes a carton a day ... but I'm not taking roles anymore unless they mean something to me."

"Yeah?"

"Yeah. What's the point? I'm already known in this industry. I don't need to take mediocre roles in films just to get my name out there. My name is already out there."

"What's going to happen when you go back to London?"

I groan into her hair. "I know I have to go back at some point, even if it's just to tie up loose ends there. I'll have to face the wrath of my entire angry team, except my publicist. Carol's a pretty decent human being. I need a new team ... agent, manager. If I want to keep doing this, I'm not doing it with them anymore."

"Do you miss it?" she softly asks. "Acting? The life? Being in the spotlight? The glamour? Do you miss any of it?"

I think about her question for a minute. "I can honestly say I miss *one* of those. Acting. I miss acting, because I *do* enjoy stepping into a different character, being a different person, but I don't miss anything else about the life I left in London. The insanity of it all, just utter chaos all the time and never having a say in what my day looked like."

Her fingers weave into my hair. "You want to be in control of your own career."

"I do."

"What was it like for you?" I can hear the hesitation in her voice as she asks. "Growing up like that? I grew up too fast. I saw things—did things. People treated me like I was an adult, when I was only thirteen."

I flash back to my life as a teenager in the entertainment industry. Alcohol, drugs, sex too soon, hearing things I shouldn't have heard—seeing things that I should have spoken up about.

"First time I got drunk was at the house of the actor playing my father in a film," I tell her. No one even cared. I was twelve. Think I've tried pretty much all the drugs out there that don't involve shoving a needle in my arm, not because I sought them out, but because I was just given them. Lost my virginity in a drunken stupor when I was fourteen to the actress who was playing my older sister. I also have a list in my head of every single actor and actress I've seen cheat on their significant other—"

She suddenly sits up and places her hand over my mouth to get me to stop talking. "I used to have this dream, Killian," she says, slowly bringing her hand back down. "This dream that I was in this cage with hundreds of other birds, and they were all the same black color, but I was bright red. Even when we all flew away together in one big flock, I stood out.

Everyone saw me, pointed, knew who I was. And I hated it. I hated being different, being the one who everyone noticed. Then one day, all the other birds got jealous of me, and one by one they started attacking until I was left shriveled up ... weak, and thinking I was better off dead than constantly being attacked by them."

"*Hazel*," I reach for her hand. I don't think this is just a dream, this is a nightmare and I have a feeling she probably lived it at some point.

"But in this dream, I realized something," she goes on. "If I'm *dead*, if I give up, who's going to fight for the next red bird? I'm not the only one out there, and someone needs to fight for the others who are still getting attacked every day." She squeezes my hand and places it on her chest. "There's going to be a moment at some point where you have to choose if you're going to sit back and let other people control you—hurt the others around you, hurt more people—or if you're going to fight back for those who are currently wandering around lost." She lifts up her shirt and points to her birdcage tattoo. "You know *you* always have the ability to be free ... why not remind everyone else that they can do the same?"

# Hazel

## -during-

I smell. I smell like sweat. I smell like vomit. I smell like failure. My arms are damp and look salty, my tears have left actual marks on my body. My stomach feels hollow, just completely empty, like the rest of me.

"Hazel?" her kind voice croons throughout the still air. Meredith.

"Your flight is getting ready to board. Can I help you to your gate? Do you know where you're sitting?"

"First class," I croak from the chair I've been curled up in for the last hour. I suddenly remember him. I remember the time he sat next to me. His fingers. His voice. His face. I spring up from my seat. The room spins as I realize how lightheaded I am. "Please! Can you make sure no one sits by me?! I don't want to sit by anyone—I don't want anyone close to me!"

"Let's go see what we can do."

I follow her over to the gate, keeping my head down and letting her guide me. I tug at the bottom of my London Underground t-shirt, trying to hide my skin, feeling a sense of comfort suddenly wash over me as I remember the exact moment this shirt became mine.

"Meredith!" I hear a man's voice say. I look up to see a large gate attendant with a balding head standing behind the customer service counter.

"Could you do me a favor?" she asks him. "Can you check and see if there's anyone sitting by my friend here today?"

"What's your name?" he asks me.

"Hazel Hemingway," I quietly respond.

He taps around on his keyboard. "Yes, the seat next to her is occupied—"

I immediately start crying.

"But there's an empty row I can move you to if you'd like?" he quickly adds.

"Yes!" I wipe away my tears. "I don't want to sit by anyone. I just want to be by myself."

I see him inspect my face further. His eyes become slightly bigger, and then just look sad. He recognizes me. His head turns to Meredith, who somehow silently speaks to him with her facial expressions.

"Not a problem, Hazel," he kindly says. "I'll move you over to the next row, empty, and make sure no one else sits next to you."

"Thank you," I manage to say.

"Are you a frequent flyer?" he asks. "Will you be coming through JFK again?"

I shake my head. "I don't know. Maybe."

He hands me a business card. "If you ever do, before you book your flight, give me a call. I'll get your flight arrangements taken care of and make sure that seat next to you doesn't get occupied. Okay? Anytime, Hazel. You just call me. My name is Harold."

# chapter twenty-three

You just volunteer here?" I ask Hazel as she drives us down a long dirt driveway.

"As often as I can," she turns to me and says.

"Can I ask, why?"

She swerves her BMW into an unmarked parking spot in front of a fenced-in green pasture. "You've never just given your time for the greater good? Never just wanted to help because you had the opportunity to?"

Deep thoughts on a random summer day.

"If I truthfully answer that question, are you going to make me walk home?" I ask her.

She starts laughing. "No. I actually want to hear your honest answer. I won't judge you."

"I've never given my free time to the greater good," I answer her. "Because I've never had free time," I follow with. "Every second of my day has always been strategically planned out by my thoughtful team, to the point where my only free moments were when I was allowed to sleep."

She keeps her eyes on me as she unbuckles her seatbelt. Then she scooches a little closer. Her hand wanders to my hair that's draped over my forehead. She moves it a little as she says, "I'm sorry. I've been in that exact position before and now that I'm not, I use my time to heal lost souls. Like you."

"I'm a lost soul?" I smile at her.

"Not so much anymore," she responds, and then she places a kiss against my lips. "But definitely when you walked up to me in JFK."

I run my fingers through the bottom of her curls. "Thanks for healing me," I say.

"My pleasure." She then points behind her to the farm that awaits us. "Ready to get dirty?"

Hazel's idea of giving her time to the greater good involves spending an entire day at a horse farm. I've never been up to my knees in horse poop before. I've never even shoveled a pile of horse poop before. I doubt I've even stepped in a pile of horse poop before. But for roughly two hours, Hazel and I are surrounded by horse shit.

At first, I will admit, I tried my hardest to keep it off my boots, my jeans, each and every small insignificant part of my body. But by the time Hazel declares we're done shoveling horse shit, it's everywhere. These boots Tim let me borrow, these jeans that probably cost more than a typical mortgage payment, will all be lit on fire and burned after today.

My hands are blistered, my arm muscles ache, but Hazel just walks out of the barn without a complaint in the world. I now understand why her abs and arms are so toned. It's from shoveling horse shit whenever she can.

"You doing okay?" she humorously asks me.

"Hell, yes," I reply. "I could go for another two hours."

"I won't do that to you," she grins. "Follow me."

She guides me over to a picnic table that's placed under a giant oak tree. On the table is a basket, and there's a pitcher of lemonade sitting next to it. She stops right before she reaches the table, where an outdoor sink is propped up against the side of a small shed.

"We definitely should wash our hands first," she declares.

"Is that for us?" I point to the basket as she starts

scrubbing her fingers with a scrub brush while the hot water flows from the faucet.

"It is," she says, handing me the soap. "Us, and Beth."

"Who's Beth?"

"I'm Beth," a voice announces as an older lady in overalls and a straw hat walks around from the side of the shed. "You must be Killian," she smiles at me. She has two long braids hanging down under her hat and looks as if she's been living the farm life since the day she could walk. "Thanks for helping today. We've missed you around here, Hazel!"

"I've missed *you* guys," Hazel says to her, drying her hands off and then sitting down along the bench in front of the table. I quickly scrub my hands clean and join her. "Killian, this farm is Beth's," she tells me. "All the horses here, they all belong to her. She rescued each and every single one."

"Rescued?" I question.

Beth opens the basket and starts pulling out wrapped sandwiches. She hands me one as she says, "Thirty-two as of right now. Each and every horse here was either abused, neglected, or set to be slaughtered."

I slowly unwrap my sandwich as Hazel pours everyone some lemonade. The horses suddenly appear behind the fenced-in pasture across from us. Galloping, so free as they trot along the grass. They're so beautiful and elegant, I find it hard to believe anyone would ever want to hurt them.

"Who would do that?" I question both Hazel and Beth.

Hazel just sadly smiles, while Beth says, "Cruel people. People who don't have a heart."

"There's a phone chain," Hazel tells me. "Beth gets calls all the time, but she can't take them all."

"I wish I could," Beth announces. "But I rely on volunteers and donations, and sometimes it's just not enough. I love my volunteers, though," she raises her glass to Hazel. "Hazel's been coming here for over a year now. We all love her here.

Especially the horses."

Hazel laughs. "The horses and I have a lot in common."

"Yes, you do," Beth knowingly responds. "Let's eat! I always make the effort to eat lunch with my volunteers," she says to me. "If you're going to help me out on my farm, I'm going to feed you. Keep you coming back." She points to the basket. "Help yourself!"

One hour of eating lunch with Beth, listening to her talk about her horses, about Hazel, about her life ... and I know exactly what I'm doing before I leave here today.

"Are you ready to go hang out with the horses?" Hazel asks me once we're done eating.

"We get to hang out with them?"

She nods her head. "Absolutely. Feed them, brush them, talk to them. Did you think I was just bringing you here today to shovel shit?"

I place my hands around her waist and give her forehead a small kiss. "You go ahead," I nod to the gate that will take us into the pasture. "I'll be there in a minute."

She gives me a curious look, but then squeezes my hand and walks away.

"That Hazel," Beth says from behind me. "She reminds me of a few of my horses."

"Yeah?" I question.

"When I first met Hazel, she was struggling," her voice is sad as she speaks. "I could tell. Depressed, just living life because she had to, not because she wanted to. She came here one day, out of the blue. Said she saw the horses in the pasture as she was driving, and she just wanted to watch them roam. She walked right up to that fence and just stood there, for an hour at least, watching them."

I turn back to look at Hazel. She has walked up to a white horse with small black spots. Her hand is gently running along the length of this horse, so careful and slow, like she doesn't want to frighten it with a sudden movement.

"That's Ophelia," Beth points to the horse. "I got her right after I met Hazel. She was a wild one. She had spent the majority of her life being bred. One right after another. Her sole purpose in life was to be assaulted by male horses twice her size, just to produce a foal every year. Then when her body had had enough and started miscarrying them all, she was set to be slaughtered."

"That's absolutely horrible," I respond.

"Isn't it?" she agrees. "Hazel overheard me on the phone, trying to get another horse owner to step up and save Ophelia. I didn't have the funds to get her here. She was out in California. I hung up with my last hope, knowing that was it and there was nothing else I could do, but then Hazel stood right in front of me. Those damn eyes, I could tell by just looking in her eyes."

"She gave you the money?"

"Every last penny," Beth nods. "And more. That horse actually belongs to Hazel," she points to Ophelia again. "She gave me everything I would ever spend on Ophelia for the rest of her entire life. And she spent countless hours with me, earning that horse's trust."

I look at Beth, who's busy watching Hazel and the horses. "She's too good for this world," I say to her. "Hazel. She's way too good for this world."

Beth looks at me now, staring into my eyes. "This world is lucky to have her in it."

"Can I make a donation?" I ask. "I don't want to leave here today without knowing I made a difference. I want to do something, anything."

"I can see that," she points to my eyes. "I can see it right there. I'd be honored, Killian. Thank you." She then turns back to Hazel. "They're bonded, Hazel and Ophelia."

"You think?"

"For sure," she places her hand on my shoulder and says. "They both know what it feels like to be at their absolute lowest, to be abused by the people they should be able to trust. Hazel was lost when she first showed up here. So was Ophelia. Lost souls, both of them."

"And now?"

"Now? Well, look at them, Killian." She points once again to the two of them. "Their souls have returned. They healed each other. Now ... they're both free."

"It's horrible to think what someone, something, has to go through in life before they're able to find freedom," I respond.

"It is," she agrees. "But sometimes life does that in order to teach a person what empathy is. Hazel, I can tell what kind of person she is just by the way she treats my horses. She's filled with empathy."

"Are you saying that whatever happened to her in the past happened for a reason?" I ask, curious.

"Maybe," she answers. "Maybe Hazel's past is the reason she now walks around trying to save every lost soul she comes across." She suddenly looks at me. "Is she saving you?"

Deep thoughts on a random summer day.

"I think she might be," I confirm.

"Hazel's not too good for this world, she's exactly what this world needs. Can I tell you something, heart to heart?"

"Sure."

She smiles a warm smile. "Hazel's energy today, her aura, it's different ... brighter. It's like her soul is finally happy. I think that's because of you." Her hand presses against my heart. "She might be saving you ... but actually, I think you're saving her, too."

# chapter twenty-four

B lake, Mum, how's London?" I ask when they pick up for our weekly check-in. I'm sitting at the bar in my basement, picking at the toast I made for breakfast.

"Dismal," my mum replies. "I have lost my purpose in life without you here."

"Mum, take up a hobby," I suggest. "Read a good book for once. Go out on a date. Find yourself an actual lover that isn't just sleeping with you because your son is me."

I can hear someone choking on the other end.

"How's Madison doing?" I ask Blake, chomping down on the dry bread.

"She left me. Gone. Moved on to someone else, someone younger," he angrily announces.

"You cheated on her literally every week," I point out, chewing noisily. "Good for her."

I hear choking noises again.

"A couple new scripts have come through," my mum tells me. "They look promising, Killian. I hope you'll consider them as you now have absolutely nothing lined up for the fall when you return from this *hiatus*."

"New scripts?" I question, tossing the toast onto my plate. "What are they for?"

I hear Blake clear his throat. "A historical romance, and

then a thriller, starring the actress who played your older sister in that movie you were in when you were fourteen."

"Oh, you mean Becki Jones?" I ask. "The girl who took my virginity after getting me plastered at the after party?"

More choking noises.

"Are you taking any of what we say serious?!" my mum cries out.

"I just told you I got plastered at fourteen at an after party and lost my virginity to someone five years older than me, and you're asking *me* if I'm taking this serious?"

"Fine, Killian. Fine. Please, tell us what you want *us* to do to get you working again," she emotionally begs.

"Really? I finally have a say in what *I* do?"

Hazel appears on the outside of the basement patio door, letting herself in with a quick wave. I call her over, placing a kiss on her cheek as soon as she's close enough.

"Yes, Killian!" my mum suddenly exclaims. "Just tell us!"

"I want a role I can be proud of," I say to them both. "Something that I really work my ass off for, something that pushes me, makes me want to be a better actor and a better person." I smile up at Hazel and pull her hand so she sits down in my lap. "And huge, massive perk if it's filming somewhere near New York."

Blake coughs loudly into the phone. "Fine, Killian. I'll see what I can do."

"Good. Thank you," I sincerely reply. "And Mum, you know … you can call just to say hi, and not just to talk business all the time."

"Oh!" I hear her make a funny noise. "Yeah, sure. I suppose I can do that."

I know she won't call. I haven't had a normal conversation with my mum since before puberty hit. "All right you two, until next week, unless you find something that ticks off all those boxes before then." And then I just hang up, because there's no need for formal goodbyes with them anymore.

"Good morning," Hazel throws her arms around my neck, placing a firm kiss on my lips.

"It is now," I reply, squeezing my hands around her back. "What's on the agenda for today?"

"Well ... I only have one week left to revise my screenplay, so I was thinking some extremely large amounts of caffeine are in order. You want to check out my favorite local coffee shop? And maybe sit across from me and tell me to keep working every time I stop?"

Hazel has been extremely overwhelmed lately with trying to change the ending of her screenplay. A month sounded long three weeks ago, but the days went by so fast, she now only has a week left before we're both supposed to head to New York together. I keep waiting for her to back out on what she had said earlier. I keep waiting for her to ask me to stay in Ohio because she's realized she's still not ready to let me into this part of her life. But our flights are booked and the only thing I can do is sit here and be supportive, and hope she doesn't change her mind.

"I can do that," I smile. "I just need to check in with my publicist really quick."

"Carol?" Hazel nods. "The only one on your team that you actually trust?"

I've already got her number dialing on my phone. "Yes. I think I might miss her—Carol! How's London?" I ask when she picks up.

"Killian! So good to hear from you," her warm voice responds. "London is wonderful, though I haven't been here much. Your summer off has allowed me to travel Europe with my husband finally. Just got back into town a few days ago from Greece."

"Greece?!" I raise my eyes. "That sounds amazing."

"It was. So beautiful. How's Ohio, and your father?"

"Really good, Carol. Thanks for asking."

"Will we be seeing you back in London soon?"

"Not quite," I answer, expecting at least a long dramatic sigh from her.

"Well, that's quite all right," she surprisingly says. "You needed the time off."

"I knew I liked you, Carol."

"People *are* asking," she then tells me. "Wondering where the great Killian Lewis has snuck off to. Is there anything you'd like me to say?"

My eyes meet Hazel's. Carol could do a whole piece on me being in Ohio all summer to bond with my family. The press would love that. But ... this town, if the press knew I was in this town, they would most likely discover Hazel. "Can I think about it?" I ask Carol.

"Absolutely, Killian. Take all the time you need. You just let me know when there's a news story you think is worthy enough to throw your name in, all right?"

"I will. Enjoy your time off."

"You too."

I place my phone next to my plate of toast. "I'm all yours now," I say to Hazel, pressing my lips to her forehead. "Local coffee shop? Get to sit across from you and stare at you for the next few hours?"

She pulls me up from my chair. "I'm very excited I get to be the one to pop your Cool Beans Café cherry."

Cool Beans Café, located in the same town as my new favorite ice cream shop, is apparently home of Hazel's own coffee drink that was named after her. It rests right in the historical area of the picturesque town of Medina, Ohio, which looks like it was plucked right out of a Hallmark holiday movie that airs on repeat during the month of December.

"I would come here probably three or four times a week when I started writing," she tells me as we walk down the sidewalk. "I always asked for the strongest iced coffee they could give me." I pull the door open to the brick building, allowing her to walk through first. "An iced red eye," she continues. "But one day I took it up a notch and asked for a pump of vanilla syrup, a splash of oat milk, and to top it off with whipped cream." She points to the menu board behind the counter. A list of all their sandwiches and baked goods line one side, with their specialty coffee drinks on the other.

"The Hazel," I read. Her drink is listed with numerous other ones, all with unique and creative names. Iced red eye, pump of vanilla syrup, oat milk, topped with whipped cream. "You really have your own drink here?" I turn to her in shock.

"I do," she grins at me.

"Hazel!" the lady behind the counter greets her. "Haven't seen you in a while."

"Been a little busy this summer," she responds. "This is Killian," she introduces me. "We're going to sit here for a bit so I can get some work done. Can I take my booth?"

"Absolutely," she smiles. "Same as usual?"

Hazel nods. "What about you, Killian?"

"I'll give the Hazel a try," I point to her name on the board. "And a few scones ... maybe a breakfast bagel with bacon, too."

The lady behind the counter laughs. "I'll bring it all over. And some waters."

Hazel walks me over to a booth that sits up against the windows of the café. "In the winter," she says, pointing outside, "I sit here and just watch the snow fall down. It's like being inside my very own snow globe."

We settle into our spots, Hazel on one side of the booth, me on the other, no one paying any attention to these two celebrities that have taken over this corner. Hazel waits for our coffees and food to arrive before pulling out her laptop, and then she gives me a firm warning.

"I'm not ignoring you. I promise. But I tend to get lost

when I write—"

"I've noticed," I grin at her, because these last three weeks I've witnessed her writing a lot. "I'll still be here when you find your way back."

She narrows her eyes. "The English accent, Killian. You're doing it again."

I point to her laptop and smile, "Get to work, Hazel."

She isn't lying. She does get lost when she writes, and an hour easily passes as she types away in front of me. But today I can tell she's just not all in. She keeps pausing, biting her lip, tapping her fingers, and her legs are bouncing in her seat. As I sit there enjoying my over-caffeinated coffee and breakfast bagel, while briefly reading emails on my phone, I watch her facial expressions as she leans back into the booth and folds her arms across her chest. Something is bothering her.

"I need a break," she declares out loud. Her eyes close and her breathing looks forcefully planned. Large, deep breaths come from her nose. She's trying to calm herself down, but *why*, I have no idea.

"Hazel?" Her eyes pop open. "You okay?" She gives me a small smile but doesn't say anything in return. My phone noisily starts to vibrate on the table as a call comes through.

Theo.

"I'm going to take this for a second," I say to her. "And when I'm done, we're going to close the laptop for a few minutes and you're going to come sit by me."

She places her head on the table and gives me a weak thumbs up.

I grab my phone, "Hey, Theo," I answer.

Hazel's head immediately flies up from the table and her hand knocks over her glass, sending ice cubes and chilled water everywhere. I jump and make a mad dash for her laptop, pulling it safely off the table as she just sits there, not moving, staring at me with this sudden look of fear in her eyes.

"Killian!" Theo's voice is loud in my ear. "I've got something to tell you—"

"Hang on, Theo," I say. "Let me call you back—"

"Call me back?!" he repeats in shock. "You better!" he quickly exclaims. "This is big!"

I place my phone in a dry spot, yanking out napkins from the dispenser as I try to soak up the water that's slowly making its way to the edge. But my eyes stay on Hazel, who is as still as a statue.

"What is it?" I ask her, confused as to what just happened in front of me.

"Nothing," she immediately says, but I know she's lying. "I just—it's nothing. I'll be right back." She quickly leaves the booth, disappearing down a long hallway and into what I assume is the bathroom.

What the *hell* just happened?

I clean up the water. I close her laptop and place it in her bookbag because we're definitely done for the day. I stack our empty plates and take them to the counter. And then I sit there, waiting for her.

She doesn't return five minutes later.

She doesn't return ten minutes later.

And when she doesn't return fifteen minutes later, I swing her bookbag over my shoulder and walk over to the door that she had disappeared through.

"Hazel?" I knock. Nothing. I press my ear against the door and can hear her softly crying from the inside. "Hazel, I'm coming in." I twist the knob and push the door open. I immediately see her sitting up against the wall, her head is buried in her knees and she's slowly rocking back and forth.

I suddenly remember that moment in JFK. What's with us and bathrooms? Why are bathrooms the place of Hazel's emotional meltdowns?

I place her bookbag on the sink and join her on the floor,

not caring in the least how disgusting it is to be sitting on the cold tile of a public bathroom. I hesitantly place my hand on her back, and she flinches.

She *fucking* flinches with my touch. My heart shatters.

"Hazel?" I fearfully say her name. "What is going on?"

She lifts her head from her knees, her face is tear stained, red and blotchy. I've never seen her quite like this before. I've seen little tiny snippets, but nothing like what I'm witnessing in front of me right now.

"I can't do this," she suddenly whispers.

"Can't do what?"

"This! All of this!"

Well, now I'm extremely confused. "The screenplay? The role? New York City? *Us?*"

Her face drops instantly when I say us, and she lets out a loud sob. "*Us?!*" she repeats. "I *love* us! But everything is going to come crashing down, and I don't think I can do it anymore! I can't do this to you, Killian!"

Just last night we were wrapped in each other's arms during another moment of heated passion in her bed. Just last night as I tried to fall asleep without her next to me, I was thinking up clever ways of asking Hazel if we could lease an apartment together in New York City. If I could join her. If she would let me be a permanent part of her life for as long as I can. And just this morning, as she walked in through my basement door, I literally could see my future with her. The future I *want* with her.

I want everything, all the baggage, all the low moments, all the high moments. But now she's falling apart on this freezing bathroom floor in a coffee shop, acting as if she's unexpectedly giving up on us, and I don't even know why.

*No.*

Big fucking no. I'm *not* letting her do this.

I pull her into my arms. "You have to let me in, Hazel. I

want you to let me in. Don't push me out because you're scared to tell me—"

"It will destroy you!" she wails into my chest. "My past, it will destroy us! I can't let them make this movie! I can't *be* in this movie! I can't write a happy ending when I know there isn't going to be one!"

I move her hair out of her eyes and hold her chin in my hand. "Whatever it is, whatever you're keeping locked away in fear of what other people will find out, in fear of what I'll find out ... I want to *be* with you, Hazel. Holding your hand and standing by your side—"

She pushes against me. "You won't! Not once everything is out—and *you*!" she cries as her fingers jam into my shirt. "You weren't supposed to find me! We were never supposed to see each other—"

"What the hell does that even mean?!"

She slams her hands into my chest. "I am the *wrong* person for you to love—for you to fall in love with! You promised you wouldn't! I will only break your heart and I realize that more now than I ever did before—"

"Then fucking break it, Hazel!" I exclaim. "If by letting me in completely, you break my heart in the process, then do it! But I'm sitting here on this goddamn bathroom floor with you, telling you I am *not* walking away from this, from you and me! I'm not scared of you breaking my heart when you finally let me be a part of those memories you keep trapped inside, I'm fucking scared of you thinking you're not worthy enough for me to love you!"

She gasps with my words, and then buries her face into her hands as she cries, not saying anything else.

I scooch in closer, enclosing her body with my own, kissing her head, rubbing her back, letting her completely break down in my arms for reasons I have yet to fully understand.

"You're worthy, Hazel," I whisper into her ear. "Whatever it is that happened, whatever it is you eventually tell me, you're worthy of every ounce of love I'm able to give you."

And it's as we sit there in that bathroom, as she slowly brings herself out of this destructive panic attack I just witnessed, I realize something extremely valuable. Hazel is not free, even though she thinks she is.

Hazel is still Birdie. Every day she's still Birdie. She's caged, stuck in that life because her past has her trapped. She relives those moments every second, those moments she doesn't want anyone she loves to know about. It's as if her mind is forcing her to wait to trust, to love, to allow someone else to open her cage because she's not able to do it herself. She's just stuck, waiting. And until that day comes, until that moment arrives when she finally lets someone unlock that door for her, she will never truly be free.

# Hazel

## -during-

This house is amazing. California is amazing. But the cast of strangers that I'm currently supposed to be bonding with, there's just something about them that screams warnings out at me. Especially him.

During the day it's easier to avoid him, it's easier to not be alone with him. But when the day is over, when the night arrives and I'm safely in my bed with my door locked as everyone else drinks and gets high downstairs, that's when the texts come through. The texts from him. More texts to add to my pathetic collection.

At first, I ignored them like I always have. I turned my phone off so I didn't have to hear the constant alerts as he sent me text after text from his own room down the hall. Then in the morning I would carefully scroll past them like they weren't even there. They're vulgar and obscene, definitely worse than what they were over the last couple weeks. I question how I could possibly be in this type of situation. Trapped, in this house with the same person sending me these messages every night.

He doesn't say anything the first few days. He acts completely normal, as if he's not sending me detailed descriptions of what he wants me to do to his body sexually. He won't say anything in front of everyone else, nor will he show his obsession over me. He knows how to play this game, and I'm almost certain he's played it before.

But when our time here is halfway through, when he knows I have no intentions of responding or acting on the erotic propositions he's been sending me ... he finally snaps.

"Birdie, you realize I *got* you this role?" his voice quietly hisses in my ear as he corners me on the patio outside. Everyone is out here ... drunk, high, but not me. One mistake and I'll let my guard down. I can't let that happen here.

I pull my cup of lemonade into my body and scoot against the wall. "You shouldn't have," I quietly say back, sarcastic but at the same time I mean every word.

He moves in closer; his body covers mine so that no one would even see me if they walked by right now. His hand rubs along my thigh and I tightly close my eyes in disgust, not realizing this is the biggest mistake I could have ever made. He suddenly brings his hand out from my skirt.

"Look at me, Birdie."

My eyes open.

"You liked that, didn't you?" his eyes look wild as he asks. "My hand on you? You liked how that felt. Trust me, I can make you feel *so* good."

I glance around. No one seems to care. They ignore the fact that this man, who is at least ten years older than me, has his entire body pushed up against mine. They've seen it before. This is normal to them. This is normal in their lives.

"Why are you acting like this?" he breathes into my ear. His breath smells like beer and weed. "You know you belong in my bed tonight. You know that's why you were cast in this film. You belong to me, until this film is over."

I gulp down the dry air that's in my mouth.

"You might as well just accept it," he goes on. "And if you

don't, you can kiss your acting career goodbye."

I twist my way out of his grasp and walk over to the couch, drinking what's left in my cup in hopes that the gagging reflex in the back of my throat will go away. I toss the empty cup to the ground, hearing the laughter of everyone else as he walks over to them. I pull my legs into my body and stay on this couch for a while, trying to be invisible as I lose track of time. It plays out in front of me in slow motion, every clip claiming minutes of my life I'll never get back.

"Are you okay?" I hear someone ask, a girl's voice, but I don't look up to see which actress in this film is standing in front of me. I just nod my head.

"Birdie is fine," he answers from across the patio. "She'll be even better tomorrow because my baby brother is coming for a couple days!" he shouts into the still night, raising his cup in the air. "You all will love him, and he's your age," he points to me. "I'll share you with him while he's here," he then winks.

Everyone laughs like it's a joke, like it's a fucking joke. I need to get out of here. I need to run while I still can. I need to go home.

I go to stand and suddenly realize the outside night is spinning in front of me.

"Are you okay?" the same girl asks again.

I grab at the couch, trying to keep my balance.

"Birdie's fine," he says for the second time. "Must have had too much to drink." He starts moving toward me. Slow motion. Minutes of my life I'll never get back.

I try to get away. I try to move so I'm not directly in the path he's walking toward, but I just end up falling backward into the couch.

"I didn't have anything to drink," my words slur unconvincingly from my dry mouth.

He laughs as he stands in front of me. "Yes, you did. You and me, we did shots earlier, in the kitchen. I think they're finally catching up to you."

I did *not* do shots, but I can't get my brain to say that statement out loud.

He places his cup down on the table and his hands are suddenly on my body. He effortlessly picks me up, like I'm his. I try to fight against him. I try to hit him with my own weak hands, but I can't move them. They're so heavy. My body feels like deadweight, like I'm drowning and just being pulled further and further under the water. I'll never reach the surface again. I can't even speak anymore, and no one does anything. This is normal to them. They've seen this before.

"I think it's time for bed, little Birdie," he says, walking us to the patio door.

I can't lift my head from where it has landed on his shoulder. I can't hear what he says to anyone else as he strolls us into the house. I can't scream as he walks past my room and instead goes to his own. I can't fight back as he undresses me and lays me on his bed. I can't tell him no as he climbs on top of me. I can't do anything at all.

I am useless.

Trapped.

Tonight I belong to him.

And in the morning, when I wake up alone in my own bed, having absolutely no memories of the night before, I question why my body hurts. I question why I'm so sore. I question the fingerprint marks I see on my arms. I question if what they tell me is true, that I drank too many shots with everyone and blacked out. I've done this before, maybe not here, but definitely before. Who's to say I didn't just say fuck it and drink with everyone? Who's to say I really wasn't carefully helped to my bedroom when they all realized I had too much? It could have happened, right?

But I question why I don't remember anything, not one single thing. And I question why my mind is screaming at me that something isn't right. And it's not until later that evening, when his younger brother arrives, when I'm standing at the railing overlooking the kitchen, that I see what he does. His younger brother, who hasn't noticed me yet, is oblivious to what's going on around him. He looks lost, sad, misplaced, like he doesn't want to be here but feels trapped.

Like me.

I feel his pain. I can almost see the emotions pouring from his soul as he sits there, wearing a London Underground t-shirt and speaking with the most beautiful English accent I've ever heard. You can see his pain, but you can also see the trust he has in his older brother, so he doesn't notice. He doesn't notice when his brother drops pills into his filled cup. He doesn't notice as they quickly dissolve into the beer before he brings it back up to his mouth.

But I do.

And it's at that exact moment, I remember pieces of the night before. Little clips flash before my eyes like someone has a remote and keeps hitting fast-forward—pause, fast-forward—pause. I remember he cornered me. I remember I closed my eyes just to get his face out of my vision as his hand wandered up my thigh. It was then, when my eyes were shut, that he must have done the same thing to me that he just did to his younger brother.

He suddenly looks up at the stairs. He looks up at my shocked face as I stand there over the railing, remembering what he did. And he knows, he knows I remember something. I turn quickly, heading back to my bedroom to grab whatever I can so I can make my escape out of this life, away from him, away from them all.

But then I hear him coolly say, "I'm going to see what's taking Birdie so long."

And it's then I know. He's not going to let me leave.

I am his for now. I am Theo's, until I find a way to fly free.

# chapter twenty-five

It's been six hours since I was able to get Hazel to follow me out of the bathroom at Cool Beans Café. The first hour was spent in almost complete silence as we took Aspen for a walk along the trails. The second hour was spent lying in the hammock in her backyard, a few words spoken between us, but mostly Hazel was still lost in her own thoughts. Hours three through five were spent with Hazel asleep in my arms on her couch while I watched her, thankful that in sleep she was at least peaceful. And now, hour six, she's finally starting to come down from this event, this attack that threw her into an entire day of hopelessness.

She's changing her clothes, as we have that barn raising party to attend this evening. Apparently, everyone in town will be there, and her tank top and jean shorts aren't good enough for this type of event. I follow her upstairs to her room, waiting by her closet as she searches for something to wear.

"We don't have to go," I remind her. I don't want her to think she has to plaster on a smile all evening, when she's feeling like this right now.

She walks out of her closet, wearing a lacy cream-colored dress and carrying a pair of brown cowboy boots. She stops where I'm standing and drops the boots to the ground, folding her arms over her chest.

"We are the sole reason this barn is even being built. We have to show up," she says to me.

I move a few steps away so I can take a better look at her. Her hair is doing its perfectly planned thing again even though I know she did absolutely nothing to it all day long. Her natural waves and curls hang all the way down to the middle of her back and look stunningly flawless. She takes this moment to slip her boots on, and then places her skinny gold rings on her fingers, throwing matching bracelets on her wrists, too. She then stands in front of me again, waiting for me to say something.

She looks like a Bohemian goddess.

"Jesus, Hazel," I sigh, tapping her bracelets with my fingers. "You look absolutely beautiful."

She gives me a small smile. "Thank you."

"But we don't have to go tonight," I tell her again.

"We don't *have* to," she agrees. "But I'm going, and I really want you to go with me."

"Hazel," I shake my head at her, saying her name in almost an alarming way. We need to talk. She *has* to know this.

"No questions," she says, throwing me back to our time in JFK. She places her arms around my neck and stares into my eyes. "Please. Not tonight."

I gently rest my forehead on hers. "*When*, Hazel?"

She sighs, her arms tightening. "How did we get so lucky, to have our paths even cross like they did?"

"Bad weather in Pennsylvania."

She lets out a small laugh and then kisses me. After seeing her fall apart today, I welcome this simple kiss. But I'm not letting her forget that we need to talk. I can't watch her fall apart again without knowing why it's happening.

I wait until her lips leave mine before asking once more, "*When*, Hazel?"

Her stormy gray eyes desperately search mine. Comfort.

She's searching for comfort. "Tomorrow, okay? Tomorrow, I promise. But tonight, we don't talk about today or the past. Tonight, we're just Killian and Hazel. Just us. Together. Can we do that?"

"Baby, we can do that tonight, and tomorrow, and the next day, too," I reassure her, kissing that perfect soft spot between her eyebrows. "Killian and Hazel. Just us. Together."

THE SIMPLE DEFENITION of a barn raising party is, "A gathering, usually providing food and drink, for the sole purpose of assisting a neighbor in raising their barn."

When Hazel and I arrive, the party is in full swing. The barn has been raised and the locals of Sharon Center, Ohio, are now in a celebratory mood. She is well known by everyone in attendance, the same people we've seen numerous times over the summer. Regulars from the café, artists who had booths at the craft fair, neighbors we see on our walks, even Beth the horse owner is here.

Hazel is respected, and loved, and beautifully protected. And as we walk around this farm holding hands and greeting all these people, I'm suddenly overwhelmed by the fact that I am now also respected, and loved, and beautifully protected by this town of people who are no longer strangers to me.

I spend the night side-by-side with Hazel, and although she's back to her vivacious, wild self in front of everyone, I know it's just an act. I can see below the surface now, and below the surface she's in pain. But her brilliant acting skills would never let that on, not to the people she so desperately loves. So, the night is spent playing with goats, eating the vast amounts of comfort food her parents have provided for everyone here, and discovering that we kick ass in some mindless game called cornhole.

The night is spent pretending everything is perfectly fine. After our winning streak in cornhole comes to an end, we get a tour of the new barn from the grateful family we had met earlier this summer. The children meet us at the entrance, and crown Hazel with a headband of wildflowers.

"You're the princess of our barn!" the little girl proudly announces to her.

A little boy then places one single wildflower in the pocket of my shirt. "And you can be her prince!"

Hazel lets out a small laugh under her breath. "Maybe I *am* an American princess," she winks at me.

There's something so pure about having these hard-working people show us the framework of what will eventually home their livestock and livelihood. And although the air outside reeks of cow shit and the smell might never leave my nose, I could stand here for hours listening to them talk about life on their farm. They eventually ask us, and Maisy, to sign a plaque that they'll keep at the entrance of their barn, reminding them every day of why it's even there.

I'll have my name, signed, next to Hazel's and my little sister's, on a plaque that will forever stay on the walls of a cow barn in northeast Ohio, and I couldn't be prouder. Screw Oscars and all other movie awards, *this* feeling is the best feeling in the world.

When daylight disappears, kids start running around with nets and jars, collecting the fireflies that now flutter around. Maisy is one of them.

"Hazel!" she shouts, running past us as her dark hair swings behind her. "Come help me!"

Hazel places a quick kiss on my cheek and follows after her, leaving me standing by the barn with my dad and Crystal.

"Killian, never thought I'd see the day you attend a barn raising party," my dad grins as he taps my beer with his.

"Neither did I," I agree. "Does it always smell like this?

How do they live here with the smell of shit constantly filtering into their house?"

"I think they just get used to it after a while?" my dad shrugs his shoulders.

"Hazel doing okay?" Crystal suddenly questions.

My head snaps to her. "Why are you asking?"

"No real reason," she holds her hands up. "She just seems a little off tonight."

"*Fuck*," I lean my back up against the frame of the barn. "Something happened today—she was working on her screenplay, working on a different ending, and she fell apart. Like completely fell apart in the goddamn bathroom of this coffee shop."

Crystal looks worried. "What you saw was probably a panic attack," she makes known. "A lot of people suffer from them, even when they act completely fine most of the time. I'm guessing that's what it was."

"I'd definitely call it that," I agree. "It's like she forgot how to breathe? And then the rest of the day she had to relearn how to function normally. All because of this bloody screenplay."

"I take it you haven't read it yet?" Crystal carefully asks.

I hit my fist on the wooden beam. "No, Crystal, I haven't fucking read it yet—"

"Killian!" my dad angrily shouts my name.

"But I know *you* know what's in there," I continue. "I know you know what she's hiding. Which makes me pretty pissed off right now. Because neither one of you will tell me."

"You know what's in there?" my dad asks Crystal.

"She was my *patient*," Crystal reminds us both, "before she was whatever you two are now. And she had the right to tell me things in private. I took an oath to not break doctor-patient confidentiality."

I watch Hazel as she picks Maisy up to grab a firefly. "Yeah, well, she said we'd talk about it all tomorrow—"

"She did?!" Crystal turns to me in shock.

"Yes?"

Her face softens and she's looking uncomfortably between my dad and me. "Just be there for her, okay? She needs you to be there for her. And if either one of you need to talk—"

"Crystal," I roll my eyes. "Even after her panic attack today, I doubt she'll need to run to you for more therapy—"

"It's not Hazel I'm worried about," she cuts me off, and then she gives my shoulder a squeeze and walks toward the field of fireflies.

I turn to my dad, raising my eyes as I question what his wife just said to me.

He takes a sip of his beer and simply responds with, "Women," as he walks away.

I stay by the barn, watching Hazel run around this open field with my little sister. I watch how she carefully secures the fireflies in the jar, filling it almost completely with a constant flicker of little lights. I watch how her wild hair seems to float behind her as the breeze from the night whispers through. I watch how carefree she is around these little kids, how they seem to gravitate toward her and her natural maternal instinct.

She catches me staring and calls me into the field with her finger. I move slowly, just so I can watch her from a distance a little while longer. But once I approach, I can't help but wrap my hands around her waist and pull her body into mine, well aware that we have small kids and an entire town watching us.

"You look beautiful out here," I whisper into her ear.

She gives me a funny look. "In a field with fireflies and the foul smell of cow manure wafting throughout the night?"

I laugh under my breath. "You're in your element, Hazel. A Bohemian goddess. Wild and carefree looks stunning on you. Minus the cow shit smell, of course."

She rubs her finger on my lips and places a quick kiss on

them. "Want to see something magical?" her eyes light up as she asks. She tugs my hand and pulls me right into the middle of the field. "All right kids!" she then calls out to them. "Everyone over here!" They all listen to her, forming a circle around where she and I are standing. "Does everyone have their jars?" The kids raise them up in the air, flickering lights now illuminating us. "Good! We're going to do a countdown. Then we're going to open them and release our fireflies into the night sky, because they don't want to spend the rest of their lives trapped in your jar. They have much more important things to do, okay?"

The kids all agree and excitedly start jumping up and down with just the simple thought of letting their hard work go. Kids are funny. They can spend all night running around catching fireflies in a jar, sweating, tripping, crying when they can't reach one. But then in one quick moment, they agree to watch their dedicated efforts simply vanish into the night sky. I wish adults could think like kids. I wish adults realized that sometimes you have to work your ass off for just one perfect second in time.

"Whisper to them," Hazel quietly says to the waiting kids. "Whisper to the fireflies and thank them for giving you this beautiful moment."

The peaceful sound of these children whispering can be heard all around us. I swear to God, even the trees, the stars, the moon ... they're all listening in right now.

Hazel's hand is suddenly in mine. She gives it a small squeeze. "Okay, guys!" she gently calls out. "Are we ready? Let's free them! Three ... two ... one!"

The lids come off and all the fireflies make their escape. Hundreds of them fly around, lighting the sky as they find their way back home. We turn in a slow circle, me and Hazel, our hands still clasped together as we watch this magnificent moment in front of us.

Her voice suddenly mixes in with the softness of the night. "Magical, right?"

I don't answer. I can't think of the right thing to say. That happens so often with Hazel. Her words or actions leave me speechless and feeling inadequate in her presence. So, I just kiss her, standing in this field as fireflies flutter around us. I kiss her, knowing I will never find anyone else in this world, that could make a barn raising party and the smell of cow shit feel this blissfully magical.

"Can I stay with you tonight?" she asks, her nervous eyes locked on mine.

I can definitely find words for that question. "Of course. Every night, Hazel."

Comfort. Hazel needs comfort. She's not asking for a night of passionate sex. She's not asking for another night of the two of us discovering new ways to make the other feel epically incredible with our bodies. She just wants comfort. She just wants to feel safe.

Later that night I bring her back to my house, officially ending my first barn raising party. We slip in through the basement door and head right to my bedroom. I hand her one of my t-shirts and watch with a sense of pride as she undresses and tugs it over her head. I pull back the blankets and we crawl in, where I immediately wrap my arms around her, not planning on letting go the rest of the night.

"I'm sorry," she suddenly whispers against my skin after a few moments of silence.

Confused, I ask, "What are you sorry for?"

"Lots of things," she responds. "There are a lot of things I'm sorry for. A lot of things I regret. But tonight was perfect," she goes on. "I just wish every night could be like tonight was. You and me, just magical with nothing to worry about."

"What are you worried about, Hazel?"

She places her hand on my chest. "I'm worried that we'll

never have another night like tonight."

I look down at her and she raises her head to meet my eyes. "I'm not going back to London after the summer," I blurt out. There. Decision made. Fuck my entire career. "And even if you decide you don't want to be in your film, or you don't even want it to *become* a film, I want us to move in together ... somewhere ... anywhere. You and me, our own place ... because I'm determined to show you that every night can be exactly how tonight was."

Her eyes light up for just a brief second, but then it's as if she remembers a hundred different reasons why she's not allowed to feel excitement with what I just declared. "Tomorrow," she calmly replies. "Let me know if that's how you still feel tomorrow."

Then she buries her head into the crook of my neck and instantly falls asleep. It takes me much longer—my thoughts are all over the place—and when I finally doze off a couple hours later, my phone buzzing loudly on the nightstand jerks me awake.

Theo.

I forgot to call him back today. I know he won't stop until I pick up. I reach for it, trying not to wake Hazel at the same time. "Theo!" I whisper into the phone.

"Why are you whispering?" he loudly asks.

"Because it's the middle of the fucking night here."

"Oh shit! I forgot about the time change!"

"It's like, midnight in California right now, too. What do you want?"

"Midnight?" he laughs as his words slur. He's obviously drunk. "Shit, you're right. Should probably go to bed—"

"Theo? What is it?" I ask, annoyed and just wanting to go back to sleep.

"You never called me back today," he reminds me.

"Okay, can I call you tomorrow—"

"I'm coming to Ohio!" he joyfully announces.

"Sure you are."

"For real, little brother. Booked my flight today. That's why I was calling."

I sit up a little in my bed with Hazel still in my arms. "You booked a flight to Ohio?" I ask in disbelief.

"I did."

"When do you get here?"

"Three days. Just for the weekend. Think Daddy Steve will let me crash with you?"

"You'll be in Ohio, in three days?"

"Yes sir."

I shake my head in doubt, wondering if I'm dreaming up this entire phone conversation. "Okay. Well. I guess that's good? I'm going to call you in the morning to make sure I'm not just imagining this, all right?"

"Sounds like a plan," he laughs. "I need to go eat something. I'm as high as a kite—"

"*Goodnight, Theo*," I groan, hitting end on my cell and placing it on the nightstand. I then turn back to Hazel. She's awake, her eyes are wide and her body is shaking in the bed. "Jesus Christ!" I exclaim, pulling her back into my arms and throwing the blankets over the two of us. I start kissing her forehead, checking with my lips to make sure she's not sick with a fever. Her skin is the opposite, though. She's freezing. "Baby, what is it? What's wrong? Please just tell me."

I hear her breathing deeply, just like she was at Cool Beans Café. She's trying to get herself to calm down. She's trying to bring herself out of another panic attack. I rub my hands along her back, over and over again, waiting for her breathing to return to normal.

"Whatever it is, Hazel, I'm right here."

It takes her a while, but when it finally happens, it happens quickly. I can literally feel the warmth return to her body. I can sense her heart beating a normal rhythm again as her chest presses up against mine. Her fingers are no longer clenched as she starts to move them along my back. And then her eyes, they lift and look up at me, searching for that comfort she's always able to find.

"There you are," I simply say, because no words will be able to properly explain how difficult it was to see her go through that again. "I love you, Hazel."

She moves her face closer to mine. Our eyelashes blink against each other. "I love you too, Killian," her voice comes out shaky but absolutely beautiful at the same time. And then she kisses me, her warm fingers cradling my chin. "I love you," she repeats again. "I think I always have." And then she snuggles her way back into the comfort of my body, knowing I won't ask any questions tonight.

I won't. I won't ask any questions right now, because she promised me tomorrow. Tomorrow is when I'll find out everything. So I hold her, I breathe her in, I comfort her. I fall asleep with her soul so tightly wrapped around my heart, knowing tomorrow will be here soon.

But when tomorrow arrives, I know something is different before I even open my eyes.

She's not in my arms.

She's not in my bed.

She's simply ... gone.

# Hazel

## -during-

**W**here are you going, Birdie?" he asks me, closing my bedroom door behind him.

*Why didn't I lock the fucking door?!*

My heart is racing, beating so loudly in my chest I question how it's possible I haven't just collapsed yet. "I know what you did," I point to my door. "What you just put in your brother's cup down there—"

"I promised him a good time. I'm ensuring he'll have one and won't remember shit the next day."

"And what about me?!" I cry out under my breath. "Last night? I didn't do any fucking shots! You did the same thing to me, didn't you?"

His eyes narrow and I can almost sense the distress behind them. "What are you going to do about it, Birdie?"

"What am I going to do about it?! How about I go downstairs and tell everyone what a piece of shit you are—"

His hand covers my mouth and he pushes me hard against the wall. He then snatches my phone from my hand, tossing it onto the floor. It slides under the bed. "You're not going to do that." His eyes are hollow. There's no emotion in them whatsoever now.

I pull his hand down. "You raped me," I say to him. Speaking those words out loud makes my body start to shake. "You put drugs in my cup and you raped me, didn't you?"

"I wouldn't be so quick to jump to accusations. You never said no, Birdie. You never told me to stop."

I jam my finger into his chest. "You're a rapist. And I *know* I'm not the first girl you've done that to."

His fingers slowly push the hair off my neck, and he trails the exposed skin with his tongue. I fight back the urge to vomit. "I know you like how that feels," he groans. "You sure did last night."

I start crying, trying to push him away, but he's too strong.

"I always get what I want," he whispers into my ear. "And you shouldn't have acted so fucking stubborn." He pushes at my shoulders, slamming me up against the wall again. "You going to fight me now? Make a scene? Scream for help? No one will believe you. Ever. Not now, not tomorrow, not next week. No one will *ever* believe you. No one in this house will even remember what happens tonight. I'll make sure of that."

"I'll remember," I say through my tears, struggling against him even though I know my efforts are worthless.

He still owns me.

I'm still trapped.

He rips my shirt right from my chest, and then slips his hand under my skirt, yanking my panties down to my ankles as his body presses hard against mine. "Good, Birdie," he replies. I can hear the crackle from the wrapper of a condom as he pulls it out of his pocket, and then he starts to push his jeans down. "I want you to *always* remember me."

# chapter twenty-six

She's not answering her phone. It's going straight to voicemail. Fuck it. I'll just go to her house. I'm going to find her. It's already after nine and I have no idea when she disappeared last night, but I know something isn't right. Hazel wouldn't just leave.

I throw some clothes on and head up the basement steps to grab the Audi keys. Surprisingly, Crystal and Maisy are at the kitchen table, eating waffles.

"What are you two doing home?" I ask them.

"Gym is getting new equipment today," Crystal answers. "And I took the day off to spend with Maisy, but she's abandoning me."

"*Mom*," she groans between bites. "The entire team is meeting at Piper's to go swimming. You have me for like, ten more years."

Crystal laughs and takes a sip of her coffee.

"Hey, did either of you see Hazel this morning?" I question them both.

"Hazel was here?!" Maisy exclaims with a mouth full of waffle. "Did you two have a sleepover?!"

Crystal chokes on her coffee.

"A sleepover?" I repeat. "Yes, sure ... a sleepover. Crystal," I turn to her, "something isn't right. I'm worried about her."

Her eyes raise and she pulls the chair out next to her. "Sit, Killian. Explain."

I do. I sit down, my legs bouncing with anxiety. "There's something really bothering her and I can't figure it out. And last night we came back here and fell asleep, and I thought she was doing okay, but then Theo called—"

"Theo called?!" Crystal grabs my arm.

I look down at her fingers as they painfully squeeze my skin, and then back up to her sudden alarmed face. "Yeah? In the middle of the night. He called yesterday while we were at Cool Beans—"

"Was Hazel with you when he called then?"

"Yes?" I respond, confused. "He called to tell me he's coming to visit, but I hung up before he could, so he called me in the middle of the night—"

"Hazel heard this?" Crystal interrupts. "She heard you two talking last night?"

"She was lying right next to me, so I assume she heard ... and then she had another panic attack after I hung up the phone. Crystal, what the hell is going on?!"

"Maisy," Crystal quickly turns to her. "We're going to be late. Go get your swimsuit on, okay?"

Maisy pushes back from the table and slowly takes her plate to the sink. She then taps my head as she stands behind me. "Next time you have a sleepover with Hazel, don't forget about me." And then she walks to the stairs.

Crystal takes my hand into hers. "I need you to think for a minute. Just sit here and think. Yesterday at Cool Beans, what happened right before Hazel had her panic attack?"

I think back to yesterday. "She was working on her screenplay. She said she needed a break and she rested her head on the table. Then Theo called—"

"Stop!" she shouts. "What happened last night right before Hazel had her panic attack?"

"We were sleeping ... *just* sleeping, and then ... then Theo called ..."

My heart. My heart has dropped right out of my body.

"Are you telling me this is about fucking Theo?!" I cry, jumping out of my seat. "Why?! Why is Hazel having panic attacks over Theo?!"

"Go find her," Crystal tries to calmly say, but her voice is quivering and I see her eyes start to gloss over. "Don't call him. Do *not* call Theo and mention Hazel. Go find her, and if you can't find her within the next hour, come back here. I'll be here and we'll talk, okay?"

I grab the Audi keys and I'm down the driveway before I even let it fully register that my brother is the reason for Hazel's panic attacks. My brother. Theo. The only person who's ever cared about me. The only person I've ever trusted before Hazel came along.

*Calm down, Killian.*

*Just. Stay. Calm.*

I head to her house first. Her BMW isn't in the driveway. Her house is completely locked up, and I can hear Aspen barking from the inside as I repeatedly ring the bell and pound on the door.

I try her cell again. Still going straight to voicemail.

I drive to her parents' café. The parking lot is filled but her BMW isn't here, either.

*Go see if her parents are inside. Go see if they know where she might be.*

I pull the door open and find Lori at the counter.

"Killian!" she warmly greets me. I walk right over to her; each step feels like I'm dragging weights behind me. "Hazel get to New York okay? Haven't heard from her since she left early this morning."

*New York?!*

I freeze, clutching the barstool as Lori pours coffee into

the empty cups in front of the seated customers.

*Don't let her know. Don't let Lori find out that Hazel didn't tell you this. Find out more from her, but don't let her know anything is wrong. Don't worry her.*

"She's good," is all I say.

"Such short notice," Lori goes on. "But she said this was it, the make it or break it meeting. That last night it came to her? She figured out the new ending to her screenplay? You want some breakfast? Coffee?"

*Last night. In my bed. She figured out the new ending?*

"I'll take a coffee to go. I've got a few things I need to do this morning."

She pours coffee into a disposable cup and hands it out to me, a curious look on her face. "Come over for dinner when Hazel comes home, okay?"

I nod my head and walk back out to the Audi without saying another word. I call Hazel again as I throw myself into the driver's seat, already knowing what will greet me on the other end.

Voicemail.

*Think, Killian.* I rest my forehead against the steering wheel. *Think.*

New York. She's in New York. She flew to New York without telling you, and she probably did it because she thinks she's going to hurt you with whatever you're about to uncover.

Theo. Something about Theo. It all make sense now, why she said it would destroy us. All along, her past ... her life as Birdie ... her horrible memories that throw her into panic attacks, they were about Theo. My brother.

I'm *done* questioning all of this.

Looks like I'm going to New York.

I turn the Audi on and drive back home, immediately running down the basement steps to throw some clothes into a bookbag. First flight. I'll just drive to the airport and book the first flight into JFK. I'll walk the entire goddamn city shouting her name if I have to. I'm going to find her.

I run back up the steps just as Crystal comes in through the garage.

"Did you find her?"

I shake my head. "She's in New York."

"New York?!"

"Yeah, I'm going. I have to get to the airport. She's not picking up, but I'm going to New York—"

My cell starts ringing in my pocket. I yank it out and see an unfamiliar phone number on the screen. As an actor, you *never* answer the phone when it's a number you don't recognize. But I'm desperate.

"Hello?"

"Killian!" his thick English accent hits my ear.

"Blake?! I fucking don't have time for this—"

"Wait! Wait!" he pleads. "Just wait! There's a script! A new one! I knew you wouldn't answer my call—"

"Blake! No! Not today!"

"Listen to me you *bloody* fool!" he shouts. "A producer called from New York! The writer—the writer of this film asked for you! She asked for you to take on one of the leads and they sent me the script! Killian, this is it—this is the role you wanted! I read it, and you need to get to New York, right now! But you have to read it first—they asked that you read it first before you meet with them. Fuck—I'm out of breath! Are you listening to me, Killian?!"

I am. But the kitchen is currently spinning in my vision.

Hazel. This is Hazel's film.

"Send it to me," I demand. "Send me the script, right now."

"Yes! Right now!" Blake exclaims. "It's sent. You come in on page thirty. Killian, this is huge, but it's hard to read, and I get this feeling you're somehow a part of this story ... so just prepare yourself—"

"I'll call you when I'm done." And then I hang up.

"What is it?" Crystal immediately asks.

"It's her film," I answer. "Her screenplay. They sent it to my agent. She's asked for me to play the other lead. He—he just sent it to me. Printer! I need a printer!"

Crystal pulls me into my dad's office and turns on the printer. I open the attachment on my phone and send the pages to the waiting machine.

"Killian, I'll be out here, okay?" she points to the foyer.

I shake my head. I feel like I need her in here with me, and I don't know why. I've never felt like this before. I've never needed a mother before, and I strangely don't want her to leave my side. "No. Please. Just stay?"

I think I hear her gasp. "Of course," she nods.

I reach for the papers when they're finally done, stacking them in a neat pile in front of me on my dad's desk. "I'm not going to like what I read, am I?" I look up at Crystal and ask.

"No, honey," she sadly responds. "But just remember, you're the good guy. You've always been her good guy, and you can still be her good guy."

I flip to page thirty and my eyes start reading the words that lie in front of me, and immediately ... I start remembering our before.

I start remembering Birdie.

# Killian

## -during-

Jesus, it's fucking loud in this house. I thought that when I came here it would just be me and Theo with the cast of the new film he's in. I haven't seen him in years, and I had an audition not too far from here, so I begged my team to give me two days. Just two days to hang out with my big brother. But there's probably thirty other people in this house, and they're all either drunk or high. Drugs are freely passing between hands, being snorted straight from side tables and counters.

Theo has disappeared, leaving me alone in the kitchen. My mind doesn't want to imagine what he might be doing, and I'm starting to think coming here was the dumbest mistake of my life so far.

He told me he plans on moving here permanently, to southern California. He's never had an actual home before and usually just rents something wherever he's filming. I was excited to hear this since now I'll always know where to find him, but after seeing the life he's currently living here, he's a bloody idiot to move here permanently. He's just adding fuel to his already out of control fire.

I stand at the kitchen counter, taking in this scene that I

swear looks straight out of an HBO series, one that throws numerous disclaimers on the screen before the show even starts. I just gradually sip on the beer Theo poured for me the moment I arrived in my Uber, wondering if I can possibly get an early flight back to London in the morning. I drink it all too quickly because what the hell else am I supposed to do right now?

My mouth is too dry. I need water. I go to get a new cup when I hear the doorbell in the distance. I don't know how I heard it, but the bells are chiming faintly in my ear. At least this will give me something to do.

I go to the front door and swing it open. There's a rather terrifying looking pizza delivery man standing on the steps, just one pizza box in his hands. I think he might be missing some teeth as his lips don't fully cover his mouth.

"You Theo?" he asks.

I shake my head. The fact that this sketchy person asked specifically for my brother makes my nose turn up. "I can go find him."

"He owes me six hundred."

"Six hundred for a fucking pizza?!"

Then it hits me, hard, and I actually hear myself groan. This homeless-looking junky is a drug dealer. My brother's drug dealer. That pizza box does not have pizza in it. *What the hell, Theo?* A lot has changed, that's for sure.

"I'll go find him," I tell this so-called pizza delivery man. "You just ... do whatever."

The stairs, I last saw Theo walking up the stairs. I head to the second floor. Most of the doors are wide open, welcoming whoever wants to get high or have sex in privacy in these vacant bedrooms.

"Theo?" I call out, knowing with all this noise there's no way he'd hear me calling for him behind a closed door. I twist the handle of the first one, only to see it's a closet filled with coats. I then twist the handle of the second and stare in. At first what I see doesn't register. It takes my brain at least five seconds to understand what is playing out in front of me, because I think my mind is trying to protect me from what's actually going on.

Theo, his jeans down to his ankles, pushing himself forcefully into a girl he has pinned up against the wall. Her wild hair is the first thing I notice about her, her naked chest is sadly the second. I'm eighteen. I'm an actor. I've had sex, lots of sex. I've walked in on plenty of people having sex at parties, too, but that is not what this is. Theo's hand is covering her mouth, she's crying, she's squirming every time he pushes himself into her, but she can't get away.

She's being raped.

She's being raped by Theo.

"What the fuck are you doing?!" I scream out, clearing those ten or so steps toward them as I push him off of her.

"Killian!" Theo says my name so casually, like what I just witnessed means absolutely nothing. He turns his back to me, pulling up his pants.

I shove him as hard as I can and he falls into the nightstand. "What the hell were you doing to her?!"

"Just having some fun," he winks as he stands back up. "She was enjoying it, right Birdie?"

I turn to her. She's now slouched down against the wall, burying her face and chest into her knees.

"Get the hell out of here!" I yell to him, furiously pushing him to the door.

He barely moves as he's gained his footing now and is nothing but muscle. "Oh, I get it," he holds his ground and smirks. "*You* want a turn with her?"

I punch him, right in his face, shocking both of us. This is not my brother. This is not the Theo I used to know. "Get the *fuck* out of here," I repeat again. "And we're done. You're a piece of shit."

He starts laughing. "Sure, Killian. We'll see about that in the morning." And then he turns and walks out.

This girl is sobbing up against the wall, and I don't know how to comfort her. I'm a stranger to her, a stranger that just walked in on his brother raping her. I think I stand there for a few minutes or so before my mind reminds me that I can actually speak to her.

"Let me call the police for you," is the first thing I say, reaching into my pockets for my phone. *Shit.* I left it on the counter downstairs.

"No!" she cries out. "Don't! Don't call the police!"

I go to move closer to her and she flinches, scooting as far away from me as she can. She has every right to be afraid of me, but I don't want her to. I hold my hands up. "I won't hurt you," I promise her. "I'm not like that. I'm not like him." I see her shirt on the ground and reach for it, only realizing once I pick it up that it's ripped right down the middle. Vomit rises into my mouth. "Here," I say, pulling off my London Underground t-shirt. "You can wear this."

She slowly takes it from my hand and pulls it down over herself, covering her naked chest.

"What can I do?" I gently ask her. "What can I do to help?"

"Nothing," she says. "There's nothing you can do. I just—I just need to get out of here."

*You and me both.*

"I can help," I tell her. "Let me help. I can find a way to sneak you past—"

"Oh, *Birdie!*" we both hear Theo's voice echoing from downstairs. Our heads snap in unison to the bedroom door. "I have something for you! Something to make this night *so* much better! You too, Killian!"

Her hands cover her ears and she rocks back and forth.

This is bullshit. I'm going to kill him. I'm fucking going to kill my goddamn brother. I need to get her out of here before he walks back in.

"There's a closet!" I quickly tell her, pulling her up off the ground. "In the hallway! Go, get in there and hide. I'll get rid of him, and then I'm going to get you out of here. I promise. Okay? I promise."

Her eyes. I swear her eyes are searching mine, searching for something to believe. She gives me a quick nod and heads out the door, and then I tensely stand there and wait for him.

He appears in the doorframe a minute or so later. A bruise already forming on his face from my fist, and a smug grin on his lips. He points to my bare chest. "Had a little fun, I see?"

I shove him hard again and he hits the wall. "Theo, what have you done?! This isn't you! Do you realize what you just did?! Do you have any idea what you just did to her?! What's *happened* to you?!"

He ignores me. I can see his eyes scan the room for her. His possessive eyes. His empty eyes. He pushes past me and enters the room. "Where is she?!" he angrily asks. He looks feral. He looks high. He looks crazed and obsessed. "Birdie! Where are you?!"

"She left."

"Bullshit!" he furiously hisses at me. "I know you're in here somewhere!" he shouts. "Just come out so we can talk! I promise, we'll just talk!"

"You need help, Theo!" I whisper under my breath.

He ignores me and hangs his head out the open door. "Fine!" his sharp voice pierces the walls around me. "If this is how it's going to be, good luck making it in this world! Acting like this will only ruin you! I'll make sure of that!" And then he turns back to me.

I step away, moving slowly into the room. He honestly looks like he's going to attack me.

"Be the hero now, Killian," he heatedly whispers. "But

tomorrow, you'll just be the same old Killian again. Come find me in the morning, when you remember who I really am to you." And then he leaves, leaving me standing there with my heart broken into a hundred pieces.

I wait until he's fully down the stairs before I even think about leaving the room. I need my phone. I need to get out of here, but first I need to get *her* out of here. I walk to the closet and stand in front of the door, praying she's behind it.

Three.

Two.

One.

And I pull it open.

# Killian

*-during-*

S he's in there. Hiding in this closet with coats thrown around her. I feel relief. Instant relief. "Is it okay if I come in for a minute?" I whisper.

She nods her head. I step inside, quietly closing the door behind me and taking a seat next to her. I hit the wall light which illuminates our bodies in a soft yellow glow. She does the same to the one on her side. Our shoulders touch and I'm afraid this is going to frighten her. I don't want her to be frightened of me, but there's no way I can scoot over any further in this tight space.

"Are you okay?" I ask her.

*Stupid question. Of course she's not okay.*

"No," she softly replies.

"Was that—was that the first time he's done—"

"No," she cuts me off.

I hear myself take a deep breath. "I won't let him get away with this. I promise. As soon as we're both out of here ..."

Her hand appears on my arm, almost as if she's trying to comfort *me*. "Killian, right? You're Killian Lewis?"

"Yeah?"

"Killian, your brother dropped drugs in your beer when

you weren't looking. Some sort of roofie. I saw him do it. He did the same thing to me last night. You have about thirty minutes, maybe a little more because you're bigger than me, before it kicks in fully. You're not going to remember any of this in the morning. You're not going to remember me at all, or what you walked in on."

I stare at her, losing myself in her stormy gray eyes. "Why the hell would he drug me?!"

She takes a minute and then bluntly says, "Probably so you'd forget everything that happened tonight. Him. So you would forget him. Everything you'd see him do."

*Are you kidding me*?! "If I'm going to forget what he did, then I'm going to fucking do something about it right now." I go to stand but she yanks on my arm.

"Please! No!" she quietly begs. "Please just stay in here with me. I'm—I'm scared of him. Of all of them. And I just—I just want you stay in here with me for a few minutes, okay?"

Of course. Of course I'll stay in here with her. I slowly sit back down. "Sure," I nod my head. "You're an actress, right? I've seen some of your films. Your name is Birdie?"

"No. Call me Hazel. My name is Hazel."

*Her name is Hazel. Remember that, Killian. Her name is Hazel, not Birdie.*

"Nice to meet you, Hazel."

She smiles, she actually smiles at me. How can she smile at me after what my brother just did to her? "Nice to meet you too, Killian."

My shoulder rests against hers again. "Am I really going to forget everything?"

Her hair is tickling my arm as she nods her head. "Yes. I have no real memories of last night. Just a few little flashes of before he snuck them into my drink. But now that I know what he did, I think I'm starting to remember more. It's like a door has been opened."

I slam my head back against the wall. I can't believe I'm in this situation. I was drugged by my brother and I'm hiding in a closet with the girl he sexually assaulted. "I'm so sorry," I say to her. I throw my hand over my face, trying to hide the fact that I might start crying. "I can't believe what he did—what I saw ... I'm so sorry."

"Don't apologize for him. To be honest with you, I don't think I'm the first girl he's done that to."

*What*?! "I'm not like him, I swear!" I find myself pleading with her to realize.

Her hand goes back to my arm. "I know, Killian. I can tell." Her eyes are on mine, searching them again. "You have really pretty eyes," she says to me. "Like the ocean on the brightest day of the year."

I hold her stare, shocked that during these moments after a traumatic event, she can still find it in herself to say something so meaningful. "And yours, they look like the ocean after a summer storm."

"He doesn't have the same eyes as you—"

"Different dads," I tell her. "I didn't grow up with him, and I actually haven't seen Theo in years—"

"Don't say his name anymore."

"Okay," I quickly agree. "I won't. I didn't realize how much he changed. Or maybe this is just how he's always been? And I just—I didn't know because I don't see him at all. I wouldn't have come here if I had known, but then—you ... he would have kept—"

"People change," Hazel stops me from saying more. "People change all the time. Humans are like chameleons, almost. And this lifestyle, it can change you pretty quick. It's not your fault you didn't know."

"I'm going to make him pay for what he did," I promise her again. "I'll find a way—"

"You're not going to remember, trust me. You're going to

wake up tomorrow and not remember any of this."

I know she's right. I'm already starting to feel different, woozy. Like I took too much cold medicine and it's quickly crashing down on me. "Then you need to remind me," I say to her. "Remind me of tonight, so he doesn't get away with this."

"You think we're actually going to see each other again, outside of this closet one day?"

Why do I feel a pang of guilt in my stomach over not seeing her again? Over not being able to make sure she's recovered from this? Over not being able to make sure she's okay?

"Maybe," I answer. "And if we do, make me remember, okay? Don't let him get away with this."

Her lips form a frown. "I'm too scared to let the world know. They won't believe me and he'll just twist it all around. He's idolized by so many people—"

"Then *I* will. I'll let the world know. His *brother* will. They'll fucking believe me. But you just have to remind me. If I forget all this, make me remember."

"Sure, Killian."

She places her head on my shoulder. I'm glad I've made her comfortable. I'm glad she knows I'm not like him. I'm glad I can be this person for her right now.

"How am I going to get out of here?" she whispers. "I need to go home."

"Where is home?"

"Ohio," she remarks.

I look down at her and our eyes meet again. "That's ironic, my dad is in Ohio."

She smiles. "Maybe we *will* meet again."

"We're both actors," I remind her. "Our paths could definitely cross."

She shakes her head hard. "I just want to be done with acting," she then tells me. "My life is being controlled by other people all the time. I don't have a say in what I do or how I feel. I just feel trapped with this life. Caged. Always on display, but never free."

I never thought about my life the way she just effortlessly explained it. But she's right.

"They cage me, too," I agree. "All of them. I get it. I feel trapped every day."

She lets out a loud sigh. "I need to get out of here," she says again.

The closet starts to slowly spin on me and I put my hand up to my head to keep it still.

"It's starting to hit you, isn't it?" she whispers.

"Do you think if I make myself sick, it would help?"

She shakes her head. "Maybe a little. But it's already hit your bloodstream."

*Think, Killian. Help her get out of here before you can't help her anymore.*

"A phone!" I exclaim. "We need a phone. We need to call you a ride. An Uber? A Lyft? Where's your phone?"

She points to the door. "I think it's in the bedroom. He threw it. I think it landed under the bed."

"We'll get it," I promise. "We'll call a ride and stay in that room with the door locked until it gets here. Okay?" I stand up and wobble on my feet. She grabs my arm to keep me steady.

"What about you?" she questions.

I pull her hand so she's standing in front of me. "He's an asshole and he belongs in jail, but he won't hurt me. Drug me, sure. But hurt me, no. I promise. I'm not worried about me right now."

"*I'm* worried about you."

That might be the nicest thing anyone has ever said to me.

"Once you're safe and out of here, I'll find my phone. I'll find my bookbag with my shit in it, wallet ... passport ... and I'll get myself out of here. I'll sneak away and get back to London tomorrow. Don't worry about me. Okay? You just need to trust me, even though you have no reason to."

Her fingers brush against my cheek. She looks so sad, so defeated, like she knows what I just said is nothing but an empty promise because there's no way I'm making it out of this house tonight unless someone carries me. I think we both know this.

"I trust you," she then whispers.

My vision is doubling and I quickly twist the doorknob, peering out to the empty hall. The noise of everyone from downstairs hits me hard, almost like a punch to the chest. I take her hand and pull her into her room, closing the door and locking it. She crouches down under the bed and finds her phone. My back is up against the door as she quickly taps away on the screen.

"Done," she declares, looking up at me. I see three of her now. "Few minutes."

"Your phone! My phone! Give me your number—"

"You won't remember it—"

"Then I'll put mine in there," I take her phone and pull up a new contact, but as I try to tap out my number, the screen grows blurry and my fingers hesitate as everything is floating in my vision. I can't recall the actual order of the numbers, either. "I don't remember my fucking phone number!" I shout, shocked.

She slowly takes the phone away from me, realizing this is pointless. She then grabs a tattered bookbag and starts throwing things inside of it. "Your shirt!" she suddenly says. She starts to pull it off her body.

"No! Keep it. It looks good on you. And it will remind you of me. Remind you that I'm not like him ..."

She slowly pulls it back down. "You're not him, Killian," she reassures me.

I start to cry, and I struggle to figure out why I'm letting these uncontrollable emotions out in front of her. The alcohol? The drugs? The memory of what I saw in this room? The memory of my brother? The memory of knowing who he really is? How can she stand there, trying to comfort *me*, after what happened to her?

"Hey," she whispers, holding onto my hands and giving them a squeeze. She's floating in front of me now. "You're going to be okay."

"I don't want to forget what he did—"

"I don't think you will. You'll remember one day—"

"Make me remember, promise me. He has to pay for this. Make me remember you, us—this night."

"Okay," she nods. "One day. When we're both ready to remember it all, we'll do something huge. Killian and Hazel. We'll be free of this night. Together. I promise."

I know she's only saying this to make me feel better, but it's working.

Killian and Hazel. Free. Together.

"I'm sorry. I'm so sorry, Hazel."

She gives my cheek a small kiss. "I'm sorry, too, Killian." She then walks over to the window that overlooks the street. "How do you feel right now?" she asks.

I'm going to black out. I can feel it coming. "Fine?" my voice slurs.

Her face looks worried. "Would you be able to make it to the car with me?"

*She's considering taking me with her. Tell her you can. Tell her you can make it.*

"No," I truthfully respond.

Her head nods, like she knew that would be my answer. "Stay in this room then, okay? When I leave? Just stay in here. Get in the bed and go to sleep. Don't try to do anything else."

Fuck no. I'm going to go find Theo as soon as she's safely in the car.

"Okay," I say in return.

She stares out the window. "My ride's here," she turns to me and says. Even with her face floating in front of me, I can see the emotions in her eyes. "The ledge, the porch. I'm just going to climb down, okay? I can jump."

I nod my head and try to open the window as my shaking fingers slip against the glass. She helps and we get it fully open. I then push the screen out and it falls onto the overhang.

*Her name is Hazel.*

*Her name is Hazel.*

Everything is swaying in my vision.

"Killian!" my name is called out. I focus my eyes, she's perched on the overhang roof now, getting ready to slide down to the porch. "We met for a bigger reason," she says. "Thank you for this—for being you. Stay in the bedroom. You've already been the hero tonight, just stay in this room."

She's crying, I think? Why is she crying? She should be ecstatic to be getting out of here, but instead she's crying as she sits on this roof.

"Hazel?" I say her name with uncertainty.

She wipes her eyes really quick. "I hope we see each other again someday," she finally says.

I reach for her hand, because I've never been more certain in my life, that I *will* see her again someday. She takes it and gives it a firm squeeze. And the last thing I say to her before she safely disappears into the night, before she disappears from my life and my memories, might be the most profound thing I've ever spoken ... and I won't even remember that I said it to her.

"Hazel, no matter how many times they try to cage us, remember ... we always have the ability to let ourselves fly free."

# chapter twenty-seven

Her name is Hazel.
Her name is Hazel.
*Her name is Hazel.*

But she was right. No matter how many times I reminded myself of her name as I stumbled down the stairs desperately looking for my phone, I didn't remember the next day. No matter how many times I screamed it out loud as I searched frantically through the crowds for Theo to confront him again about what he did, I didn't remember the next day. No matter how many times I cried it out as I crawled into the closet, feeling lost and helpless as the drugs overtook every ounce of my body, I didn't remember the next day.

Her name and everything about that night, had left my memory by the time I was found the next morning, curled in a ball on the closet floor, coming down from whatever he had slipped in my drink.

"Damn, Killian," Theo self-righteously pounded my back when I was brought into the kitchen. "You sure know how to fucking party."

And because this was Theo, because this was my brother, someone I had looked up to from the moment I was born ... I believed him. I believed him that I partied too hard and blacked out, because it's happened before. I believed him that the bruise on his face and my sore hand were both due to a drunken wrestling match in which I won, because it's happened before. I believed him that the drugs that were passed around like candy again later that night had been consumed by me twenty-four hours earlier, because it's happened before.

And when he dropped me off at the airport the next morning, laughing about my hungover state and how neither one of us would ever clearly remember our short weekend together, he told me how proud he was of me. And I believed him, because I couldn't remember a reason why I shouldn't.

It had left me. Everything about her. What I saw. Our moment together. Her promise to me. My promise to her. The way she looked. All the comfort we both had found in our brief encounter. It had left me. It disappeared like it was never even there. It was all a dream that simply faded away the moment my eyes opened the next morning.

And only once she reentered my life, once our paths crossed due to the simple fact that fate knew we were always going to find each other again in this world, did I remember everything so clearly. It had been there all along, trapped. Just waiting for the moment she came to finally unlock that bolted cage door.

And when that moment happened, when she turned that key and released me from the memory I didn't even realize I had been chained to this past year, it all came flooding back. The moments, that night, images suddenly flash in my mind like clips of a movie. And I remember it all.

I remember our before.

I remember what I promised.

Her name is Hazel.

And I'm the one who's going to set her free.

# chapter twenty-eight

When the memories start to come back, the first thing my body does is expel everything I've consumed in the last twenty-four hours. The vomit flies out of my mouth with such force, I don't even have time to stand up.

Crystal is there with a trash bin, catching what she can, trying to reassure me. But she's crying and her shaking voice is the opposite of reassuring. Her words are punctured with emotion over what she's witnessing, and that makes me feel even worse. I hate what I'm putting her through.

When the vomit has stopped, I push my chair out and stand, but I don't make it far. The second thing my body does as the memories start to come back is go into shock. I hit the wall with my back, the office spinning in my vision, and I slide down onto the floor.

Theo's face is floating like a hologram in my mind. Theo's body, pushing up against Hazel's as she cries. Hazel wearing my t-shirt. Our shoulders touching in the closet. Watching her get into the waiting car. It's all coming in bursts, like lightning, and I throw my hands over my eyes to get it to stop. I don't even realize I'm thrashing my head up against the wall until Crystal's arms protectively act like a barrier.

She pulls my entire body into hers and holds me so tight, I struggle to breathe. But then I realize it's not her hug that's depriving my lungs of air, it's the third thing my body does as the memories start to come back. It graces me with a full-blown panic attack. My breathing is coming in large puffs from my nose and I honestly think my heart is just going to stop beating. Death is coming, which is actually better than reliving over and over again the images that are now bouncing around in my head.

Crystal is whispering into my ear, but I can't understand what she's saying. There's this loud ringing that has overtaken every small sound in this room. It's a death train, and it's obviously coming to take me to my hellish afterlife. But just as I start to feel the dark cloud of nothing overtake me, it evaporates into a whisp of clear air. I start to feel my body come out of this uncontrollable panic attack, and I realize that ringing was just my mind screaming at me to fight through it.

The fourth and final thing my body does as the memories start to come back is remind me of every single moment I've had since I walked up to Hazel in the JFK airport. Every moment with her, every moment with my family, every moment in this small town.

They say your life flashes before your eyes before you die, and I have to say this was an eerily similar concept. I wasn't dying, I wasn't being reminded of the best parts of my life because my soul was leaving my body for good ... I was being reminded of the best parts of my life because I needed to fight for them, for those moments. I was being reborn. I was being reminded of what I wanted my life to look like.

Before, and after. My life has always been a before, and an after. Which part of my life do I want to fight for? The before, or the after?

I can hear her now. Crystal's voice has thankfully turned calm. Her voice is now reassuring me as I silently concentrate on what I need to do next. Her voice, it's the voice of the mother I didn't know I had. It's the voice of the mother I didn't know I needed.

I focus on her face. On her eyes. She's calming me down with just her steady gaze.

"Why didn't she do anything?" is the first thing I ask her when I'm finally able to speak. "Why didn't she report this? Why didn't *you*?!"

"She was scared no one would believe her," she quickly tells me. "She was scared by speaking it out loud, it would make it worse. It would throw all this attention on her; attention she knew she couldn't mentally handle. Attention she didn't want you to have to take on either. And I had to professionally respect her choice, even though I didn't agree with it at all."

"Why didn't she tell me? All this time?"

Crystal's face suddenly lights up, like what she's going to say next will have the ability to fix everything. "Because she loves you, Killian. She knew it would come down to this at some point. She knew you'd remember when she told you, and she knew you would have to make a choice. She loves you enough to respect that, even though losing you to this has been her fear from the moment she let you in."

Hazel's not going to lose me. I refuse to let that happen. I wipe at my eyes, freeing myself from the tears of these memories. Freeing myself from the year I spent without these memories. Freeing myself from that life, and freeing myself from Theo.

"He's not getting away with this. I need to get to New York," I bluntly say in return, a sense of urgency in my voice. "Right this minute."

Crystal kisses my forehead. "I knew all along you were going to be the one to show her that good guys do exist in this world." She pulls me up. "What can I do to help?"

I already have my phone out, calling the number that Blake had reached me with earlier. It doesn't even ring before

I hear his voice in my ear. "Killian, your flight to JFK leaves in ninety minutes from Cleveland. I'll text you all the info. Will you make it?"

"I'll make it. How'd you know I'd take the role?"

"Because I've been your agent for over a decade," he calmly replies. "And actually, everything was already booked when they sent the script over. This script, it's you, right? This story is about you? About your brother? Those couple days in California ... you came back a different person. This is why, right? You just didn't know ..."

"I think it is," I answer him. "I'm not coming back to London, Blake. You know that, right?"

"I figured. But I'm still your agent right now, and I'm going to give you some rather quick career and personal advice."

"What's that?"

"Get off the fucking phone and get to the bloody airport. They said you'd be taken care of when you arrive in New York, okay? Just get there."

"Got it. Thank you for being a persistent asshole. Don't tell Mum any of this, not yet, okay?"

"Wouldn't even think about it. She's a scary woman and I don't want to be around when she finds this out. Go, Killian. Get to New York."

I don't wait any longer. I shove my phone in my pocket and look up at Crystal. "I need to get to the airport, quickly. My flight leaves in ninety minutes."

"I'll drive."

The Cleveland Hopkins airport is approximately thirty-two minutes away from the house. Crystal gets me there in twenty-four. As she swerves the Audi up to the curb, she suddenly grabs my shoulder. "This might be hard," she says. "What you and Hazel are going to do together, but just remember, it's the hardest things in life that are the ones worth fighting for. I'm *so* proud of you, Killian. For the amazing man you've been, and the amazing man that you continue to be."

I open the door and step out, leaning my head into the car one last time. "Thank you, Crystal, for everything today, but especially for showing me what a real mother looks like."

Security is busy like always but I have one full hour. I can make it. TSA PreCheck helps, cutting the time in half so when I get to my gate, I still have a few minutes to spare before my plane starts boarding. I have a phone call I need to make, not to Hazel because I know she won't talk to me about this until we're face-to-face. But I also know that once this story gets out, heads are going to roll and I refuse to let Hazel become a victim again. I need some advice, some legal advice. I need someone to be our backbone, someone who's not afraid to stand up for her, for us, when we light the entertainment world on fire.

"Dad?" my voice is wobbly as he picks up.

"Killian? What's wrong?"

My emotions become even more evident by the simple fact that he can sense something is wrong with just one spoken word.

"Dad, I need your help."

He doesn't hesitate. He listens to me talk, and he tells me to get to New York, to bring Hazel back home. He promises he'll have everything figured out for us before we even get off the plane. I knew I could trust him. I've known this all along. I just never gave him a chance.

By the time our conversation comes to an end, I'm the last passenger at the gate. I pull my baseball cap down firmly on my head and bring up my boarding pass on my phone.

"You're Hazel's friend?" the gate attendant asks as she scans it. Of course Hazel would have a team of people she trusts in the Cleveland airport, as well.

"I am," I nod.

"Nice to meet you, finally," she smiles. "Hazel has told me all about you." She then nods to the breezeway.

I walk down, staring at my phone to see where I'm sitting as I haven't paid attention to this minor detail yet. First class. Right up front.

"Killian?" someone says my name as I buckle my seatbelt. I look up and recognize the flight attendant hovering over me. She was on my first flight to Cleveland at the beginning of the summer. That flight with Hazel.

"Claire, right?" I question. Another person in Hazel's family of trustworthy people.

She nods. "I was told I might see you today."

"Yeah?"

She sits down in the seat next to me. "Hazel was on the early flight this morning into JFK. I've gotten to know her really well over this last year, and you were the first person I've ever actually seen her with. She told me a few things this morning ... the flight was pretty empty, we got to talking. Girl talk and stuff. I am *really* happy to see you on this flight, Killian. You let me know if you need anything, okay?"

"I will, thank you."

The flight into JFK is short, but long enough that I have time to sit in my seat and read the entire script. I start at the beginning this time, and get further than I did in my dad's office. At home I stopped when she got into the waiting car. But on the plane, I read up until the very end which actually isn't even an ending. Hazel left it unanswered and has stopped at the exact moment she fell back asleep in my arms last night after her panic attack.

Everything else is in there. Every single second of her life as an actress. Every detail on her encounters with my brother. All the people in her life she trusted, who just repeatedly let her down. Her JFK family, how she met each and every one of them. What happened after she got in the car, after she left me. And exactly how she felt when I walked up to her a year later in the airport, not remembering her at all.

Then comes all the moments we've spent together since finding each other again. It's beautiful, and heartbreaking all at the same time. But now she's waiting to see what I do, how we end this story of ours. I can't help but think she purposely did this. She didn't write an ending because she needs to see how it actually ends first.

When I step off the plane, the very first person I see is Harold. He's actually waiting for me on the breezeway. His arms are folded and he truthfully looks rather intimidating, almost like a hitman with his large frame and bald head. I had this strange feeling Hazel's entourage of JFK trustworthy people would be guiding my way to her, but I didn't think I'd be frightened in their presence like I am right now.

I walk right up to him though, and he pats me hard on the back, harder than necessary, but I think this is his subtle way of warning me that Hazel is important to him. "Glad to see you, Killian. Follow me."

He takes me through the open door and past his counter, straight to Sammy, who's waiting for me with his electric cart.

"Killian!" he greets me warmly. "Hop in."

I shake my head a little, as only Hazel could pull all this off. "How are you doing, Sammy?"

"Perfectly fine, now that you've arrived. Was sweating all day," he tells me as he starts up his cart.

He drives me straight down the terminal, where we slow down as we approach Fred's pub. Fred is standing at the entrance, obviously knowing I was going to be cruising by with Sammy at this point of the day. He salutes me with his fingers, giving me a little nod as I turn my head and watch him walk back inside.

"Did Hazel tell all of you I was going to be flying in today?" I ask Sammy.

"What Hazel tells us is between us and Hazel," Sammy responds. He then starts to slow down his cart as we approach another gate.

Meredith.

Where ... is ... Meredith?

She sneaks up behind me and hops into the empty seat. Sammy keeps driving like nothing has happened.

"Hi, Killian," she kindly smiles. "You doing okay today?"

"Honestly, no. But I'll get there."

"I'm going to let you in on a little secret, all right?" she throws her arm around my shoulder. "I don't know everything that happened in Hazel's past ... and I don't know how you're connected to it all. But she's told me that you're one of the good guys. I was here when she hit rock bottom. I *saw* when she hit rock bottom. I don't want to see her like that again."

Sammy stops his cart by the entrance of baggage claim. I glance around to see if there's anyone waiting for me now. A man in an all-black suit holding a sign catches my eye. It's a sign that says *London*. In JFK, I'm not Killian. I'm London.

I know the man holding that sign can only be one person. Neil. It's definitely Neil.

I turn back to Meredith. "I won't let her hit rock bottom again. I promise."

"Her family here in JFK will hold you to that promise. I hope you know that," she delicately warns. She then gives my arm a small push. "Go. She's waiting for you."

# chapter twenty-nine

I take it you're Neil?" I ask the man holding the sign.
"That I am," he grins. "I take it you're London?"
"Killian," I reply. "You can call me Killian."
"Well, let's go, Killian. New York City traffic is a bitch."
Neil's black Mercedes is waiting outside. The way he weaves in and out of traffic as we leave the airport is rather impressive, I'll admit. I find myself closing my eyes a lot, waiting for the impact of him hitting another vehicle, but it never comes.

"You hungry?" he looks through the rearview mirror and asks. "I picked up some bagels. Hazel likes everything, the occasional asiago, but she says those make her breath smell. I have a variety in there," he points to the brown paper bag in a basket on the floor. "What's your bagel preference?"

No one has ever asked me that before. I look into the bag and pull out a salt one. "Salt," I lift it to show him. "With chive and onion cream cheese."

"Good to know," he smiles. "I'll keep that in mind."

Neil talks nonstop the entire drive. He points out every New York City landmark that we pass and tells me the history behind each one, like I've never been in this city before. He also tells me the best place to get a good burger, a good steak, a good cupcake, and where I can find an impressive deal on suits and watches. I don't plan on going shopping while here, but I'll keep his suggestions tucked away for the next time. Then, when he announces we're less than three minutes away, his delightful tour guide tone changes.

"Killian?" he quickly turns to me while stopped at a red light. "Did Hazel tell you I have triplets?"

"She did," I nod. "Teenagers, right? In school?"

"Pretty close to your age. Seventeen. After years of fertility issues, God blessed us with three at once. Two boys and a girl. Good kids, they mean the world to their Mama and me." He pulls up to a curb and puts the car in park. "I would have no problem killing for my babies," he abruptly says. He turns his body around to face me. "I know some people, some good hiding spots. Hazel is like my fourth baby. Just wanted to make sure you knew that." He then points to the entrance of the building we're parked in front of. "Twenty-fifth floor, Killian. Let me get the door for you—"

"That's okay, Neil," I hold my hand out to stop him from moving. "I've got it. Thanks for the ride." I step out of his car and close the door, but quickly knock on the passenger window. Neil rolls it down and I hang my head inside. "Your kids ... Hazel said we'd get an invitation to their graduation party next summer? I'm looking forward to it."

Neil throws his head back and starts laughing. "That you will son ... that you will."

I walk through the doors of this skyscraper and head straight to the elevator. It shoots me up to the twenty-fifth floor so fast, I don't even have time to mentally prepare myself for what's waiting for me when the door slides open. I clutch the straps of my bookbag and feel my stomach drop as the elevator comes to an abrupt stop. Lights, lots of lights are the first thing I see. This reception area is lit up with the most stunning chandeliers that seem to reflect streams of light perfectly off the exposed brick walls. It makes me feel like I'm suddenly thrown into a royal dining hall.

I hear the clunk of heels hit the wood floor, and as I step out of the elevator, I'm met by an extremely tall woman in a tight business suit. Her hair is pulled back into a slick ponytail, and although she immediately comes across to me as a pompous bitch, her warm smile suddenly makes me regret ever thinking that thought.

"Killian!" she says my name as if she's known me forever.

"Evelyn. I'm Evelyn. I'm part of Hazel's team—"

"Team?" I question.

"Manager, agent, publicist," she lists. "We all do a little bit of everything here since Hazel formed our agency."

*Hazel formed their agency?* That definitely wasn't in the script I just read. But ... Evelyn. This name. I'm almost certain I'm staring at the same Evelyn who helped Hazel escape from the movie awards last year.

My words stutter out of my mouth, "I didn't realize she had formed an agency."

"Six months now," Evelyn smiles. "She handpicked all of us, and we've got a few actors already signed, including her, of course." Her hand suddenly appears on my shoulder. "You doing all right?"

Her dark eyes are pure, trustworthy, caring. Definitely not a pompous bitch. "I am, Evelyn. Thanks for asking."

"Good! Follow me, I'll take you to where Hazel is." Her thin heels echo as she walks me through the open reception area and to a corridor lined with steel doors. "She's in the last one on the left," she points to it. "She's alone," she adds, like she felt the need to share that small piece of information with me. "We're glad to have you here, Killian." And then she promptly leaves, walking back to the reception area, echoing as she goes.

*Breathe, Killian. Deep breaths. In and out.*

I move to the door. Knowing Hazel's behind here has my

emotions sputtering out like a pot boiling over. Every thought is bursting, flying in a different direction, and I'm not sure if I'll be able to contain it all once I open that door. But I need to open it, because standing here and staring at it isn't going to solve anything.

I need to open it. So, I do.

Hazel's standing by a window, her back is to me as she stares out into the New York City landscape. Her hands are clutching the wood below the glass so firmly, her fingers almost look transparent in color. I close the door and carefully place my bookbag on the table that's in the center of this large, exposed beam room.

"Hazel?" her name immediately soars out of my mouth.

She slowly turns. Her arms fold protectively around her body. Her wild hair is hanging down and covering her chest as if shielding her heart. She almost looks afraid to see me, not at all like she's looked these last two months. I silently tell myself not to panic yet. It kills me to think I'm making her afraid, and why do I suddenly feel scared to even touch her?

These negative thoughts are rapidly taking over my mind, but then it's as if someone new appears. My conscience. It decides I'm not smart enough to figure this out for myself and it needs to do it for me.

I'm swiftly overwhelmed with the realization that Hazel's not scared to be touched by me, she's not afraid of *me* ... she's scared I'm not going to want to touch her. She's scared that I'm afraid of *her*.

*Hell no.*

My feet clear the vacant space between the two of us in three massive steps, and then I'm pulling her directly into my arms. My body melts into the familiar shape of her. My head buries into the dip of her warm neck. Her fingers start to run delicately through my hair, and it's at that simple moment, that subtle embrace, that my emotions rapidly take over like I knew they would.

I drop down hard onto my knees, squeezing my arms around her perfect waist. "I'm so sorry!" I sob into her shirt, my hands gripping at it from the back, twisting it tightly in my fist. "Hazel, I'm so sorry! I didn't remember—I swear I didn't remember!"

She slowly brings herself down so she's kneeling in front of me. She holds me for a minute as I cry, her hands gently clutching my head as she massages it with her fingers. She then lifts my face from where it's now resting on her chest. "Killian, I know," she simply says, her eyes are filled with tears. "I know you didn't remember."

"Why didn't you tell me?!"

The tears drop from her eyes. "When, Killian?! At the airport? On our walks? At the craft fair? In my *bed*?! Every single time I thought about telling you, my body would panic! I felt like it was completely shutting down, like my happiness would vanish if I reminded you of that night! Those memories ... I knew what they would do to you, and I didn't want you to have to share that pain with me!"

"I should have done something!" I cry out. "I should have gone with you! We should have gone to the police together! I should have done more!"

Hazel grabs my face and shakes her head, obviously disagreeing with what just flew from my mouth. "You did *everything* you could have possibly done that night! You saved me from him—from what else was coming! You were drugged! He drugged you and you didn't have the ability to do anything else but just be there with me!"

"No! I could have done *something*!" I feel like I can't breathe. I actually think I'm gasping for air at this point. "I didn't do *anything*!"

"Stop!" she pleads. "You can't blame yourself! Do you know every single time I thought about him this last year, I remembered *you*?! Remembering you actually made me smile! *You*, Killian, you were my comfort that night even when you could barely stand up straight! Even when you didn't remember me at all, *I* remembered you! I remembered everything you said and how you made me feel! And the second you walked up to me in that airport, I knew that was it! I knew you were showing up in my life again for a reason and I wasn't going to be able to just walk away from you again! But I was scared to let you in because I knew I'd have to tell you everything! I knew you'd have to choose between me and your brother!" She lets out a deep breath, and more tears fall from her eyes. "I didn't want to hurt you, but I also selfishly didn't want to lose you."

I carefully wipe her tears with my fingers. "How you could possibly think for even a second that I would choose *him*? After what he did? How could you think that I would walk away from you?"

"Because I walked away from *you*," she softly replies. "That night. And I shouldn't have. I walked away and took all our memories with me. Your memories, that you had a right to own."

I bring my hand to the back of her head and guide my forehead to hers. "No, Hazel. You didn't take them, you guarded them until you knew I was ready to remember them."

Her tears drip onto my legs. "Do you, Killian? Do you remember them?"

I wrap my arms around her back because I need her as close to me as possible. "Yes, but they come at me in bursts, almost like a flash of light I can't control."

"*All* of them?" her voice cracks as she asks.

I won't lie to her, even though I know the truth is going to hurt her. "All of them."

She starts to quietly cry, and I squeeze my arms tighter around her like this will make a difference. "Only think about the ones of you and me that night, okay?" she begs, her hands pull on my t-shirt. "*Please?* Not him. Not what he did. Just the memories of you and me."

"Always, Hazel. Just you and me." I then cautiously place my lips on hers, as gentle and delicate as I possibly can. "I'm so sorry," I whisper into the air between us as I bring my forehead back to hers. "I'm so sorry for what he did to you."

"I know you are, Killian," she whispers back. "But that is the *very* last time you're going to apologize for him, okay?"

I nod my head against hers. "I love you," I then say. I want her to hear me say it, even though she's heard me say it before. I need to make it clear to her that how I feel hasn't changed.

"I love you, too."

It's instant, it's beautiful, and it's almost like these words we just spoke to each other are already paving the path of where we're going to go from here.

Minutes pass as we stay like this, in silence now, just the sound of our breathing filling the air of the room. Just the sound of our hearts beating one right after the other. The calmness is welcomed. It's needed. Our minds are heavy, pierced with memories that have obviously changed both of us. But this quiet embrace that we're currently sharing is the universe's way of reminding us that we're still here, together. We still have something worth fighting for, and I'll be damned if we don't give it our all.

"Hazel?" I finally say. My voice sounds odd in this room after so many minutes of silence.

"Yeah, Killian?"

I lift my head from hers. "You created an agency?"

She faintly smiles. "Good people do exist. These people here are kind, and caring, and protective. This agency is a family and anyone who joins, they're not just another face in the industry. They're an actual person whose feelings and emotions are validated every day. People need to feel safe. I want people like us to have a place to feel safe."

"You're going to change the world, Hazel," I declare. "People are going to know who you are not because of your past, but because of what you're doing right now."

"I hope so," she quietly replies.

"You didn't write an ending," I then point out. "Your screenplay, the script ... there wasn't an ending."

"No, there wasn't," she agrees. "I'm honestly not sure how it's going to end. I was hoping you could help me with that, if you wanted to."

"You want me to help you write your ending?" I feel my heart flutter in my chest as I ask this question.

Her eyes search mine like they always do. She's searching for comfort, for something to believe in. "I can't make this movie without you. It's about you, just as much as it's about me. And I won't do that to you. I won't throw all that on you, if all you want to do is forget about it. And I'll understand, trust me, I will."

"But then we're still trapped, Hazel. Trapped in the memories of that night." I push her hair off her shoulder, gently running my fingers along her cheek. "Trapped with knowing he thinks he got away with everything. You promised me if we ever met again, you'd make me remember. And I promised you that I'd make him pay for what he did."

She holds my wrist with her hand as my thumb caresses the side of her face. "It's not about revenge, Killian. It's about protecting people who don't know who he really is, and reminding everyone like us that they have the ability to fly free, too."

"But *we're* not free, Hazel," I push my finger against her bird tattoo. "Not really. Not unless people know. Not unless we make people see. And people need to see."

"I can't play this part without you by my side," she quietly tells me.

"I'll be by your side," I confirm. "The entire time."

She smiles with my words. "We could just go home. We could just write a new story, one that starts the moment we leave this building."

"Or ...?" I question.

"Or, we walk out that door," she points to it, "and go tell everyone that's waiting for us that we're ready to write the ending to this one."

I kiss her again. And I hold my lips on hers as long as I can before I pull away. Her stormy gray eyes are waiting for my response. "But we already wrote the ending to this one, Hazel. We just did. Right now. You and me, in this room together. And it's beautiful."

Her arms wrap around my neck and she grins as she asks, "Well, then tell me. How does it end, Killian?"

I kiss her one more time, tugging on the ends of her wild hair, knowing that all along, this was the ending that was supposed to happen. This was always going to be the ending to her story, to *our* story, even if it took over a year to make it happen. Even if I had to completely forget her and everything about that night in order to get us to this exact moment in time ... this exact perfect ending.

"Like this, Hazel," I confirm, pulling her back into my arms. "Exactly like this. The two of us, ready to do something huge, ready to be free of those memories ... together. Like we promised each other the night we first met."

My name is Killian.

Her name is Hazel.

And this moment right here, this exact second in time, is the ending to our before.

# chapter thirty

Twenty-four hours. Hazel and I spent twenty-four hours in New York together before we flew back home. What did we do during those quick twenty-four hours?

First, we sat down with her team and the producer who bought her screenplay. She introduced me to everyone in the room as if they didn't know who I was, and then she pitched them the new ending. It was met with instant praise and acceptance, just like I knew it would be. Although it might not be apparent to Hazel, it's very apparent to an observer that she calls the shots when it comes to her screenplay.

This producer, an up and coming one who I recognized from an indie film that won a few awards last year, is determined to keep Hazel involved with the entire process. This is *her* story after all, and everyone there was well aware that the entire script is based off of true events. The director was also in the room, and invited both of us to sit in on all pre-production meetings between him and the producer that will take place over the next couple months.

I knew as soon as I was asked for *my* opinion on certain scenes and dialogues, that Hazel had struck gold when she found these people who were all quietly watching me and waiting patiently for my response. Where were these people ten years ago? Five years ago? Last year? Hazel has definitely found her tribe in New York City, and it looks like they want to recruit me as a new permanent member. After some lengthy discussions, things are moving forward for filming to start in a few months. Hazel and I will spend the rest of the summer bouncing around between Ohio, New York, and California. Roughly five hours after I had gotten off the elevator on the twenty-fifth floor, unsure of what my future with Hazel would look like, I walked back onto the elevator on the twenty-fifth floor with Hazel's hand in mine.

We spent the rest of our time in New York City ordering room service to our hotel room, as neither one of us wanted to make the effort to actually go anywhere. We also escaped to Central Park for a few hours the next morning, where we found solitude as we strolled along the peaceful paths together. It's ironic that in the heart of the loud and busy city of New York, you can find yourself in the quiet tranquility of a park that stretches over a mile long.

We could have stayed longer, days, even the entire week. I know both of us would have enjoyed that, just the two of us in New York, leaving real life behind for a little while. But I needed to get back to Ohio. Theo was set to fly into Cleveland soon, and I needed to make a phone call to him before it was too late. I didn't want to do that in front of Hazel, nor did I want to do that alone. I wanted my dad to be with me. I needed his support.

Twenty-four hours after arriving in New York, Hazel and I are back at my house in Ohio.

"It shouldn't take long," I softly say into her ear. My arms are wrapped around her as her head presses on my chest.

"You sure this is what you want to do?" she questions. Her voice is hesitant, like I'm going to change my mind.

I lift my head from hers. "Hazel, I should have done this a year ago." Then I place a kiss on her lips. "You stay down here, and I'll be back down in just a few minutes."

My dad is waiting for me in his office. He puts his hand comfortingly on my shoulder as I sit down in his chair, and then I place my phone on the desk that he and I had built together. I don't need encouraging words from him. I just need *him*.

I could sit here for hours staring at Theo's contact info on my phone, but I'm not allowing him to waste another minute of my life. I firmly press down on his name, turning my phone on speaker as I wait for him to pick up.

"Killian! You've been MIA the last day or so," is what he says when he answers. "Thought maybe you got lost in a corn maze or something."

His voice which I used to seek out for reassurance, now just makes me want to vomit. I actually have to swallow hard before I speak.

"I was in New York," I then calmly say.

"Oh yeah? With that girl? She finally tell you what she's doing there?"

"She did, actually," I tell him. "She wrote a screenplay. It was bought. She's starring in it, so am I. We're working with the production team to get everything rolling."

"Jesus, Killian!" he exclaims. "You picked a good one. You going to tell me her name now? I mean, I'll meet her tomorrow, right?"

Here we go. More vomit rising in my throat. "You actually already met her."

"Oh yeah?"

My heart has stopped. I'm pretty sure I'm clinically dead right now. "Her name is Hazel. Remember that, Theo. *Her name is Hazel*. But when you met her, she was called Birdie."

Silence. Absolute silence. There's no comedic response that will fix this moment. There's nothing he will be able to say to fix what he did in the past; what he is now realizing I remember. So he doesn't say anything at all.

I keep going. "Last spring ... I remember now. I remember my two days with you last spring—"

"Killian!" his alarmed voice breaks through my phone.

"I remember what I walked in on. I remember what you were doing to her—"

"It wasn't like that!" he cries out.

*Stay calm.* "You're a fucking liar, Theo. You're a liar, and you're a rapist."

Silence. More silence.

I feel my dad's hand pressing firmly on my shoulder. My voice is steady. My voice is blunt. "You also drugged me when I got there. Which is why I didn't remember any of this. But I remember it all now. She helped me remember what a piece of shit you are."

"You're going to believe *her*, over me?!" he shouts. "I'm your brother, Killian—"

"You're not my brother," I tell him. "You're a shell of the brother I used to know—"

"How can you believe *her*, over me?!" his shocked voice asks. "You realize when she walked out on that movie, half the cast left, too, and the director! That movie never got made because of what *she* did."

I actually find myself laughing with what he just said. "Do you even hear yourself? You're honestly blaming her for walking out on a movie that *you* were in. You're her rapist, Theo. Fuck you."

"You're going to regret choosing her—"

"No, I won't," I boldly say. "I regret ever trusting you, I regret thinking I could look up to you, I regret not leaving with her that night, and I regret waking up the next morning not remembering what I saw you do to her. But I will *not* regret her. Never."

Heavy breathing. The silence is replaced with heavy

breathing, and then his voice is shaky as he speaks again. "Where does this leave us?"

"*Us*?! There is no us anymore."

"We're brothers—"

"By blood, yes," I agree. "But I don't want you in my life anymore. You're a rapist, Theo. You sexually assaulted her. You have no shame for what you did, and I have a feeling she wasn't the first girl you've done that to. How many people *have* you drugged? How many people are walking around right now, missing memories of a night that you were involved in? How many girls, Theo?"

The silence is back.

"I know you're not going to answer me," I say to him. "And I hope that's because you're humiliated over your younger brother finally calling you out for being the fucking piece of shit that you are. Don't call me anymore, okay? This conversation is the last one you and I will ever have together."

His voice cracks through the phone. He's crying, and I feel nothing for him. No sympathy, no emotion, nothing at all ... "I'm sorry, Killian! I'm sorry!" he theatrically sobs.

Time to end this call. "No, you're not, Theo. You're just acting a part right now. You're fake, but I can see right through you. You're not sorry for what you did, you're just sorry that I remembered." I look up at my dad, who's standing over my shoulder, and I nod to my phone. "Don't call me again," I remind Theo. "I'm going now, but my dad has a few things to say to you."

I then stand up and walk out of the office, closing the French doors behind me. I don't need to stand there and listen to what my dad tells Theo. I trust him, and I trust that whatever he tells him will ensure that Theo never contacts Hazel or me ever again.

She's waiting, sitting on the edge of my bed. I'm sure she was sitting exactly like this the entire time I was upstairs. She doesn't ask how it went. She doesn't ask how I'm doing. She just looks up at me, searching my face for clues on my emotions. I take her hand and crawl into my bed, pulling her with me as I go. I then just lie there with her in my arms, the two of us in complete silence for a while.

Two months and some odd days. I've known Hazel Hemingway for two months and some odd days. But in actuality, I've known her for over a year. Life suddenly feels different, like there was this fog I had been trying to walk through since last spring. My brain was struggling with the absence of those memories, and I was stuck trying to live life without them. And now that they're back, my life is finally moving forward. I'm not trapped anymore, wandering around aimlessly trying to figure out why I felt so lost to begin with.

Hazel. It was Hazel. She was the reason I felt that way. And I'm not going to lie here right now and say that my life is now whole, that at nineteen, I know she and I will be together forever and *that* was the reason I felt so lost. I wasn't lost because my soul was searching for the one person that completes me. I was lost because together was the only way for the two of us to ever be free.

Minutes pass by in my bedroom before I lean down and give her head a kiss. My own silent way of saying we can talk now. She glances up at me, her eyes actually looking like moving storm clouds as she stares into mine.

"I think I love this," I tell her. "You right here, an entire future of endless possibilities."

She smiles. "It's a really good feeling. Sort of like a brand-new chapter has started?"

I nod my head in agreement. "Not a new chapter," I suddenly say. "The old story ended. It's a new one now. An entirely different book."

She places her head back on my chest. "I think I love *that*," she then says. "An entirely different book. I wonder what's written in it ... what the story is about?"

That's easy. Although I don't know all the details, the plot twists and the surprises that might come our way, I know the general synopsis. And I'm more than confident as I wrap my arms tighter around her and softly say into her ear, "Killian and Hazel. Proving to the world that no matter how many times someone tries to cage you, you always have the ability to let yourself fly free. Like us."

She lifts her head, placing a tender kiss on my lips before declaring, "Now *that* is a story I can't wait to read."

# five years later

Neil!" Hazel greets him as she pulls open the Mercedes door. "Long time, no see."

"I saw you both yesterday," he points out.

"She was joking, Neil," I confirm, climbing in after her.

"Ah. It's too early for jokes," he laughs. "I got us some bagels," he points to the brown paper bag in the basket on the floor. "An everything with light cream cheese, and a salt with onion and chive."

"I love that you always have bagels for us," Hazel declares, handing me mine. "No matter what time of the day it is. Early morning, afternoon, dinner, middle of the night. You always have bagels."

"I love it, too," I agree. "Hey, did your daughter accept the internship at our agency?" I ask him. "Evelyn said they offered it to her yesterday."

"She did," Neil smiles through the rearview mirror. "Thanks for pulling some strings."

"No strings pulled, Neil," Hazel quickly tells him. "She deserved it."

The rest of the drive to JFK is rather quiet. It's too early to form a proper conversation of more than a few sentences here and there, and I find myself dozing in and out of sleep on Hazel's arm. When we arrive, Neil pulls up to the curb and gets out to help with our bags.

"All right you two," he says, giving me a few fatherly pats on the back. "Enjoy yourselves, okay? When can I expect to see you again?"

"Not too sure," I answer. "We'll call you?"

"I have a big meeting with the producer of my next film in a few weeks," Hazel reminds him. "So we'll definitely be back for that."

"Looking forward to it. Make sure you wear sunscreen if it's someplace warm!"

Hazel and I check in our baggage, and then find Sammy patiently waiting after we get through security. "Let's get this show on the road!" he hollers.

We climb into the empty seats of his electric cart, and I throw my arm around Hazel. She leans in, resting her head on mine. "Sammy," she yawns as she says his name. "When are you going to retire?"

"Do I look old or something?" he questions. "Shit. I still feel like I'm in my twenties."

"You need to retire before it's too late," Hazel tells him. "Your wife is waiting to travel the world with you. She told me that at our wedding."

Yes, you heard that correctly. *Our* wedding.

Hazel and I got married a month ago. It was quite possibly the very best moment of my entire life, and everyone was there to celebrate with us. Both of our families, of course, the entire trustworthy crew from JFK, even our team at Hazel's agency here in New York, of which I became a partner with. Carol as well, who I kept on as my publicist, and Blake, who I fired as my agent but surprisingly became friends with over the last few years. Oh, and every single resident of Sharon Center, Ohio, because that's where our wedding was.

It was elaborate, because Hazel deserved to feel like a princess, yet she insisted we hold it at our own house and not anywhere else. Hazel and I have a farm now, less than a mile away from both of our families. It's not the kind of farm you're thinking of. We don't raise cattle or grow corn that we harvest every fall. I do *not* own a tractor.

We actually bought twenty acres of land and had a beautiful white farm house built. We even had our own barn raising party because we did indeed buy a couple goats, but it's the horses that take up most of our land. Rescue ones, and Ophelia, of course. There's something so beautiful about waking up in the morning with Hazel in my arms, and walking outside together with our coffees to go feed our horses.

The reception was held right in our barn. Just imagine vaulted ceilings, twinkling lights, wooden tables, a live band playing in the distance, and no foul smell of cow shit. The best part was the dance floor. It was placed right in the middle of a field that fireflies took over as soon as the sun went down.

It was perfect. It was beautiful. It was everything. It was us, with everyone we love.

Who was *not* there? Theo. But did you think he would be? I haven't spoken to him in over five years. And Mum, well once I told her everything, she didn't talk to me for almost two years. I was more than okay with that, though, and I sort of knew that was going to happen. I had my dad and Crystal ... and Hazel ... and Tim and Lori. I honestly have the most amazing tribe of family and I'm lucky to call them my own.

It wasn't until shit hit the fan with Theo after our movie came out that Mum finally reached a breaking point. I don't think she had realized the extent of Theo's actions, nor do I think she had realized the extent of her own actions all these years. We definitely don't have the typical mother-son relationship and we never will, but we have something. And as long as there's something, I'll keep trying. She *did* come to our wedding, just in case you wanted to know.

So ... our story, our movie ... once everything got going it took about six months to film. It was hard, I won't lie. Probably the hardest thing we've ever purposely put ourselves through. Filming those moments almost felt like we were living through them for the very first time again, but we did it together. We leaned on each for support, we held onto each other at night as we cried, and we both sat down with counselors who helped us get through it all. And the day the film finally wrapped, it was almost as if we could actually visualize ourselves flying free.

It was another six months in post-production, and during that time Hazel and I did absolutely nothing but wander around Sharon Center. That town is our comfort, and the residents protected our delicate souls as if we were wounded birds trying to heal.

Did our movie turn heads? Did it shed light onto issues that were always quietly swept under the rug? Did we win awards that we now display on our fireplace mantel next to pictures of us and our family?

Yes.

Yes.

And yes.

What about Theo? What happened to *him* when this movie hit the theaters? Although names were changed and we never confirmed if this film was based on actual true events, people knew. People talked. People made the connection. Girls came forward, *so* many girls, and they all told their stories. It was only then, surrounded by her new family of warriors, did Hazel feel comfortable confirming her own tragic tale. The floodgate had officially been opened and I'll just say, Theo got what was coming to him.

Where are we now? Five years later? Married, of course. Living in Sharon Center most of the time, but we also have an apartment in New York. We were here often enough when we started filming our movie that we found it necessary to have a permanent place to call home in the city. We always seem to come back here for one thing or another, so we've kept it all these years. It's nice to have this little space. It overlooks Central Park, and sometimes it's just calming to throw on our NYC t-shirts and hats, and stroll along the city as if we're exploring it for the very first time.

I still do roughly one film a year, but I very carefully consider my roles now. I'd rather be at home with Hazel and our horses, and I have no problem making that well known. We're a team, Hazel and I, and we're rarely seen without each other. I tend to choose roles that keep me closer to her, and when they don't, Hazel is a familiar face on each and every set.

What about Hazel? Well, the last film she starred in was the one she wrote. She *has* sold three other screenplays since then. Do I think the world will ever see her in front of the camera at any point in the future? She's brilliant, an amazing actress. She has the awards to prove it. But she absolutely shines when she's writing. Sometimes I just sit there and watch her in wonder as these stories come to life under her fingertips. But never say never. Hazel likes to do the unexpected, and I love that about her.

What are we doing today? Why are we in New York again? Hazel and I had a few loose ends to tie up here. Just a few days to wrap up some projects before we head out for a couple weeks. Her new movie is going to start filming soon and it involves a younger cast. She likes to be on hand for each and every meeting with them, to ensure they feel safe and comfortable. She's like the mother hen of this industry and everyone flocks to her, knowing they're well protected when she's around.

"Fred!" I hear Hazel squeal. Sammy slows his cart down outside of Fred's pub. "What are you doing here? It's six in the morning!"

"Obviously, I'm not going to miss the chance to wish you

two a happy honeymoon day," he responds.

Yes, today Hazel and I are *finally* heading out on our honeymoon.

"Us, too," Meredith announces her arrival as she and Harold appear from inside the bar.

"You guys!" Hazel jumps out of the cart and throws her arms around them all.

"Get in here, Killian," Meredith swiftly waves her hand at me. And I do, because Hazel's family of trustworthy people in the JFK airport are also my family of trustworthy people in the JFK airport.

"Still not telling anyone where you're heading?" Harold questions us. "I see your layover is in Charlotte, but after that you cease to exist."

I start laughing at his determination to figure out our plans. We have a private jet picking us up in Charlotte that only one other person is aware of. "Just one person knows," I tell them all. "And unless you have my thirteen-year-old sister's cell number, you're not going to get very far."

We told Maisy our honeymoon plans, because even when you want to completely go off the grid for a while, you should at least clue one person in on where you'll actually be. We promised to check in every two days, and she swore not to tell anyone where we are going unless we go missing for longer than forty-eight hours. We trust her completely, and promised to bring her back an elaborate souvenir if she holds up her end of the bargain.

"One last hug," Hazel suddenly declares. "We need to get to our gate."

We say our goodbyes and get back in Sammy's cart where he safely delivers us to our first plane of the day. Six o'clock in the morning and the gate is already packed. Hazel finds two empty seats along the window overlooking the runway, and throws herself down into one. We don't hide anymore, not like we used to, that is. Gone are the days when we felt the need to be completely invisible. When we get recognized now, people respect our privacy more. Being together helps alleviate any unwanted anxiety, too.

I stand over Hazel. "What?" she asks me. "Why are you staring at me?" I didn't even realize I was doing this until she called me out.

I smirk, tugging on the ends of her untamed hair. "Is that seat taken?" I point and ask.

"You're hilarious," she laughs, and then she yanks on my hand and pulls me down into the spot next to her. She rests her head on my shoulder and keeps my hand in hers.

I'm Killian Lewis. I'm in the JFK airport with the American actress formerly known as Birdie. The screenwriter that everyone now knows as Hazel, who also happens to be my wife. Five years ago as I walked up to her in this exact airport, I had no idea which direction my life was heading. All I knew was that I felt lost, trapped in a life that made me miserable, and I was frantically searching for someone to save me.

Little did I know as she dragged me around this airport that day, that *she* was the one who would save me.

We board our flight, sitting side-by-side in first class, the arm rest pushed up so that Hazel can rest her head against the familiar comfort of my shoulder. Every time we're on a plane together, my mind flashes back to that first flight we shared. I remember how I felt watching her sleep next to me. I remember how I felt thinking that would be the last time I ever saw her. I remember how I felt so protective over this person who I thought was a stranger.

My life ... it's always been a before and an after. I always struggled with where to put the split, where the before ended and where the after began. I used to think the split came the moment I met Hazel. That every second before was my miserable life without her, and every second after were the perfect moments of us together. That's not true, though. I know now that the before was everything that happened up until the very moment we walked out of that office together on the twenty-fifth floor in New York City. The after is this amazing life we've created since then.

Hazel's hand appears on my neck. Her fingers start twirling my hair as she rests her head against mine. "Do you remember that first flight?" she quietly asks me as our plane lifts into the air.

"I do," I respond.

"Do you remember that moment?"

She doesn't need to explain the details. I know which moment she's talking about. The one where she woke up from a nightmare, thinking I was someone else sitting next to her. "I do, Hazel," I answer.

She looks up at me and smiles. "When I heard your voice, and I turned around and saw you right here, and you lifted your arm, welcoming me back into that comfort I needed ... I knew, right that second."

I give her forehead a kiss. "What did you know?"

Her stormy gray eyes raise, and she stares directly into mine as she says, "That at some point, you and I would be sitting in the same exact spots, heading off on our perfect honeymoon together."

I start laughing. "Want to know what I knew that day?"

"Sure," she grins.

I kiss her forehead one more time. "That I had just met the person who was going to change my entire life."

She snuggles her way back onto my arm. "I'm extremely grateful for that day, for *both* days, actually—for both times we met for the first time. I think life just has a funny way of making sure the story ends the way it's supposed to, right? Like maybe that day, in the closet, maybe you *were* supposed to leave with me. But had you done that, would you be sitting next to me right now?"

She doesn't say anything else, just takes my hand in hers and wraps her fingers around mine, the same way she wraps herself around my heart. I never asked myself that question before. Had I gone with Hazel that night, had I remembered everything the day after it happened, would we be where we are right now?

Happy. In control of our own careers. Married. And undeniably in love.

Possibly. But also, maybe not.

Sometimes fate just knows the outcome. Sometimes you have to get through the dark shit in life first in order to understand what actually matters as the years float on. Life flies by too fast. We need to grab onto those good moments as often as we can, and that is what I do. That is what *we* do. That is what our before has taught us.

Don't settle for a life of *just* brief moments.

So, where are we going on this honeymoon of ours? I'll give you a few clues. Someplace tropical. Someplace where we sleep in wooden bungalows along the ocean blue water. Someplace where little wild monkeys run around stealing the fruit that's floating in our drinks with those tiny umbrellas. It's somewhere no one knows who we are. It's somewhere we won't be bothered. It's somewhere we can disappear and just be Killian and Hazel.

Killian and Hazel.

The two people who wrote the perfect ending to their troubled before.

The two people who live every day to the fullest in their beautiful after.

Killian and Hazel.

Just us.

Uncaged ... and free.

Together.

No matter how many times they try to cage you, remember ... you always have the ability to let yourself fly free.

Have you read all of Sarah Forester Davis' books? Check out the Confession Series!

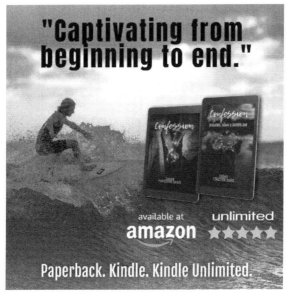

Follow Sarah Forester Davis on social media for all her latest book news!

Printed in Great Britain
by Amazon

13740597R00169